3/3

SUNRISE
SHOWS LATE

SUNRISE
SHOWS LATE

a novel

Eva Mekler

BRIDGE WORKS PUBLISHING COMPANY
BRIDGEHAMPTON, NEW YORK

Adam Mickiewicz is quoted from *Selected Poems,*
ed. Clark Mills, trans. Robert Hillyer and Donald Davie
(New York: Noonday Press, 1956).

Library of Congress Cataloging-in-Publication Data

Mekler, Eva.
Sunrise shows late : a novel / Eva Mekler. — 1st ed.
p.   cm.
ISBN 1-882593-17-0
1. Landsberg am Lech (Germany)—History—Fiction. 2.
Holocaust survivors—Germany—Fiction. 3. Jewish women—
Germany—Fiction. 4. Jewish women—Poland—Fiction. I. Title.
PS3563.E423S86   1997
813'.54—dc20   96-43464
CIP

2   4   6   8   10   9   7   5   3   1

Jacket design by Eva Auchincloss

Printed in the United States of America

FIRST EDITION

For my mother and father. All stories begin with theirs.

And for Julia, who spins her own.

Acknowledgments

I wish to thank University Seminars at Columbia University whose generous support is greatly appreciated.

I am deeply grateful to Nancy Weber and Joshua Karton for their invaluable counsel and friendship.

Thanks to Alexandra Shelley and publisher, Barbara Phillips, for their editing and kind, respectful support.

To my agent and friend, Al Zuckerman, who made it possible.

To Catherine Hiller, Mark Alpert, Johanna Fiedler, Steve Goldstone, Dave King, Melissa Knox, and Cheryl Morrison whose advice and support made the writing process a joy to share.

To Carla Stevens who started it all.

Any finally to my husband, Michael Schulman, for his ideas, patience, and relentless encouragement.

SUNRISE
SHOWS LATE

CHAPTER I

Manya checked the number on the slip of paper and looked again at the house. Twenty-four Sienkiewicz Street. The building appeared intact but scarred, like so many others in this section of Warsaw. Twisted wrought-iron spokes dangled dangerously from a balcony on the second floor and a wedged wooden beam supported a side wall with a large, ominous crack down its middle. Scorch marks from the fires that had swept the city during the last months of fighting blackened the surrounding buildings. It was October, 1946, almost two years since the Germans had left, yet much of Poland still lay in ruins.

Manya scanned the streets for any sign that she was being followed. She searched the faces of the few people strolling by, trying to decide if they belonged in this quiet, residential neighborhood. She looked for a head disappearing behind a newspaper, a shadow moving in a doorway.

She heard quick footsteps and swung around. A woman with a parcel clasped to her side rushed toward her. Manya stood paralyzed, her vision blurred by fear. The woman passed and disappeared around the corner. Manya took a deep breath, pretending to read the piece of paper she clutched in her hand while she waited for her body to stop shaking. A thin web of moisture broke out above her lip.

There was still time to go back. She could act confused, then walk to another house. She could knock on the door and say she was looking for an old classmate. She could even stop at a nearby bookstore and buy a text she needed for her next university lecture. She plotted the moves, watching herself go through the motions as though performing for an invisible audience. A passing car startled her. She took in the street, empty, indifferent, and knew it was too late to turn back.

Mounting the steps of the house, she lifted the brass knocker. She tapped once, paused, then tapped three more times as she had been instructed. The lace curtain at the window moved and she heard a soft scuffle. When the door opened, a female face, half hidden in shadow, peered out at her. "*Amchu*," Manya whispered, using the Hebrew word for "our people." The door swung open and a slender woman, about thirty years old, stood before her. She wore a simple skirt and sweater, both of gray wool. Short, curly black hair framed a tired face, one that was rather plain except for the eyes, almond-shaped and thick-lashed. A Jewish face, Manya thought, until she saw the crucifix that hung from the woman's neck. She froze.

The woman put her fingers to her lips and beckoned her to enter. Manya followed, cautiously, and stopped for a moment inside the dim corridor while the woman slipped the crucifix inside her sweater and smiled.

She followed the woman down a hallway to a small parlor. The room was bare except for a desk, a few chairs and some maps and papers strewn on the floor. A window looked out onto a dusty courtyard. Scraps of Polish drifted down from other parts of the house, and then something that sounded like Czech. Surely, this was the headquarters of the Brichah, the Jewish underground, yet Manya's heart pounded as if she were being led to the Gestapo.

"I'm Tzili," the woman said and walked quickly to her desk. "Doctor Miskowski told me to expect you. How do you know him?"

"He was my family's physician before the war."

"And now?"

"And now what?"

"Is he still your family's physician?"

"My family is dead."

"The camps?" Tzili asked, leafing through her papers.

"My parents, yes."

Tzili looked up, waiting to hear more.

"My husband died six months ago."

"I know. The Doctor said you both worked for the Communists and he was killed by them shortly after the takeover."

"No, it wasn't an official killing," Manya said quickly. "There was a man in Joseph's group who hated him, hated Jews. He was jealous . . . some of the Jewish comrades got important jobs, he resented it . . . he became crazy . . . " She stopped, confused by her sudden outburst. She was still defending the Party, trying to convince this stranger that Joseph's death was not a conspiracy, but an aberration, the work of one man acting alone. Why, when she was through with all that, did it still matter?

"You want to leave then," Tzili said.

"Yes."

"Good." Tzili returned to her papers. "Europe is no place

for Jews. We'll get you to the Allied Zone and then to Palestine." She smiled briefly. "You came at a good time. We have a group leaving today. The borders are getting tight and we're trying to move as many people as possible." Tzili looked up. "Your face is white. Shall I go on?"

"Yes, go on," Manya replied. "I need to hear this." She reached for a nearby chair and sat down, holding on to the seat with both hands. There seemed not to be enough air to breathe. When she touched her damp forehead, she felt her hand shake. Tzili sat down next to her, her brown eyes momentarily filled with concern.

"Dr. Miskowski said you were very brave during the war."

"I'm not so brave now."

"You'll have to be. A long-time Party member. Someone who was with the Polish Underground. A teacher at the university, right? If you get caught, they'll be tougher on you than on an ordinary Jew." Tzili touched Manya's arm. "We have a good success rate. Hundreds of Jews are smuggled out every day. We've bribed the border guards and the worst thing the Americans will do is keep you in a shoddy DP camp before sending you on to a better one. They're not sending Jews back to the East anymore."

Manya gazed past Tzili to the window behind her. Outside a solitary elm rustled gently, breaking the sunlight into tiny gold fragments. Something urgent rose up within her and she wanted to talk. During the last six months she had moved like a stranger through the city she loved, speaking to no one, not even her friends, as though preparing herself for this inevitable separation. Now she wanted to free herself of the wordless weight she carried. "Leaving is not that easy."

"I would think it's staying that's hard. The Doctor told me someone tried to shoot you."

"Nationalists from the anti-Communist underground. They shot at me through my dining room window."

"Of course," Tzili said. "They hate you more than they hate the Russians. A Jew *and* a Communist. Not a winning combination in Poland."

"There's nothing for me any place I go," Manya said, unable to stop the words. "It was all lies, everything I grew up believing."

"Of course," Tzili said again.

"We were going to change the world, Joseph and I. That's what kept us going throughout the war. I thought when it ended, once the Soviets came, everything we had worked for would happen. Equality, justice, all those big words would start to mean something. But it didn't happen." She remembered the faces of the men who came to tell her Joseph was dead, and the look of relief that passed between them when they turned to leave. They had worked with her in the underground, those two, and now, when they were all free, Joseph had become expendable, one less Jew among their ranks. They never would have said so out loud, maybe not even let themselves think it, but she had seen it in their eyes. So what had the Communists changed?

"And now there's fear everywhere, spying," she continued. "People disappear every day for no reason — devoted people. Last week at headquarters I overheard a comrade ask for permission to go to Lvov to look for his missing father. My supervisor told him, 'Stalin is your father now,' and refused to give him a travel pass." She paused to swallow the tears that filled her throat. "It was going to be a new world for everyone." Tzili's face darkened, but Manya went on. "I'm not ashamed of it," she said, her voice rising. "I won't let people like you make me ashamed. You have your Palestine, I had my

5

beliefs. You think I was naive, and you're right. I'm no longer naive. So where does that leave me?"

"You want me to tell you that everything will be all right? Well, I don't know if it will. It's not all right with me. We're all in mourning, we all have the same nightmares. I choose to put aside the dead thoughts because I want to live, but I struggle every day," Tzili replied.

"But I don't want to go to Palestine."

Tzili stood up abruptly and walked to the desk. "Where do you think you can live? America? Argentina? Do you know why the Americans aren't sending back Jews from the Allied Zone anymore? Because they want to force England to let us into Palestine. And can you guess why? Because they're great humanitarians? No. Because they don't want us coming to America. Argentina? Haven't you heard about the warm welcome we get there? Any place you go, you'll be a Jew. You may as well be one in Palestine."

No, she couldn't go there. She wouldn't fit in. She was not a Jew, not really. Her parents had abandoned their religion when they moved to Warsaw to join the Party after their marriage in 1918. Palestine was not her fight. Nothing was now. "I don't know where I want to go. I just can't stay here."

Tzili slapped the papers down on the desk. "Enough! We have a group leaving today. Once you're out of Poland, you can decide."

A dark-haired young man suddenly leaned in the door. "Samuel finished the passports," he said. "We have fifteen."

"What's the route?" Tzili asked, all business.

"Danzig, Stettin. The trucks will meet us at the usual place in Berlin."

"How long before the train to Danzig?"

6

"Two hours. I'll tell Megged to get the group ready," he said and disappeared down the hallway.

Manya sat in her chair, alert, while the house suddenly came to life. She heard the man's footsteps bound up the stairs to the floor above and other steps rush to meet him.

Tzili began to move around the room, gathering papers from the floor and opening files. "Go home and pack a small bag," she said without looking up. "Take warm clothes. Germany is cold in October. And don't bring anything personal — and no photographs. You'll be searched by customs at all the checkpoints. Your passport will say you're Greek. Don't speak Polish. If the officials find anything, you'll be sent back." She got up and riffled through a folder, in a hurry now. "There's room for fifteen in this group, but each of us travels as if we're alone. If you're detained, no one will help you."

Manya stood up. "I can't leave in two hours," she said, filling with panic. "My things, my apartment. I've lived here all my life. No, I'll wait for the next group."

Tzili stopped for a moment. "Two hours is enough time to leave a cemetery."

A silence fell. Manya looked around the room for something to anchor her panic and found nothing. What was there, after all, to keep her in this country? Everyone she loved was dead — Joseph, her parents, her grandmother. She felt something stir and looked at her hands. There was still a pale circle on the finger where her wedding ring had been. Tzili was right. Two hours was enough.

CHAPTER 2

SHE SAT UP abruptly and rubbed her eyes. How long had she slept? No seam of light came through the truck's canvas flap. It was still night. A bolt of terror rammed her. It was taking too long to cross into the Allied Zone. They were going back to Poland and would all end up in prison. Heart pounding, Manya lay back in her narrow spot on the crowded floor. The man cradled next to her coughed and shifted position, scraping her cheek with the cuff of his heavy wool coat. The other refugees lay motionless, locked together in the blackness, unable to speak, barely able to move.

She closed her eyes and willed herself to relax, breathing slowly until her body grew calm. The pungent smell of sweat and old leather floated up and then the warmth of bodies, their heat rising through the grimy coats and blankets. From one corner, she heard someone's rasping breath, regular, even. From another, a soft moan rose above the sound of the wheels. And then stifled sobs. Night was the most difficult for her, for all the refugees. Trapped by the darkness, they travelled through space with nothing to ground them but their fear.

During the war Manya had discovered a way to calm herself whenever she felt the first wave of panic. She would lie in bed and listen for her neighbors — always strangers, since she moved to different parts of the city when she thought someone was becoming suspicious of her identity. It soothed her to think that others, so close, might be leading normal, ordinary lives and she tried to visualize their beds, soft and yielding, the smoothness of the enfolding blankets, their bodies moving over cool sheets. In a few moments she felt she had joined them. Calmed, she would fall asleep. Now, she closed her eyes and let her mind search for a comforting presence. An image presented itself: a man in the far corner drifting off to sleep and she beside him, her head cradled in his arm. Manya settled back and dozed.

The man next to her coughed again and jerked his blanket up to his mouth. She had noticed blood stains on it yesterday, when the truck stopped to let the refugees take a stretch. Each time he coughed she saw him glance nervously at Megged, their Brichah leader, who sat in the center of the floor. At the last train stop in Stettin, just before they had piled onto the truck that would take them through the Russian Zone of Germany into the American sector, Megged gathered them together for last-minute instructions. "Absolutely no sound," he said, repeating the sentences in Hebrew, Yiddish and Polish. "From now on we go through dangerous checkpoints. This truck is supposed to be carrying UN supplies to Landsberg in the US Zone. If we're caught now, we all get sent back to end up in a Russian jail." He glared at them while Tzili repeated his instructions in Hungarian. "Samuel will be sitting with you in the back. There is to be no sound. If anyone loses control, he has been instructed to knock them out. We can't risk the operation." Both of them delivered their speeches simply. There had been no words of encouragement, no reassurances, no apologies. None were needed.

The guides had told the refugees it would take two to three days to reach Berlin from Warsaw. There, a truck would be waiting and within one day they would be in Landsberg. But the trip had turned into two nights of silent terror, straining everyone's nerves, especially those of the people in charge of the mission. Something unexpected had happened. The truck had stopped every few hours and she'd heard fragments of conversations, sometimes in Hebrew, sometimes in Russian. The last time Megged had shouted angrily in English that he was a UN worker, and Manya knew they had been detained at a Soviet security post. After that, the truck sped along briefly, then screeched to a halt and she'd heard the scramble of feet on the road. New voices had barked exchanges in Hebrew. Then they had turned around and headed back in the opposite direction.

The truck came to a halt again. Manya sat up and rubbed her aching shoulder. "A short stretch," Megged whispered and the floor of the truck came alive. The man next to her tried to stand up, but began to cough as he staggered to his feet. Manya took his arm and helped him, then pulled him aside to let the people behind them jump down. He was too weak to walk and while the others took their silent march down the road, she stood with him and chewed the black bread and cheese Tzili handed them. He did not eat, this ashen faced, middle-aged man, but he did drink some of the water she urged on him. He sipped obediently, but he was beyond caring, unaware of the food or even her presence most of the time. She knew too, that none of the refugees would speak, even if allowed to. They were cut off from each other by terror and too many years of suffering. And what was there to say? Manya thought as she watched the disheveled group slowly moving through the autumn dusk. They were all going to the same place for the same reason and the answer to every question was there in the worn, desperate faces. Perhaps this was where the little they shared would end, in a remote village in Germany, moving further and further away from the dead past that bound them.

They had stopped in the middle of farm country. A small house and barn surrounded by fields of ripe corn stood in the distance. There had been no aerial bombardment here, and there were no signs of the terrible war that had been fought in this country. Manya had lived through the destruction of Warsaw by the Germans, endless nights of bombing and fire, and each day she had emerged from the shelter to find another piece of her city reduced to rubble. During that last year when she worked at the University, she had grown accustomed to moving through the broken, rubble-strewn streets until the chaos of the landscape became commonplace, normal. The serenity of this untouched countryside soothed and anguished her at the same time.

She walked toward the group, a faint outline in the failing light. For a moment, she heard the soft rustle of hay being spread in a nearby farm. She stopped. Her senses quickened and she could feel animals, cows probably, steaming in their wooden stalls as they settled their lumbering bodies. She could smell fertilizer, human and animal, mingle with the yielding earth. She was caught off guard by this tranquility and for a moment forgot her fear. She let herself listen to the earth, alive and brooding.

"Back in the trucks!" Megged said. "We're behind schedule." The refugees began to pile in. Manya grabbed a rope suspended from the canvas covering and hoisted herself up. She settled down again next to the coughing man. Then the wheels screeched forward and she sank into the familiar darkness.

The truck stopped abruptly. Heavy footsteps came towards them and they heard a scraping sound. The canvas flap whipped open and voices shouted to come out. Beams of light poured over the refugees. They bolted up, blinded and confused, clutching their blankets and small bags. Then they pushed toward the canvas opening where outstretched arms waited to lift them down. Once on the ground, soldiers motioned for them to keep moving. Soldiers were everywhere, their faces blurred by the searing lights. One came into focus and Manya made out an American uniform. They had made it.

The man she had helped suddenly appeared. "Where are we?" he whispered hoarsely. "Are they Americans?"

"Yes," she said breathlessly, filling with relief. "And see? These are UN people." She looked around at the barrack-like buildings barely visible under the dim street lamps. "We must be in Landsberg."

"Oh, my God" the man cried and fell to his knees. Once more, Manya helped him to his feet and holding on to his arm led him past the line of soldiers into the building.

Inside the barracks, the refugees huddled together in silent, waiting groups. A long table at one end of the room held a large urn and plates piled high with doughnuts. Manya ran her fingers through her hair, disentangling bits of straw, then smoothed down her coat collar. She watched a young soldier fill metal cups with steaming coffee and pass them to the refugees. Something in his impassive face riveted her, and she watched closely. This was just a job for him, she thought, one he had done every night for months, and he had grown used to seeing misery. He handed her a cup, but she just stood there, some of her old boldness returning, and waited for him to acknowledge her. When he glanced up, she was startled by his impersonal gaze. He made her feel invisible, reduced, as if all she had been and all she had lived through had left no mark. She had never considered herself beautiful, but she knew that her hazel eyes were appealing and her hair, even disheveled as it was now, fell in soft brown waves. In the soldier's eyes, she was not a young woman; she was just another refugee with no identity except her Jewishness. She grabbed the extended cup and pulled it sharply toward her, but the soldier moved on without noticing.

The man from the truck still held onto her. He gulped down his coffee while he scanned the room with nervous eyes. "I've lost my glasses," he said. A few minutes later a uniformed woman carrying a clipboard approached them. She was middle-aged and robust, and had an air of authority about her. The badge clipped to her lapel read, "Eleanor Weiss, UNRRA Staff."

"Your name and country of origin," she asked Manya in broken Polish, her pencil poised.

"Manya Gerson. Warsaw, Poland."

"Date of birth?"

"June 20, 1919."

"So that makes you twenty-seven," the woman muttered, jotting down the information. "Living family members?"

"None."

The woman looked up briefly, appraising her. "Were you an inmate of a German concentration or labor camp?"

"No," she replied, enunciating the words clearly. "I had

forged identity papers and I lived as a Pole in different parts of Warsaw during the war. I worked in a paint factory."

"How did you manage that?"

"The underground got me working papers."

"Any distant relatives who might be looking for you?"

"No."

Miss Weiss turned toward the man, but before she could speak he blurted out, "My name is Isaac Flamb and I was born in Vilna, Lithuania." He spoke quickly and began to cough. "My wife might still be alive," he said, still holding onto Manya for support. "We were both in Theresiendstadt when the camp was liberated." Miss Weiss tried to interrupt him, but he rushed on, his hands shaking with excitement, coffee splashing down the front of his coat. "I went back to Vilna right away, but I couldn't find her. Please, do you have a Hinda Flamb on your list? Hinda Flamb. Please, write it down. She is a small woman, only so high, forty years old . . ." He turned to Manya. "I know she survived, they didn't take her on the march because she was too sick."

"You can go to the Tracing Bureau in the morning and they'll help you," Miss Weiss said and patted his arm. "Just let me finish this and everyone will be able to rest." She lifted her clipboard and continued. "Date of birth?"

"March 14, 1900."

"Any other relatives who may be looking for you?"

The man looked at the floor. "I don't know. We have such a large family, maybe. There are the Rothmans and the Danzigers on my mother's side. Write that down! Rothmans, Danzigers. Do you have them on the list?" He straightened up, trying to see the clipboard.

"Yes, yes, it will all be taken care of tomorrow," Manya said, firmly.

Miss Weiss gave her a grateful smile, moved on to the next person and repeated the same question over and over. Toward the end of the line she stopped in front of a tall, pale man wearing steel-rimmed glasses. He spoke in a quiet, but distinct voice that caught Manya's attention. He had an accent and when she heard him identify himself as "Emmanuel Kozak," she guessed he was Czech. He looked as tired as the others, but he leaned in solicitously as he spoke to Miss Weiss, giving the interview the air of an easy exchange rather than an interrogation. Something in the rhythm and intonation of his speech reminded her of Joseph, who had always commanded authority without needing to raise his voice.

An hour later, they were all led to an adjoining room filled with cots. A few of the refugees lay down immediately, but most remained seated on the edge of their beds, as tense and alert as if they might be summoned to return to Warsaw.

An hour later Miss Weiss returned, positioned herself in the middle of the room, and lifted her hand for attention. "This displaced persons' camp is administered by UNRRA, the United Nations Relief and Rehabilitation Agency, and the US Military Government," she announced in English while a partner translated into Polish and Hungarian. "In the morning you will be processed at the camp's military head-quarters before you can be officially admitted. Then you will be issued a ration card and assigned a place to live and the JDC, the American Joint Distribution Committee, will give you supplies and a monthly stipend for as long as you are here." Manya saw her stop to take in the weary faces dutifully turned toward her. She looked sympathetic but tired, as if she had witnessed this scene too often and it was losing its drama. Something about her reminded Manya of the Soviet woman who had taken over the university in the early months after the German defeat. Miss Weiss looked official, humorless, sensible. She looked like someone who expected people to behave. Manya realized this was the first American woman she had ever met, and yet she seemed all too familiar.

Miss Weiss strode quickly to the barracks door. "It will be daylight soon. Sleep if you can." She hesitated as if she had forgotten something and turned back to look at the group. "Everything will be all right," she said, addressing the doubt in their faces. Then she turned off the overhead lights and left.

Manya lay back on her cot with her arms beneath her head and stared into the anonymous darkness. Sighs filled the room and then some muffled sobs as though the refugees were still afraid to cry out loud. "It's good to cry," she remembered her grandmother saying when the village children made fun of Manya because she didn't understand their Yiddish. "Tears clear the eyes," she had said smoothing Manya's hair from her wet cheeks, "and then you can see better."

The room fell quiet. Somewhere a door slammed and the murmur of voices dissolved into the night. She slept.

CHAPTER 3

MANYA HAD BEEN WAITING for several hours before the soldier called her name. She missed it at first, unused to the American's strange pronunciation, and when he repeated it louder, as if all the refugees in the small room were deaf or stupid, she jumped. She straightened her creased skirt, looked around the crowded anteroom of Landsberg's Military Headquarters and stood up.

The GI held open the door to the adjoining room and she saw an officer seated at a desk. He was middle-aged with gray hair cut close around an equally gray face. He was trying to smooth out the make-shift identity papers that she had given to Miss Weiss the night before. He was not having much success.

"I'm told you speak English."

"Yes, a bit."

"Where did you learn it?"

"At university. I was good at languages and I hoped one day to . . . "

He cut her off. "Why did you leave Poland?"

"Because the Poles were still killing the Jews. They killed my husband. I thought everyone knew about the pogroms."

"That's what all the Jewish refugees say. But you went to work for the Soviets right after they occupied Poland. That means you had privileges, money. A year later you leave. Why?"

She closed her eyes for a moment to let her fatigue settle itself. She would have to tell it all again, how the first year of the Soviet regime had changed nothing, how she could no longer live among the Poles with their ancient hatreds. It made no difference to her neighbors that she was Comrade Manya instead of Mrs. Gerson. They hated her just the same — even more.

She looked at the officer's impassive face. She knew he had heard too many of these stories and was weary of them. He was looking for Communist spies infiltrating the American Zone. That's all the officials were interested in — something exciting to break the monotony of their jobs. He could easily send her back to sit in a Russian jail forever.

"I left Poland because I was afraid for my life," she said. "Before the war, the Poles hated me because I was Jewish, and then they hated me because I was a Communist. Now they hate me for being both."

The officer leaned back in his chair and took her in for a long moment. She saw him run his eyes down her body. When he saw her color, he barked at her.

"Where's your family?"

She paused to contain her anger. "Where do you think?" she muttered between her teeth.

He leaned towards her. "All I did was ask you a simple question and you spit back an answer as if we were personally responsible for killing your family. Who do you think you are, streaming into this zone, getting fed and clothed, charity cases all of you. If you want a ration card and papers, just answer my questions."

"I'm told my parents were in Belzec."

"Where's that?"

"An extermination camp in central Poland. They all died there. I survived the war with false identity papers."

"How do I know you're not a Pole who collaborated with the Nazis? Or maybe you're working for the Soviets. You have no official papers. The Brichah people take out anyone who says they're Jewish. If you want to stay, prove you're a Jew."

For a moment she wanted to laugh. After years of hiding her Jewishness from the Nazis, she now had to prove she was a Jew. But she had nothing, no number on her arm, no Yiddish expressions, no prayers she could recite. Her family had been assimilated, more comfortable reading Polish translations of Karl Marx than Sholom Aleichem. They had not been Jews or Poles, and their only devotion had been to the Communist Party line.

"Why should I prove I am Jewish? Jews can be spies too," she said. Suddenly, she felt everything slipping away. She knew what she had to do. She opened her hands slowly, as if to offer him a gift. Their eyes locked in a silent exchange. "But I am nothing now," she said softly. "You tell me what I am."

A soldier brought in a sandwich of chipped beef and a bottle of wine and placed a long-stemmed glass on the edge of the desk near her. Manya watched him slowly fill the goblet to the top with a beautiful burgundy liquid. The officer was standing at the window with his back to her.

"Dismiss the others," he said. "Reschedule for tomorrow."

Manya ate and drank in silence. During the war, even

when she was numb with terror, she was able to eat, as if her body knew better than she what it needed. She bit into the crusty white bread and savored the moist layers of warm beef. It had been a long time since she had tasted meat. And the wine helped. The officer must have known it would and she was grateful to him for that.

He turned to face her. "There's a hotel in town," he said. "I'll bring the clearance papers."

His words were jagged, without warmth, without any acknowledgment of her as a human being. She could feel him watching her, but she didn't hurry. When she was finished she slowly wiped her mouth on the cloth napkin, then toyed with the wine glass while she considered her next move.

He walked toward her and stood next to her chair with his hand on the desk. She could feel his impatience.

"May I have another glass of wine?" she asked.

He hesitated a moment, then picked up the bottle.

"Just a little bit," she said touching the glass and keeping her eyes averted. "Won't you have some too?" Her voice sounded strange, even and strong, with just the right hint of flirtatiousness. She swallowed hard. Where did this come from?

"No," he said. "I don't drink."

She sipped the wine, then got up. No, she wouldn't let them send her back. "Shall we go?" she said. She walked toward him and the officer took her by the elbow. But she shook him off, straightened herself and headed toward the door alone.

The covered jeep sped over the Karolinen Bridge, which connected the Landsberg DP camp to Landsberg itself, a medieval town surrounded by the Lech river. Manya leaned back in the seat and watched the streets go by. The officer sat with his head turned toward the window, his dry, freckled hands resting on his knees. The skin on the back of his neck was wrinkled and red where his hair had been clipped. "It'll be over quickly," she thought, surprised at the steadiness of her own hands as she smoothed back her hair from her face.

By the time they arrived at the small, neat hotel discreetly tucked on a side street off the main plaza, she had grown accustomed to the quiet. The driver opened the jeep door for them and they walked into the lobby. The walls were covered in old wallpaper of barely discernible hunting scenes and a ragged Persian-style rug lay in the center of an otherwise empty room. A young German woman at the front desk stood up abruptly when they came through the door and, without saying a word, handed the officer a large brass key. Manya followed him up a flight of stairs and into a room that seemed to be all bed. He put his arms around her awkwardly and closed his eyes, ready to kiss her mouth. She turned her head away and he ended up kissing her on the cheek instead. There was something intrinsically affectionate about the kiss, even if unintended, and for a moment tears sprang into her eyes. But the officer pulled her onto the bed without comment and made no further attempt to disguise the nature of their exchange. He was hungry to get inside her and be done with it. She heard a tearing sound and looked away while he slipped on a condom. Throughout the brief, tortured transaction, she lay still, afraid that if she moved or spoke, she would hit him and ruin her last chance for shelter. She tried to control her racing thoughts, to conjure up another time or place, but felt herself riveted to the man's body, not just by his weight but by the medicinal smell of the army soap that permeated his clothes, his hair, the clumsy hands that groped at her breasts.

Nothing about this act was familiar to her, not the rough skin rubbing against her, nor the quick hard thrusts that made her wince.

The American began to moan. Manya squeezed her eyes shut and tried not to think of Joseph. She had never been frivolous about sex and had slept with only one man, a fellow student, before her marriage. Now, she surprised herself. She could eat when she was afraid and she could let this contemptible American force himself on her. Her body seemed to have a will of its own that bypassed thought, fear and her hatred of the man who was moving on top of her. She wondered how many refugee women were willing to do this, how many he had used. Didn't he get enough from the German women who were said to like the Americans so much?

The officer grunted once and rolled over. She pulled her dress down and sat up while he fumbled with his belt. Afterwards, he seemed too embarrassed to face her and slipped the stamped papers and taxi money onto the night table while she was in the bathroom. When she realized he was gone, she filled the tub and methodically scrubbed his antiseptic odor from her skin. Then she lay in the warm water, relieved. She felt no shame, only anger. And, suddenly, weariness. She closed her eyes and leaned back against the cool porcelain. When she looked again, the grayness had deepened in the small window above her.

CHAPTER 4

THE TAXI LEFT MANYA at the entrance to the DP camp. She stepped up to the two guards posted at the gate and handed them her papers. "Where is Number 4, please?" she asked in her best English.

The GIs leaned in to examine her pass. They looked so young with their fresh, smooth faces, like boys playing soldiers. "About five blocks that way," the taller one said and pointed behind him.

"Blocks?" she asked.

"Streets," he added and flashed the straight set of white teeth all Americans seemed to have.

Manya looked behind them at a cluster of official buildings. Most were dark. Further off, she could make out lines of barracks separated from each other by narrow walkways. "Thank you," she said and walked through the gate.

Both soldiers stepped aside and touched their hats. "Any time," they said. There was a cheerfulness in their tone that caught her attention. She looked back for a moment, and the tall one winked. Manya turned away quickly, startled by this forwardness, and hurried toward the barracks.

The street lights came on, casting an amber glow across

the two-story brick buildings. Manya walked the deserted streets until she found Barracks Number Four. For a moment she stopped to look at the homemade banner hanging across the front. It read, "Weizmann House." She opened the heavy door and entered. The building looked like a make-shift hospital ward crammed with army cots. Small windows, many of them broken, lined the walls, and bare bulbs dangled from the ceilings. This was her new home.

Some of the refugees had strung blankets and sheets around their beds to create a little privacy. At the far end of the room were the communal bathrooms and toilets, filthy from over-use. Thirty cots in one room. Thirty people living together in a space intended for ten. She walked over to an unmade bed and stood a moment to take in what she assumed would become her corner: a narrow cot and straw-filled sack for a mattress, a wooden footlocker, like a coffin, standing on its side and a metal crate with a single dirty glass on top of it. She sighed and sat down.

"Welcome," someone behind her said in Yiddish. A thin woman, about sixty years old, materialized beside her. She wore a flowered dress several sizes too big and a tattered black shawl. Her short, gray hair was pinned to each side of her head. She looked like a school girl disguised as an old woman.

"Thank you," Manya replied in Polish.

The woman's eyes hardened. "This is an all-Jewish camp," she said in heavily accented Polish. "Do you belong here? What are you?"

"I belong here," Manya answered, "but I don't know much Yiddish. We didn't speak it at home. Only my grandmother." This seemed to reassure the woman and she smiled, exposing broken brownish teeth.

"You will learn. You will have to, you know. People don't

like to hear too much Polish," she said. She motioned toward the open room and looked about with pride. "Do you know what house you're in? 'Weizmann House.' We named it. Isn't it wonderful?"

Manya looked again at the dilapidated room filled with worn bedding and the pitiful accumulation of displaced lives. "Wonderful," she said.

The woman paused, trying to decide what to make of Manya's irony. Finally, she nodded. "I know it isn't perfect. It isn't Palestine, it isn't my house in Feilda," she said firmly. "But it isn't Auschwitz."

Auschwitz again, always Auschwitz. There had been so many ways of killing Jews, so many ways to die, so many camps just as monstrous, but this one had become the most prestigious, as if it were a renowned university. Her parents had died in a remote crematorium in central Poland. Belzec wasn't the famous Auschwitz, but they had ended up the same way.

The woman spoke again. "My name is Rochel Mandelkern. I'm from a village near Lodz. You see, I can speak Polish. We had a notions store in town and many Polish customers. Yiddish we spoke at home. It was a nice home, I kept a kosher home and every shabbos . . . " She stopped. "Forgive me. I won't tell you everything about me in five seconds. You just came. You need supplies and you have to eat." She sat on the cot next to Manya's. "It's nice to have a pretty young face to look at. What is your name? Where are you from?"

"Manya Gerson. I'm from Warsaw."

Rochel nodded as though she had known this all along. Then she reached out to clasp Manya's cold hand in both of hers. "Let me finish praying and we'll get you some things from the supply room. Then we'll go to the dining hall. That's why nobody's here. It's dinner time."

Rochel quickly turned and picked up a torn prayer book, draped her shawl over her head, and began to sway. Manya averted her eyes as the strange, ancient murmuring filled the barracks. She fixed on one of the grimy windows nearby and watched the first dim stars appear in the east.

Manya pulled her thin coat across her body and stepped out into the cool dusk with Rochel. Small groups of refugees, mostly men, clustered at corners. They looked so much alike in their caps and brown trousers; they could have been in uniform. They were gaunt and unhealthy looking, although it was over a year since the liberation of the concentration camps. A few turned and gazed at her impassively, while others made their quick appraisal with suspicious eyes. The older woman pulled Manya past them without a glance.

Rochel stopped at a wooden building a few streets from the barracks gate. Inside a man with a deep scar on his forehead greeted them and began chatting in Yiddish. Rochel urged Manya forward and said something that made the man nod and disappear behind a counter.

"Benjamin is a very good man," Rochel said, "He makes sure everybody gets what they need. Tell him if you want more supplies. He'll get them for you."

"It's all right."

"No," Rochel insisted. "You mustn't be shy. Tell him, my child. He has to be careful because of the regulations, but he tries to help us. He got me extra blankets because my blood is not good since I came out of the camps and I always feel the cold."

Benjamin returned, carrying a large cardboard box which

he ceremoniously placed before Manya. Inside was a ration card for the mess hall, a coarse blanket, a towel, a toothbrush and tooth powder, a cake of yellow soap, and a comb. She stared at this small collection of toiletries. How little we need to start a new life, she thought, just a few things to make us clean. The antiseptic odor of the American officer came back to her. "It's behind me," she thought. "I'll never think of this afternoon again." She resolved, not to draw attention to herself, to be like the others, to blend in. For five years she had worried about passing for Aryan, about smiling back at the German soldiers who patrolled the streets of Warsaw. And even when she worked for the Party, she worried if a new hair style made her look too frivolous and vain, not enough like a committed comrade.

"This will do," she said.

Rochel saw her dejected face. "Don't worry," she said. "When you're settled, you'll see. There are better things you'll get, a lipstick, some powder. You can trade with the Americans. They get things. And you'll be able to buy things in town with your monthly stipend from the JDC. We get packages from them, too. We'll find you something pretty." She stood back and clapped her hands together. "You have such a nice figure, the dresses will look good on you. Don't worry."

Manya gazed into Rochel's eager eyes and knew exactly the life that lay behind them. She remembered women like her from her grandmother's village. Crowded into her grandmother's small kitchen they would pick over her life, as if it were a garment whose merits they were debating. They argued about how she should live, berated her for not visiting more often, and scolded her for wasting time at the university. Then they would pat her hair and push a plate of crumbling honey cake toward her, muttering how pretty she was and what a shame to be without a husband. Their relentless bustling wore her out, but she always sat quietly, out of love for her grandmother, and let them have their say. Their lives were hard, limited. But she also felt in them a generosity of spirit. She knew that all they needed was one word, one signal from her and they would try to transform an urbane, irreligious young woman into a proper Jewish child.

"This will do," Manya said again and picked up her box.

When Manya and Rochel returned to the barracks, the women of Weizmann House were preparing for bed and the room was filled with the sound of muted female voices. Heads turned when they entered and hands extended in greeting as Rochel ushered her from cot to cot. "This is Manya Gerson," Rochel said, slightly breathless with eagerness. "She's from Warsaw. She was a professor at the University." All the older women looked much the same — brittle, gray-haired, their bodies covered with random pieces of clothing. Those who had lived near Warsaw questioned her excitedly, hoping for a scrap of news about a missing relative. Where did she live, did she know so and so, was she one of the Gersons who owned a furniture store?

"No," Manya replied over and over again, "I'm sorry I don't know those people." "No, I didn't attend synagogue." It was impossible; she still wasn't part of the group, even here. They mistrusted her Warsaw Polish. She was a stranger still: a Jewish woman who had stayed behind in hateful Poland, living somehow, while they and their families suffered death and abomination.

She began to spread the linens that had been left for her on a nearby chair. One of the younger women drifted toward her cot and stood shyly watching. "It's not so bad here once you get used to the waiting," said Tovah, round-hipped, petite, with black eyes too big for her face. She seemed eager to talk. "You'll see," she said, patting Manya's arm. "The British will say yes any day now and we'll be on our way to Palestine." Manya nodded wearily and continued to spread the frayed sheets across her lumpy mattress.

Rochel sat and watched Manya place her comb and toothbrush on the night stand. "Would you like some more bread?" she asked. "I'll get some from the dining room. You're thin, you have to keep strong." She stood and began to help smooth the blanket. "There are nice men here, educated, good Jewish men you'll like. You'll find someone. You have time, you can make a family."

"I'm not hungry and I'm not interested in finding a man." Manya took the blanket from Rochel, shoved a corner of it under the mattress, and slid into bed. Despite herself, she sniffed antiseptic soap again.

"Don't say this, child. You will see how they will flock to you. One day you will have children. You are healthy and you must stay healthy." Rochel turned toward the entrance. "I'll get you something for later. I'm always hungry at night when the cold wakes me up. It's nice to put a piece of bread in your mouth."

"Stop it. I don't want anything," Manya whispered, not wanting to make a scene in front of the others. She turned to Rochel, the heat rising in her cheeks. "Please. Leave me alone. I am not like you. I never was." Her voice rose. "I am not waiting to go to Palestine. Can you understand this?"

The murmur of women's voices stopped and a silence filled the barracks. Rochel looked startled, then waved her hand dismissively. "Just sleep, Manyale. Tomorrow I'll ask

29

Benjamin for another blanket. It's cold here at night and it's hard to sleep." She turned toward her own bed. "Here. Take this one for now. I have many. Put it over your shoulders. It will help."

Manya lay still while Rochel fussed with the blanket. The room filled again with the sound of rustling clothes and the creak of cots as the women undressed and got into bed. One by one, they turned off the lights and the barracks fell into darkness. In a few minutes, she sensed the older woman's presence hovering near by, coming closer until she could smell her stale breath. As she turned her head away, Rochel bent and kissed her lightly on the cheek. Manya pulled the covers tightly around her neck, twisted herself into a ball, and tried to sleep.

A tug at her arm woke her and she opened her eyes. Standing over her, Rochel looked older in the harsh morning light, her sunken cheeks a mass of fine lines. "Wake up, dear, you'll miss breakfast. We have to eat, then you can go to the office," she said. "You have to list your name with the Tracing Bureau so your people can find you."

Manya sat up. The barracks was filled with light and disarray. Women's clothes were everywhere, slips, bras, panties hanging on lines strung across beams. These lines were their closets, exposed for everyone to see. Most of the undergarments were of rough cotton, but a few satin pieces, washed to shreds, looked as if they had once been costly. The gray light cast an institutional tinge over everything. She glanced up at the high ceiling and saw that it was spotted with water stains.

She had slept deeply, without dreaming, but not enough, and now she felt leaden. She pushed herself off the bed, gathered her toiletries, and stumbled to the washroom, her bare feet cold on the wooden floor. Inside, she glanced at the small mirror on the wall and stepped back abruptly. She was not vain, but her sleep-swollen face made her catch her breath. It was gray and puffy. She touched a large, red spot on her cheek where the American officer's beard had chafed her. She recalled one evening at a student café when she had been introduced to an overly intense young poet, a minor celebrity among her Warsaw circle. His studied detachment had annoyed her so much that she made it a point to capture his attention. She had finally let him kiss her in a darkened corner of the café even though his stubby beard irritated her mouth and cheeks. Once he was trapped, she had lied to him in order to go home alone. She was not given to these kinds of bourgeois theatrics and afterwards she felt deceitful, cheap — just as she did now. When she met Joseph a few months later and knew that she loved him, she had been relieved that she would never be tempted to betray herself again. Now, she pressed her cold fingers to her inflamed cheek. She would not regret the American officer.

She washed quickly, splashing her face and neck with cold, rusty water. She returned to her cot, pulled her suitcase from under the bed and changed into a plain blue dress. She was suddenly very hungry.

"Do we eat in the same place as last night?" she asked, turning her back to Rochel to slip on the dress. There would be no privacy from now on.

"Yes. We take all our meals there." Rochel smiled coyly. "When you get to know the place better you can bring some things in for snacks. But you have to be careful," she said, lowering her voice. "They don't like us to eat here. They say it dirties the place."

"Who were *they*," Manya wondered. Everyone she had seen last night had been in uniform, the soldiers, the UN people; even the refugees in the dining room had worn military coats. Something about the way the men carried themselves told her it was the fashion as well as necessity. She slipped on her own thin brown coat, nodded to Rochel and walked toward the door.

Outside a metallic-gray sky hung thick with clouds. She could smell snow. The two women bent their heads against the November wind and walked the cobblestone street in silence.

The Landsberg Camp was big. Row after row of orderly brick-red barracks lined a square mile of streets. The buildings looked clean and well maintained, at least from the outside. The Germans had designed these quarters for their cavalry officers before the First World War. They were meant to be simple and functional, but they had an air of imposing authority as well. As they hurried past the installations, Manya saw all had white banners boldly strung across the front. One read "Herzl House", the next "Ben Gurion House." She smiled at "Roosevelt House" — he was a man of mythic proportions among the DPs. Well, at least they still had heroes. Rochel explained that right after the war ended all displaced people had been housed together. But conflicts had erupted almost immediately between the Eastern European gentiles and the Jewish survivors. The Jews had demanded separate quarters, and the Americans, as well as the British, decided it would be best for everyone if the two groups lived apart. Landsberg was an all-Jewish camp, she said, one of many throughout the Allied Zone.

Rochel led her up the steps to the mess hall and pushed open the door. A rush of noise engulfed them. The room was filled with the clatter of metal plates and trays, hundreds of people yelling to be heard above the din. Men and women sat at long wooden tables strewn with empty coffee cups, discarded scraps of bread, and overflowing ashtrays. As Manya walked down the crowded aisles, scraps of different languages floated toward her, like pieces of interrupted music. It reminded her of the summer camp she had attended as a child, a political camp for young Communists. She smiled at the thought.

"You see, I said that you'd feel better in the morning," Rochel chirped. She steered Manya to an empty chair. "Put your coat on the seat," she ordered, "or we won't have a place. There's not much work so people sit here all day long, and there's not enough room for everyone."

Rochel was in her element. Pulling Manya after her, she elbowed her way past a woman about to reach for a cup and grabbed two plates. She stacked them with black bread and stale-looking doughnuts and, scooping up little patties of margarine, placed them on top of the pile.

"What's this?" Manya asked, peering into a large metal can filled with tan-colored goo. She looked at the label. "Peanut Butter?"

Rochel made a face. "Have you ever seen such a thing? And look at this." Rochel pointed to another can full of corn kernels floating in a whitish liquid. "They tell us it's healthy, but no one eats it. They think we'll get tired of plain bread. No one does. You can't have enough bread, can you?" She sat down. "Tell me," she asked, "was your mother a good cook?" She paused, as though the question might offend.

"I don't really know. She didn't cook much." Her parents were always running out to Party meetings and it seemed as if she had spent her childhood sitting at their dining room table, alone, waiting for them to come home. And when they did return, it was usually late, her mother arguing loudly over the merits of the lecture they had heard, her father shushing her, afraid the neighbors would learn of their Communist affiliation. Even as a child she sensed the bond between her gentle, thoughtful father and the tempestuous woman whom he adored but did not respect. She had been a force, her big-boned, athletic mother, and it was the very danger she posed, so contrary to her husband's diffident nature, that repelled and drew him at the same time. They would sit with their glasses of tea and haggle over their ideological differences, and only when their argument got heated would they turn to her, always with questions about school. What were they teaching her? What did her teachers say about the Soviets?

When she was quite small, they decided they couldn't trust themselves to teach her proper Marxist theory and sent her to summer camp on the outskirts of Warsaw. Every year until she was seventeen and entered university, they shipped her off to learn the Party line and do outdoor calisthenics no matter what the weather. But in truth, she loved it. She willingly grew into the daughter they wanted, and she would not blame them now for her bitterness.

"I wish I could make some good soup," Rochel said absently. "They give us something watery and call it soup. But you had it last night, remember? Terrible, terrible! How can anyone get healthy with food like this?"

Manya had been too distracted with fatigue last night to notice much of anything. She did remember Rochel putting a full plate in front of her and a cup of hot brown liquid called "Ovaltine," and then she became sleepy. Manya rubbed her neck. For a moment the officer's face rose up before her again, but she pushed it away. She spread some margarine on a piece of bread with the back of her spoon and turned to Rochel, glad to have someone near.

"Do you pray every night?"

"And every morning," Rochel replied, eager for conversation.

"And your family?"

"A brother in Argentina. He went there in 1933, to make a living. He was going to send for his wife and two children when he had enough money, but they were all deported and died in the camps. Last month the Landsberg Committee found him in Buenos Aires and I wrote to him that I want to come. After all, we are the only ones left of the whole family. But I don't know yet. I am waiting for papers."

"I thought you wanted to go to Palestine," Manya said.

Rochel swallowed hard. "I would have gone right after the war, if the British had let us. Now, I have no fight left. I don't want to die on an illegal boat. You have read about them?" She spoke quickly, not waiting for a reply. "And what kind of life would I have? I have no family. I can be of no use. It's too late for me." She paused and turned to Manya, her eyes shining. "But you can go. There are people here who can help you. I'll introduce you."

Manya finished her coffee and stood up. "Thank you for your help. I think I'll go back now." She started to move toward the door when a tall man in a cap and a leather jacket approached them.

"Rochel," he said smiling. "Is this someone new? Did she come with the Polish group the other night?"

"Manya," Rochel said. "Come meet someone. He's a big wheel here. He works for the Joint in the immigration office."

Manya stopped and retraced her steps. The man extended

his hand and she took it. He shook it hard, surveying her face.

"Bolek Holzer," he said. "Welcome."

"Thank you."

"Are you settled yet?"

"I think so." She looked at Rochel. "I've been taken to the warehouse and I'm being looked after."

"I hope the Joint people treated you well."

"The Joint?"

"It's our nickname for the Joint Distribution Committee, the American Jews who take care of us."

"But she hasn't registered with the Tracing Bureau yet," Rochel interjected.

"I'm not looking for anyone. I tried to locate an uncle right after the war, but no luck. Everyone else is dead."

Bolek pushed his cap back off his forehead and ran his hand through a mass of black curls. "So many deaths, so many people alone. But you never know, someone might have survived, a distant cousin perhaps. Put your name down, just in case." He began to button his jacket. "Come. I'll take you."

She thought of her Uncle Jacob and the endless papers she had sent out looking for him, all returned stamped "Fate Unknown." She would not go down that path again. This Bolek was waiting to escort her and Rochel was hovering at his side. Manya wanted to run. Since the moment she arrived she had not been alone. She was tired of people ordering her about, asking her questions without caring about the answers. She turned to both of them. "No thank you. It's not necessary," she said and pushed her way down the crowded aisles. At a nearby table a group of breakfasters turned their heads, their cups suspended, as she rushed past.

The clouds had broken up and sunshine fell in warm circles on the street. Manya breathed in the cold, fresh air and walked, letting her anger subside. Ahead she saw the same groups of men as last night standing on the street corners, cigarettes dangling from their lips, each with a newspaper tucked under his arm. A few people on bicycles rode by, small paper-wrapped packages protruding from their baskets. She passed a group of men and women crowded around a bulletin board in front of the Red Cross office. Surprisingly, there were no soldiers. She bent her head against the wind and walked, stomping from corner to corner, as if the simple act of putting her feet on the pavement would drive out the strangeness of the place and make it her own. After a while she found herself following the endless rows of barracks to see where they would lead.

She came to the Karolinen Bridge she had driven over the day before. It was old and ornate and curved gracefully over the river. She walked across. There were few cars except for an occasional army vehicle, and some pedestrians, refugees she imagined going to do business with the Germans who needed special passes to enter the DP camp. On the other side, all the streets seemed to fan out from the Hauptplatz, the main square. She headed up a narrow cobblestoned lane, turned a corner and stopped. Before her were several shops and a café. On the opposite side of the street stood small, single-family houses, their curtains neatly drawn against the sun. People hurried past her, bundled in warm clothes, moving with purpose. This was the real Landsberg, a small German town where life went on just as it had before the war.

Manya stepped up to the café and stared through the steamy window. She longed to sit down and drink coffee and think. Her head would clear, now that she was alone, now that she had nothing to fear, and she would make sense of the present. She walked inside. A few women sat chatting in subdued tones, their coats draped over their shoulders. Behind the counter a heavy-set man in a dark blue cardigan poured steamed milk into a cup and carefully placed a slice of sugared pound cake onto a plate. She went up to the nearest table and squeezed into a chair. The world seemed almost normal.

"Bitte?"

A waitress in a flour-streaked apron was standing over her.

"Kaffe," Manya replied. Suddenly she realized she had no money. She stood up abruptly and pushed passed the waitress to the door, shaking her head and patting the empty pockets of her coat. Outside, she scanned the streets, confused and disoriented. When she spotted the Karolinen Bridge, she looked past it to the dim outline of the barracks in the distance. The buildings stood on a rise above the town, silent, defiant, a self-designated ghetto. Two women in the café's window seat gazed out at her as she hunched her shoulders and slowly started back toward the camp.

CHAPTER
5

BOLEK PICKED UP SOME PAPERS from the pile on his desk and swung his chair around, letting his eyes adjust to the writing on the application. Another refugee applying for immigration, this one to South Africa. Each day there were more requests for visas to the US, to Argentina, to Australia. The DPs were becoming desperate. It worried him. At this rate, there would be no one left to go to Palestine. He looked at the empty desk across the room and wished that Yankl was there. Yankl had arrived in Landsberg with the first transport of survivors from Flossenberg, a nearby Nazi labor camp, in May 1945. Bolek had come with the Brichah that same week. A month later they were both working for the Joint. At first Bolek was not happy sharing an office with an orthodox Jew who wrapped *tfillin* around his arms and head in the morning and swayed at the east window three times a day. But Yankl was funny and smart. If he were here now, Yankl would cheer him up. He would dismiss his fears with a wave of his hand, and tell him again not to worry so much. "So what if this DP went to South Africa instead of Eretz Israel?" he would ask. "Within a week, he'd own a diamond mine, give his wife the gaudiest gem first, then send the real beauties, the most valuable stones to Palestine." But Yankl was in Munich picking up new Joint workers and wouldn't be back for two days.

The previous year, when Bolek first started working for immigration, there had been few visa applications. The refugees expected the Palestinian blockade to end any day, and they searched the newspapers and bulletin boards for some sign that the Allies, in their infinite wisdom, had worked out a plan to let them into Palestine. He could not walk down the street without being surrounded by DPs demanding he tell them what he knew. He never told them he knew as little as they. Instead, he always said the same thing: "Why do you need permission? Are you waiting for the British and Americans the way you waited for them in the death camps? Leave. Now!"

At first, when he delivered his little speech, he would see a reaction, at least temporarily: a certain straightening of the body, a slight lifting of the chin that told him he had stirred what remained of their courage. But things had changed. The newspapers were full of details about how the British were now seizing illegal boats full of Jews trying to land in Palestine and dumping passengers into bleak holding pens on Cyprus. Stories drifted back about the unspeakable conditions on the island, the heat and lack of food, the typhus epidemics. Now, whenever he gave his speech, refugees stuffed their hands in their pockets and stared at their feet, as if their shoes were suddenly of great interest. A few continued to question him out of politeness, but because he could no longer bear to see the shame on their faces that told him they planned to go elsewhere, he ignored them.

A jeep pulled up outside and Bolek heard two GIs leap out and head toward the PX. He could make out a few

English words amid their laughter: beer, sweetie, Jerry girls. It was late morning and they were returning from overnight leave. They would go to buy chocolate or nylon hose, perhaps extra cartons of cigarettes, little gifts for the friendly Fräuleins they had slept with the night before. It stung him, not so much because he felt betrayed by the Americans — he understood their needs — but because it reminded him of his own youth when he had made love to Polish girls who didn't know or care that he was Jewish, when he still believed that class and race didn't matter, and that love could make everything possible. In his adolescence, he had had a fondness for American novels because they were filled with those romantic notions. The English were more realistic. They didn't mix classes, even in their fiction, or if they did, they made sure the endings were tragic.

From where he sat, Bolek could watch the soldiers romp down the street, nudging each other. They acted as if the Allied Occupation was a party and only the refugees were spoiling the fun. He thought of them with the Fräuleins and his throat tightened. Children, idiots to believe they could be admired by women whose husbands and brothers had been their enemies. When he slept with the Fräuleins it was because he wanted to degrade them, to convince them he found them irresistible, beautiful, and then to bed them as if they were the lowest prostitutes. He couldn't keep himself from hurting them. He squeezed their upper arms too tightly and left bruises on their soft thighs, and when they cried out, he pretended they liked it and gripped even harder. He thought punishing them would ease the rage that had consumed him during the early months after the war, but it had not. His encounters with German women had been like purges that gave him momentary relief, but no lasting satisfaction.

41

He tossed the application onto his desk and stood up to stretch his legs. He had been working since early morning. It was his habit to work nonstop, without interruption until he could tell by the shadows on the building across the street that noon was approaching. He knew if he stopped before then, fatigue would overtake him and he would grow cynical, then morose, and the rest of the day would be wasted.

He walked outside and headed for the mess hall. Several Joint workers were unloading supplies from a truck, and he stopped to watch them. They lifted huge cardboard boxes and tossed them onto the sidewalk, dislodging clouds of dust from inside. Clothes from America probably. The shipments were often mildewed and rotted after sitting in damp warehouses for months before some official remembered to have them transported to a DP center. But sometimes the garments were quite good, almost new, and then there would be a scramble to get them. Bolek joined a group of refugees who had positioned themselves nearby to watch. He knew that within ten minutes the entire camp would know a new shipment was in. He remembered the last time clothes had been distributed. The refugees had arrived on that Sunday morning, as the camp memo had instructed them, and quietly stood on line waiting to enter the warehouse. When the doors opened, they broke into a wild run, pushing and shoving their way inside. He and several Joint officials ran in after them and watched them fall on the piles of clothing. Women tore dresses out of each other's hands. Men hurled fists to keep a jacket. The sight had so sickened him that instead of trying to calm things down, he had spun around and hurried away.

A few doors down, a line of refugees had gathered at the entrance to the Tracing Bureau. They must be the group that arrived last night from Hungary, he thought. They had probably been there since dawn waiting for the office to open, driven by the hope that somewhere on a list or in a document they would find the name of a relative who had survived. He stepped inside the building to survey the disheveled crowd on the staircase. Weary, they leaned against the wrought-iron railing that snaked its way up the center of the building to the second floor landing and ended in front of the "Graffiti Wall." It was famous, this wall, covered with hundreds of names and dates hastily scribbled by refugees who had passed by it. The writing was smudged but legible, and Bolek watched the newest group press with outstretched hands to touch the fragile writing. Now and then someone stopped to underscore a name. Hope, Bolek thought, as he turned toward the street. It was as palpable as the smell of human sweat in the crowded corridors.

When he entered the mess hall, the first thing he saw was a line of hot plates filled with stew along the entire length of the counter. And the kitchen help, usually a sullen lot, looked cheerful for once. Since the army started requisitioning meat from the local German farmers last week, everyone's mood had improved.

Miriam Gold stood behind the counter looking crisp and freshly scrubbed in her white coveralls, her usually unruly curls held flat against her head by a fine mesh net. Steam from the hot plates engulfed her face and gave her cheeks a pleasingly moist sheen. Bolek greeted her with a touch to his cap and put out his plate.

"It's good," she said with a conspiratorial smile. "I heard they had to force the Germans to hand over this week's quota. Obviously the army doesn't pay as well as the black market." She piled his plate high with stew.

43

"Thanks," he said and took the food. "Did Paul speak with you?"

Miriam lowered her voice and leaned forward, pretending to adjust his plate. "Yes. We put the meat in a metal bin outside the door. It's covered with boxes so it looks like trash. Paul's men pick it up before the garbage trucks get here in the evening." She opened a tin and poured bloated green peas onto a serving dish. "Will it stay fresh long enough?"

"He made a deal with a German canner in town. It'll be vacuum packed before they ship it to the Haganah in Marseilles. It can sit on a boat for weeks; it doesn't need refrigeration."

"Good. I was worried." Her voice rose. "Okay, I'll see you tomorrow," she said and gave him a quick wink before beaming a smile to the next in line.

Bolek scanned the crowded tables for a seat. He spotted Rochel's friend, Manya, and an empty chair beside her. He had seen her several times since the first morning she had sat with Rochel. He had caught a glimpse of her disappearing into the Joint warehouse a few days earlier, and then a day later she had been on the street wearing a new coat, a heavier one, with a flowered scarf curled around her neck. Even from a distance, she was appealing. She was tall, and her stride was graceful and loose-limbed. When she stopped and threw back her hair to tie the scarf under her chin, something in her air of self-absorption captivated him, and he had stood on the street and watched her until she disappeared from view.

Bolek headed toward Manya. A look of apprehension swept across her face, as if she feared he might bring her bad news. He knew the look. It was the kind of flinch he'd seen on the faces of many survivors, as if they couldn't help preparing themselves for the worst. Then it struck him how out of character this was for someone of her background. Rochel had told him about her: no ghetto, no concentration camp. She had procured German work papers and survived the war by passing as a Pole. Yet now, more than a year later, she was still afraid. Of what?

He stopped at her table and smiled. "So, are you all settled in?"

She glanced up at him and nodded, looking solemn and preoccupied. She hunched back in her chair, clutching her coffee cup, her eyes tired and unfocused.

"Do you mind?" Bolek asked, preparing to sit down.

"No, it's all right," she said and returned to the tray in front of her.

He slid in beside her and began to eat quickly, as was his habit. He stopped and pointed his knife at her plate. "This precious meat comes from the Germans. How do you like it?"

She studied him as if considering a surly response. Then she seemed to think better of it and picked up her fork. "Oh, it's fine." She jabbed at the meat, then gave up the pretense.

"Tell me," he asked after a moment, "what will you do until you get a visa?"

"Do I have to do something?"

"You should, otherwise the waiting seems longer. Working helps pass the time. It also helps people forget." He stopped drinking and took her in. "It seems to me that you're not succeeding at either."

She gave him a small smile. "Is it so obvious?"

"Yes."

She held his gaze, but remained silent.

"You seem educated," he continued now that he had

her attention. "There's a lot you can do here. Do you write Yiddish?"

"No. Nor do I speak it."

"Why not?"

"We were Communists at home," Manya sighed impatiently. "Any more questions?"

"Most Communists spoke Yiddish," he replied. "Sorry, if this sounds like an interrogation. New people interest me. They can be of help, especially the young ones."

"What kind of help?"

"Do you know anything about the organizations in the camp, the Palestinian groups?"

"No. Just the Brichah people who got me out of Poland."

"That's not where it stops. Most people are only on their way some place else. It's a lot of work getting them there." He finished his coffee and waited.

"I don't see how I can be of use to you. I'm not a Zionist."

Bolek watched her poke at the food while her pale amber eyes strayed around the room. There was a contradiction in her appearance that he liked. Her skin was smooth, almost sheer, the kind that burned easily, and her unruly light brown hair softened her features, giving her the look of someone who had just awakened. Yet there was a boldness in her eyes, a firmness in her gaze. For a moment he thought she was about to speak, but she retreated when she caught him watching her and nervously ran her hand through her hair. She adjusted her collar and stood up to button her coat. He put his arm out to stop her and felt her shoulder.

"It takes a while to get used to this," he said. "We're all waiting. It's good to wait together." He released her and sat back, surprised himself at what he had said.

"Forgive me. I didn't mean to be rude." She avoided his eyes. "You're right. It takes time." She picked up her tray and left.

Bolek watched her weave her way down the aisle to the door and when she opened it, a burst of light briefly filled the room. He sat staring for a moment, then he grabbed his tray, tossed it on the counter at the entrance and flung open the door again.

He heard the commotion before he was outside. Then he saw her, frozen on the barrack steps, clutching the railing. He was beside her instantly, before he knew what was happening. They both stood this way, suspended, as the scene before them came into focus.

Bolek saw a group of men standing in a circle, screaming "Kholere! Schwein!" and kicking something. Manya stretched her neck to see. Suddenly, a band of DPs came careening around the corner, shouting and waving sticks and clubs. Benjamin, the refugee who worked in the warehouse, was among them, his face so inflamed that he would have been unrecognizable were it not for the scar on his forehead. "Kill him," he screamed, "Tear him apart." Another man yelled, "Dirty German," and the circle parted to let them in. Bolek saw a man huddled on the ground trying to cradle his head with his twisted, broken arms.

"Can't you stop them?" Manya asked, her eyes tense with fear.

He looked at her, surprised. "Why would I do that?"

"They'll kill him."

"He's a Nazi, probably a guard from one of the camps. Someone must have recognized him and lured him in from the German sector."

"You act as though this happens all the time."

47

"Sometimes. Not often enough, frankly."

A jeep pulled up. Two MPs jumped out and pushed through the crowd of refugees. One soldier knelt down and hoisted up the man whose face was bleeding so badly it was impossible to make out his features. He dangled in his coat for a moment, trying to get his footing while blood and mucous poured from his smashed nose. Both arms hung unnaturally at his side. One of the refugees pushed his way closer and wrenched out a fist of bloodied hair, screaming, "You killed my baby, I saw you. Animal! Monster!" Another refugee grabbed one of the broken arms and yanked it hard. The German shrieked and fainted. A shot rang out and the crowd froze, confused. The taller of the soldiers threw the German over his shoulder and ran while the other waved his gun. The MPs jumped in the jeep with the bleeding man and sped away as the crowd hurled stones and sticks.

Bolek and Manya moved cautiously onto the roadway and watched the DPs disperse. Some ran after the jeep as if they could catch it; others broke into small groups and slipped down the side alleys. A few bystanders gathered to stare at the site of the beating, at the pools of blood that had already begun to coagulate on the cobblestones.

"We both need some schnapps," Bolek said, touching Manya's shoulder. "There's a café run by DPs a few streets from here. Come."

The Landsberg Camp Café was nothing more than a store-front in one of the buildings incorporated into the DP enclave. It had been a military carpentry shop before the war and the smell of wood still lingered in the air. The proprietors had nailed together whatever odd pieces of wood they found to create counters and tables. They had not taken the time to treat the raw wood, and the smell of pine and birch was everywhere. Nothing in the café could compete with the wood scent, not even the freshly baked poppy seed loaves and chocolate babkas, or the honey cakes encrusted with caramelized sugar. The cakes sat unadorned on the same tin plates the refugees ate off in the mess hall. The smaller pastries were truly home-made, hand-shaped rather than pan-molded, and impressive given the shortage of fresh butter and eggs. It was the only restaurant in the camp, but so good that it was always filled with DPs willing to spend some of the money they got from the Joint.

Several men sat at the small, rough-hewn tables, their heads buried behind newspapers, cigarettes dangling from their lips. Two women in their mid-twenties were sipping coffee at a table by the window and waved gaily at Bolek when he entered. He nodded in their direction but steered Manya to a corner on the other side of the room. The women threw each other knowing looks, then turned to study this unfamiliar female.

Bolek and Manya had not spoken during the brief walk after witnessing the beating. Her face was still pale, and she shivered and rubbed the goose bumps on her arms.

"I'll ask Meyer to dig up some whiskey from the back. It'll warm you up." Manya looked puzzled. "Refugees aren't allowed to sell liquor," he informed her. "The Americans are afraid their GIs might get involved with the black market. And that's exactly what they do. It keeps the German economy going." He rose.

"I don't want any whiskey, just a coffee."

"You're still shaking. A whiskey will help."

"Just a coffee."

"It will make you feel better."

"No."

He shrugged and walked toward the back, pulling aside the flowered curtain that separated the café from the back room. In a few minutes he returned holding a tea cup filled with whiskey.

"Meyer will bring you coffee in a minute." He sat down and faced her squarely, as was his habit when he felt unsure of himself. Her rebuff had flustered him. He was accustomed to giving orders and being obeyed, and he was surprised both by her resistance and his vague feeling of regret at having displeased her. He took a sip of whisky and watched her. He noticed that a hint of color had reappeared on her cheeks. He wanted to know more.

She spoke before he did, "Why don't you hand the Germans over to the Americans? Why did you let them beat him that way?"

Bolek frowned, incredulous. "Hand a Nazi over to the Americans? Why should I? They let them go. It's the Jews they throw in jail for daring to hit a German." He drank his whisky and studied her. "Haven't you learned anything since the war ended? Oh, I forgot. You were in Warsaw. Well, Bolshevik justice is a bit different. The Americans don't shoot Germans just because they gassed a few million people. They look for witnesses, gather evidence, give them a nice trial. Then they let them go." He felt the old anger rise. "You're surprised, aren't you? You've never seen Jews do this before, have you?"

"Do what?"

"Fight back."

"No," she said quietly, and stopped to gaze over his shoulder at some distant memory. "They always let themselves be beaten . . . especially the Yeshiva boys. Jewish Party members used to defend themselves, but it wasn't really the same thing. The only time they fought back was during the ghetto uprising."

"That was suicide, not resistance."

She looked surprised. "You were there?"

"No."

"Then how do you know?"

"They didn't have enough guns. They knew they were outnumbered. There was no question that they would all die. It was a question of how." He remembered the first time he had heard of the uprising and all it had meant to him. He was twenty-five and had escaped from a forced labor camp. He found a group of exhausted, half-starved partisans in a forest near Vilna, barely subsisting on berries and roots, on "forest garbage" as he called it. It had been a low time for him, after what he had seen, but when the news reached the little band that Jews were killing Germans in the streets of Warsaw, they became, at least briefly, delirious with hope. Afterwards, when he learned all the facts, he felt different.

"I saw them," she shot back. "I went as close as I could to the ghetto during those last days in May. We all did, and I saw them. It was horrible, but they were brave."

"They waited too long to get brave." He did not want to talk about this, he wanted to find out more about her. But, as always when the subject of resistance came up, he got carried away. "Well, it's a new Jew now," he continued. "We don't wait for anyone, anymore." He sipped the remains of his whiskey, enjoying the burning sensation that seeped into his chest. She had to have a story. "What happened to your family? Where were they?"

"My parents were caught with their partisan unit near Lvov in '43. My grandmother went to Treblinka." She rattled it off like a list of accusations. "My husband was killed six months ago."

He raised his eyebrows. "Six months ago?"

"Someone who had been with us in the underground shot him."

"A Pole?"

She nodded and looked down at the small plate of pickles on the table.

"How did it happen?"

"Joseph — my husband — had just been promoted in the Party. It was the second time in only a few months. We knew Tadeusz from before the war. He had always been marginal, fanatical, always ranting that the Jews would sell out Poland someday. Everyone put up with him because he had been a good fighter. He and my husband were on their way to a town about sixty kilometers from Warsaw to organize the local farm committee there. Tadeusz shot him and left him on the side of the road."

"So, you know for certain that your husband died?"

"They brought him back." She pushed her plate away. "I buried him."

She was luckier than most, Bolek thought. At least she had a grave where she could go to mourn. And she would not turn into one of those "temporary widows" who hung around the bulletin boards waiting for survivor lists to be posted. The grapevine that had sprung up among the DPs was often just as accurate as Army records, but people wanted something official, a conclusion, an ending. Despite his connections to UNRRA and the Americans, Bolek could not get legal verification that his own wife and son were dead, although he had known this since last April. He even knew they had perished on the very day they arrived in Birkenau in early

1943, and that his wife, refusing to be separated from their son, had been dragged away, clutching two-year-old Abraham in her arms, and thrown into the gas chambers at the last minute without even being shaved. People had seen this and they had told him. Eyewitness information was so reliable that Bolek never consciously questioned it. He knew it was true. But every few nights he dreamed he was walking past the Tracing Bureau and spotted the names of his family on a list of survivors. He would peer at the paper for a long time, letting the wonderful, new knowledge sink in, and then, just as he moved his shaking finger to the adjacent column to see where they were located, the ink on the document blurred and he couldn't read it. He always awoke in a panic.

"I'm sorry about your husband," he said. "Is that why you left?"

"Partly. And because it was no longer safe for me."

He met her level gaze. "Do you feel safe now?"

She picked up the tin spoon lying on the table and caressed its curved surface with her thumb. When she looked up, everything about her had softened: The space where her aquiline nose met her forehead was no longer pinched white with tension. Her mouth looked supple, the lips now relaxed into their fullness.

"It's a beginning I suppose," she said. "After my husband's death everything started to change." She shook her head. "No. It started to change before that, the day in October '44 when the Soviets arrived in Warsaw. That's another story. But one night, a few weeks ago, I came home from a university staff meeting and someone shot at me through the window of my apartment. I know it was the Home Army, the anti-Communist Nationalists, and that I wasn't the only

Jewish Party member they tried to kill. But I thought the Soviets could protect me. Then I found I wasn't even safe from the bureaucrats. What had I been fighting for? What had Joseph died for?" She tossed the spoon onto the table where it clattered to a halt against her cup. "My old comrades kept saying, 'Wait. *They* have to be strict with us because we need the discipline.' We, who had been in the underground, we needed discipline!"

"And your husband? Did he feel the same way?"

A quiver passed across her face. "He was more patient. With each promotion he became more optimistic that he could make a difference. And he was trusting. That's why he died." She placed her hands on the table and clasped them so tightly the knuckles formed a white ridge across the fingers. "Afterwards, there was no longer a reason to stay. I went to the Brichah and left."

Bolek felt grimly self-righteous. He had little sympathy for her or anyone who believed Communism could cure the world of its congenital hatred of Jews. Yet, she stirred him. She had learned her lesson the hard way.

Manya unclasped her hands and spread them out on the table. They were large, slender, with scars, thin ropes of puckered skin along the sides of her fingers and on her palms. She caught him looking and held them up for inspection. "The paint factory I worked in ran out of rubber gloves early in the war."

Bolek was about to take her hand when Meyer, one of the proprietors, approached carrying a cup of coffee and a slice of honey cake. Meyer placed these in front of Manya and gave Bolek a big smile. "Here you are. For the pretty stranger," he said in Yiddish.

"Thank you."

Meyer frowned hearing Manya's Polish words. "Prosze, Pani," he replied with mock gallantry, then gave her a contemptuous little bow and left. Manya looked embarrassed.

"He's only joking," Bolek said. "Meyer means well."

"He does not," she said, stating it as a simple fact. "They hate me. I'm not comfortable among these people and they sense it. And they're not comfortable with me. I don't speak Yiddish, I have too many goyish mannerisms. In the week I've been here I feel more foreign ... You're the first person I've met here who speaks proper Polish."

"That's because I had hoped to have a proper Polish education, but of course, as a Jew, I wasn't allowed to attend Warsaw University."

"You're from Warsaw? Where did you live?"

"On Ulica Proczeski. My father owned a small furniture factory. I worked with him until the Germans came." He looked around the café. "Maybe that's why I always come here. The smells in this place remind me of home."

Manya smiled at him for the first time. It was a strange smile, more of relief than of pleasure.

Bolek felt a rustle at his side and suddenly his cohort, Paul, was standing next to him. As usual, Paul did not introduce himself. He was small and wiry and his misshapen clothes were too big for him. His cap was pulled low and the eyes under the visor were opaque and humorless.

"What is it, Paul?" Bolek asked without ceremony. Even though he had known him for over a year, he was always unnerved by Paul's style. He had a way of appearing out of nowhere and waiting silently until he was noticed.

"I need to talk to you. It's important." Paul did not look

at Manya. He just hovered by the table as though standing in his own personal shadow.

"Can't it wait a little while? I'll stop by later."

"No, it's important," Paul replied. Then he pivoted, walked outside and stationed himself at the door.

Bolek turned to Manya, considering what to do. He thought he heard something unusual in Paul's voice. And for all his coarseness Paul would not have intruded upon him in the café unless it were urgent. Bolek stood up and began to rummage through his pockets for money.

"I'll walk you back to the barracks. Or you can stay and finish your coffee."

Manya glanced through the window at Paul's stiff back and then at Bolek. Her smile had disappeared. "I'll stay here," she said and picked up her coffee cup for the first time.

Bolek tossed some change on the table and leaned towards her. "I'll be finished in a little while. I'll look for you later."

She nodded and looked toward the entrance again. "Someone you work with?"

"Yes."

"It sounds serious."

"Everything is serious these days."

Her face turned somber. "You work for the Brichah."

"Among others."

Paul started walking the moment Bolek stepped outside. He shoved his hands in his pockets and cast his eyes on the ground. He walked quickly, but spoke in slow, even tones. He did not look up.

"Another lady friend?"

"Someone new. Just arrived with a Brichah group. What's the rush?"

Paul's face remained vacant. "A shipment of guns just turned up in Bratislava and there's no one to receive it. It's the biggest shipment this year; one hundred and fifty M1's, two hundred Browning automatic rifles, fifty handguns — all rounded up by our people in France. Anton, our check link, was found dead in his room at the Jelen Hotel. His mistress found him after she broke down the door. Nobody knows for sure what happened. It might have been a heart attack, but the Czech unit is not ruling out poison." He spoke without inflection, as if he were reciting a grocery list, and Bolek found himself growing irritable. Although his mind raced ahead anticipating the details, part of him still resented this intrusion. He had felt a buoyancy in the café that he hadn't known for a long time.

"All our people in the area are away with a convoy headed for Italy," Paul continued. "Headquarters can't locate anyone close enough to the Czech border to arrange to move the guns. We want you to work out a route and get the shipment to Bari. Anton's mistress, Celia, will help you."

Bolek was all attention. Paul was with the Haganah, the defense force of Palestine Jewry that operated throughout Europe and the Middle East smuggling Jews and arms into Palestine. He also coordinated Brichah operations in this sector of Germany. He had his hand in all aspects of transporting weapons, and when a vessel was scheduled to leave, he knew exactly how many people would be on it and how much space was available for arms. He was a methodical worker, dedicated and highly valued. And he had the authority to recruit Bolek.

"Why was there only one man waiting?" Bolek asked. His own work was limited to getting refugees on ships and coordinating supplies for the vessels leaving French and Italian ports. The people who smuggled arms took much greater risks. And they did not die of heart attacks.

"The guns showed up early. Our French dealer got nervous and wanted the arms out of the country quickly. He's afraid DeGaulle might get pressured by his pro-British faction and decide to clamp down on smuggling."

When Paul stopped talking, they were standing in front of the immigration office. He nodded toward the doorway. "Give them your cover story and let's go," he said. "You can get on an UNRRA truck headed for Vienna and hook up with our people there. They'll get you across the border."

"How long will it take?"

"About four days."

"If Anton was poisoned, who did it?"

"The British. There was a ten thousand pound price on Anton's head. He was a member of the Stern Gang."

CHAPTER
6

LATER, MANYA HAD JUST RETURNED from the Joint warehouse and was folding a pullover when Tovah poked her head through the blankets that hung around her cot. "You have a visitor," Tovah said and motioned toward the barracks entrance where Bolek was leaning against the door, his hands in his pockets. Manya peeked out and Bolek lifted his hand in greeting.

"I've seen him around," Tovah continued. "He works for the Joint, doesn't he?" She tilted her head to take a better look and grinned. "Very nice." Tovah was enjoying this, Manya could tell. In the week since she first met the young woman, Manya had seen her around camp with three different boy friends — two GIs and one young refugee — and had looked equally happy with them all. Manya knew Tovah found her distant and withdrawn, and that this new development would please her. Most of the refugee women thought of men as a panacea and would assume that a new beau was sure to make her happy.

Manya stood up quickly and slipped on her shoes. She smoothed her hair, straightened her blouse and pulling back the blanket, stepped out into the room. Bolek remained leaning against the wall, but he followed her with his eyes as she approached him.

"I thought you might like to take a walk," he said when she was standing before him. "To make up for leaving you so abruptly earlier. We won't have many evenings like this before the snows."

She hesitated. He was very appealing. He smiled and tugged playfully at her sleeve. "Come on. The conversation was just getting interesting. And I have to leave tomorrow."

"Work?"

"Yes, but I'll be back in a week." He held open the door. "You don't even need a coat tonight. Just a little daring."

It was November, but warm and humid. Fog rose and drifted over the street and the air felt thick and sultry. They headed toward the main section of the camp, where the administration offices and recreation halls were clustered. As they neared the center, groups of people appeared, laughing and chatting as they passed. During the day everyone seemed worried or listless. It was a pleasure to see a different mood in the evening. Manya fell in with Bolek's easy gait.

They strolled for a few minutes. "You're a bit confusing," he finally said.

"How so?"

"For a Jew. You don't speak Yiddish, and you felt sorry for that Nazi who was getting beaten up before."

"You miss the point. I don't like the Germans, but I don't like to see people acting like animals."

"The Germans were animals."

"So, we should be, too?"

"We? Does that mean you include yourself."

"I'm not a Jew in the way you think."

"And what way is that?"

"I hardly know myself. You probably think I converted to Catholicism or that my parents did — which they didn't. Or that I'm ashamed — which I'm not."

She stopped herself. Why was she arguing with this man who was practically a stranger? He was forcing an intimacy she wasn't sure she wanted. She fell silent, and they continued past the offices to where the buildings thinned and the pavement turned to road. They were heading toward the river. In the distance she saw the lights of the other Landsberg glimmering like small halos through the rising mist. Suddenly she felt drops on her cheek. "It's raining."

Bolek looked up at the clouded sky and listened, alert. There was a clap of thunder, and then came the downpour. They were both immediately drenched through, so suddenly, in fact, that Manya burst out laughing. He smiled and, grabbing her hand, scanned the area for shelter. "This is serious," he said while she continued to laugh. Turning back in the direction of the camp, he pulled her after him, darted into the entrance of a nearby building and pushed against the door.

Bolek took off his cap and shook it out, then ran his fingers through his damp curls. "So much for that." He pulled at the front of his soaked shirt. They had run the last few steps and she was breathing hard. He reached out and wiped a few drops from her cheek, but when he saw her surprise, he took a handkerchief from his pocket and handed it to her.

"Thank you," she said. The thin cloth felt smooth against her face.

They were standing inside a small, one-story wooden structure with a rough cement floor. She thought she smelled polish and leather and wondered if this had been a shoe shop that had catered to the soldiers billeted in the nearby barracks.

No German Army left to service now, she thought, and few people could afford resoling these days. Most of the DPs wore their shoes until their toes rubbed the pavement, and then they slid in endless pieces of cardboard to cover the holes.

Bolek pushed on the heavy wooden door. "Let's see what's going on." They stood under a gable and watched the storm. Great gusts of rain blew down the street, turning the debris that had accumulated around the gutters into small whirlpools. There was a flash of lightning and the street trembled in white light. Then came a crack of thunder. A memory enclosed her of autumn storms in Komorow when she was a child and how her grandmother would come and stand next to her to watch the downpour as though it were a drama being performed just for the two of them. She sat down on the step and stared out at the grayness.

"It wasn't a conscious decision, not to be a Jew," she began abruptly. "I didn't even think about it. It was the way I was brought up."

"It sounds like your parents renounced it and you just followed suit."

She shook her head. "No! You don't understand. My parents weren't Christians or Jews. Their religion was Communism." She drew a long sigh and leaned forward with her elbows on her knees to peer into the dreary street. "When they moved from Komorow to Warsaw, everything they had been just fell away from them, dissolved. I grew up more than assimilated. We were our own club. I knew my parents had been brought up Jewish, but all my friends were Communists. We were taught it was a great privilege to devote ourselves to something bigger than our own lives. And because the Communist Party was illegal, we had to keep it a secret. That made it more exciting.

"Then there was my grandmother, my mother's mother. My mother loved her very much and never stopped visiting her. Every Sunday she went to Komorow, sometimes with my father, always with me. I remember on those visits, after the dishes had been put away and the table cloth shook out, my grandmother would sit me on her lap and braid my hair in the style of the village girls, and even when I got too old for braids, I used to wear them home and even sleep in them. For years, the last thing I remembered before drifting off was the feel of her hands gently gathering up my hair from my neck. After I went to university, I would visit on my own. There was a tenderness I needed from her I never felt from my parents.

"My mother and I had an unspoken agreement that we would protect her against what we had become. I was always ready to brand my mother a hypocrite, but not in this case. For years, we kept up the pretense that we were living as Jews in Warsaw." She smiled. "Not very honorable for Communists."

"Would she have disowned you?"

"I don't know. But she made it easy to keep the secret. She never questioned me, just listened and smiled and shared my joy. Later, I realized that she had been part of the conspiracy. She didn't ask me to go to synagogue. She didn't ask me to light candles on Friday night. She let me stay outside that part of her life because she didn't want to lose me or my mother."

The rain had tapered off to a fine drizzle and the sky brightened into an early evening luster. Manya felt tired, yet glad to talk.

"This afternoon, when we spoke of those men in the street, I realized that I never associated my grandmother with the Jews of Warsaw. The people who haggled at the markets and embarrassed me with their vulgarity. They were in no way connected to me or to her. I thought of them as victims, as an oppressed group like any other in a capitalist society, and when the revolution came they would be liberated along with the proletariat. And now . . . " She trailed off for a moment, then stopped.

"And now?" Bolek asked.

"I no longer have those beliefs."

He had been resting his head against the door frame, watching her while she spoke. Now he sat up. "You could go to a non-Jewish camp if you feel uncomfortable with us." There was an edge to his voice.

"I don't feel uncomfortable here. Just different."

"But you're not. That's why you haven't left. You know that if you said you were a Pole, you could get a visa anywhere. But you know that wherever you go someone will be there to tell you you're a Jew. You saw how easy it was for everyone to step aside while the Germans shoved us into the gas chambers. Someday someone will want to try it again. We can't let that happen."

She bristled. He was so sure of himself while she felt so fragile. "What simple answers you have."

"It's the questions that are simple. You don't have to be a Zionist, just realistic."

"Is that what you are?"

He smiled. "Aren't they the same thing?"

The rain had stopped and it was suddenly colder. She stood up and tried to smooth out her damp skirt, then turned up the narrow collar of her pullover as though it would warm her. It had not occurred to her to leave Landsberg although people changed camps all the time. She couldn't imagine being with Poles now. She felt safe here. The Jews mostly left her to herself.

They walked back through the diminishing light. The sky had turned clear and crisp, and she could see a star sparkling on the horizon. As they approached the main cluster of barracks, the lamps came on, illuminating the deserted streets. People were still inside after the downpour, the storm having disrupted their pre-dinner stroll. The refugees relished their walks and spent as much time as possible outdoors. During the afternoons when Manya sometimes passed a small park on her way from the offices and warehouse, there was always a group of young women sitting in the sun. With winter coming, what could people do but wait in their cramped quarters and grow more morose?

They reached the steps of Weizmann House. Bolek seemed to consider something. "So . . ."

"So . . ." she echoed.

He put his hands in his pockets and looked down at a piece of paper he was nudging with his shoe. "I'll be gone about a week. I hope you get better service at Meyer's next time you go."

"I doubt I'll be spending much time there." She paused. "Be careful."

His face softened. "I'll be in touch."

"I'll be here."

He stopped and turned back for a moment. "I know," he said. "You wouldn't go anywhere else."

CHAPTER

7

MANYA PUT OFF unpacking. In the first days, she wore whatever piece of clothing was on top of the pile in her suitcase for the endless rounds of appointments at the agencies and welfare organizations that ran the camp. Now, she sat down and regarded the tangle of skirts and blouses she had quickly gathered before leaving Warsaw. She had not chosen wisely. The garments were lightweight, warm weather clothes she had grabbed from a hallway closet, avoiding the bedroom with its pictures of Joseph, her parents, her grandmother, the room where she kept her winter clothing. At the last minute she had seized an old shawl, the one her grandmother had handed to her the last time they were together, just before she had disappeared with her village into Treblinka. Her grandmother had offered it shyly, this lace shawl she had worn for as long as Manya could remember, saying she had a new, warmer one that would serve her better when the time came for her to be deported, and that Manya should take it and give it to someone who might need it. Manya had accepted it silently, without protest, already sensing she would be unable to help her, unable to risk hiding an old, sick woman who spoke broken Polish, knowing that she would have to let her go and that she would spend the rest of her life grieving, not only for the woman who had loved her so absolutely, but even more for all that she, Manya, might have done to save her. Now, she carefully spread the shawl across her cot and ran her hand over the fine lace that had softened with age to a satin finish. She held the delicate, almost weightless fringe in her palm for a moment, then folded it neatly and put it back in her suitcase.

Someone called out her name and she swung around, startled. Tovah, who was lying on her cot nearby reading a newspaper, looked up sleepy-eyed. She got up late and usually stayed in the barracks until one of her boyfriends picked her up in the evening. "Relax Manya," she said over the top of the paper. "It's just UNRRA, not the secret police."

A woman in a uniform approached, clipboard and folder under her arm. Her heels made a hollow sound on the wooden floor. "Come with me for a moment, will you," she said. "You haven't been to the doctor for a physical."

"I'm all right," Manya replied, slipping her suitcase under her cot.

"All new DPs have to be screened. I'm surprised it's taken this long. Usually, everyone is processed the first week, but we've been backed up with new refugees." The woman took her by the arm. "Come."

The medical offices were two streets away in the UNRRA building. The clinic, as it was called, had a large waiting area with several smaller examination rooms adjacent to it. The woman walked her in and after speaking with an attending nurse, gave her Manya's papers and left. The space looked freshly painted and clean, its white walls covered with posters. One said, "Clean Your Latrine." Another outlined the steps necessary for maintaining personal hygiene and stopping the spread of venereal disease. The room was crowded with tense and silent refugees sitting on benches against the wall. Manya recognized Isaac Flamb from the truck. He was leaning forward in his seat, not coughing now but nervously picking imaginary lint from his cap. Next to him sat a girl with huge eyes and a long, thin face whom Manya also remembered. She had had a feverish quality throughout their harrowing flight across the border, as if the effort to hide her fear made her slightly sick. Manya recalled how surprised she had been one night when the canvas flap was momentarily thrown open, and she glimpsed the girl clutching a doll hidden under her coat. Watching her gaze out into the waiting room, her face pale and expressionless, Manya was confused about her age. It was impossible to tell how old these child survivors were. The war had stunted them so and they all looked like weary, undersized adults. She could have been 10 or 20. The girl continued to stare at a Zionist poster of farmers cheerfully plowing desert fields while she folded and unfolded her hands.

A nurse opened the door to one of the examining rooms and called out a name. A small, hunched man took off his cap, stood slowly to attention, and followed, leaving a narrow space on the bench. Manya sat down and squeezed between two people. The woman on her right turned toward her briefly. She had blond hair and pale, almost transparent blue eyes. She sat cross-legged, one shapely calf swinging rhythmically against the other.

"It will take all day, you know," she said, casually. "Everything always does." She looked at Manya with interest. "You're new?"

"Yes."

"You just arrived?"

"Last week."

The woman leaned away from her, alarmed. "They waited so long? They should have screened you right away. We have to be careful. It's easy to start an epidemic."

"What do you mean?"

"Typhus. I had it in Bergen-Belsen. That's why I'm here. I have to come for a check-up every month." Her voice was clear, high pitched. "Where were you?"

"Warsaw. I hid during the war."

A look of relief passed over her face and then some second thoughts. "Any lice?"

Manya burst out laughing. "I don't think so," she said. It had been a long time since she had really laughed, and she felt as if something tight had dislodged inside her. She leaned back in her chair, relaxed.

"Don't think you'll escape it," the woman said, playing to her new audience. "They'll delouse you anyway. They treat us like dirty clothes and spray us with something that smells like camphor. It reminds me of my mother cleaning house at Passover. She was very serious about that, my mother. Everything had to be packed away and in order, every crumb swept out. Even after I got married, she would come with bags of camphor. Some mothers bring food, mine brought moth balls." She turned away for a moment. "When I first came here, they used to put all the new refugees together in a special room and spray them, just like in the gas chambers. Can you imagine the intelligent person who thought up that? You should have seen how hysterical people got. They ran out screaming. What a sight! UNRRA finally got a little smarter and now they do it one at a time." She glanced at Manya and rolled her eyes. "Oh, come now. You

have to laugh about these things. You can't take it all so seriously or you'll never recover." She extended her hand and
smiled. "Leila Weissberg." Manya shook it and introduced
herself.

"I'm from Radom," Leila continued. "I used to go to Warsaw before I got married. I bought my trousseau there. What
beautiful shops they had." She grew quiet for a moment. "I
hear it was all destroyed."

"Yes. Most of it is gone."

"I can't say I'm sorry for those stinking Poles," she said.
"I went back to Radom after liberation, but nothing was left.
My father's factory was gone. Our house was occupied. Do
you know, I was standing in front of my house when I met our
old maid, the Polish woman who raised me. She cried like a
baby when she saw me. 'Leila,' she said, 'it's your house, kick
those people out, take it back.' But I couldn't. I was afraid
they would kill me. I just wanted to see who was left alive and
then leave."

Manya watched her with interest. There was something
vital in Leila's face, in the impetuous but graceful movements
of her body. Most of the young women in the barracks were
polite, one or two even friendly, but she sensed in them a
remoteness, not unlike her own, as if they were carrying on
a private conversation in their heads. This woman seemed
sure of herself, sure of what to do and why she should do it.
And there was something honest in her directness and in the
assured tilt of her chin.

"Your husband, did he survive?" Manya ventured.

Leila threw up her hands. "I don't know. We were separated in Majdanek. I don't know where they took him. People tell me he survived, but nobody knows where he is. He
didn't go back to Radom. Someone would have seen him."

Leila took a long sigh. "Every day I think I will hear something, and every night I go to bed afraid that in the morning his name will show up on one of those casualty lists. When can you say to yourself that you've waited long enough and it's time to start again?"

"I suppose some people never do."

Leila looked surprised. "And spend their lives lighting *yurtzeite* candles?" She shook her head. "No. That's not normal. People want to live. They go on, they have children, a home. You never forget, but you build a new life. Or what's the good of having survived?" She lit a cigarette and leaned back on the bench. "It's the waiting that can make you crazy," she said. "And the hate. You know, sometimes I think if I had only killed a German with my own hands, it would make me feel better."

Her words brought Manya back to more memories better forgotten. In the early days of the German occupation in 1940, she and Helena, a childhood friend, had been sent by their underground unit to collect rifle cartridges at a munitions dump on the outskirts of Warsaw. Some of the comrades who worked on the assembly lines managed to plant some cartridges in empty boxes before they threw them away in the back of the factory. It was one way the underground got ammunition for the few German Mauser Kar rifles they managed to steal. Neither she nor Helena had been on a real mission before, and although their assignment was routine, it became, for both of them, a personal test of their courage. Helena, though she was petite and delicate, had a bravery that bordered on recklessness. She would do well. It was her own courage that Manya doubted. There was a terrible shortage of guns in the underground, and the only weapons she and Helena had been trained to use were switchblades. Even so,

Manya had never struck another person in her life and her gentle father, for all his talk of revolution, cringed if someone raised a voice in anger.

The night before they were to go, Manya was in a panic. Even Joseph, reassuring her with his soothing voice and steady hand, could not calm her. She went, of course, wondering, as she and Helena trudged across the dark field behind the munitions factory, if her trembling legs would support her. Everything went uneventfully at first. They were quietly sifting through discarded boxes for cartridges when suddenly a German sentry appeared — standing over Helena. Manya, who was crouched behind a large cardboard carton, saw him first. In profile, he had a pug nose and an innocent, babyish face and looked even younger than the two women. Before the sentry got out "Was ist . . . ," Manya pulled out her switchblade from her pocket, jumped on him from behind, and then, as she had been so carefully taught, used the force of her entire body to push the knife into the space between his shoulders. The soldier fell forward, gagging, as she clung to his waist with one hand, her clothes drenched in blood, terrified to let go, stabbing him until he stopped struggling. He slumped and she felt the exact moment when his life ended. She had never been near something dead before, and she was stunned by the finality of its stillness. She never knew how Helena got her home, and even later, when Helena described the event to their unit in all its heroic details, Manya remembered almost nothing. But often the last thing she saw before falling asleep was the profile of a young soldier, his youthful features frozen in the moonlight.

"It wouldn't help, you know," she heard herself tell Leila. "It would be just another ghost to haunt you."

Leila stared at her. "It sounds like you've said more than you intended."

"I was with the underground in Warsaw," Manya said after a moment, hoping that this would satisfy Leila's questions.

They sat for a moment in silence. "Well," said Leila, "I'm sorry for you if it didn't help." A pause and then, "I'm sorry for me, I'm sorry for all of us." She shrugged her shoulders with comic irony. "Aren't we all tired of being sorry?"

The old woman on the opposite bench looked up abruptly as their laughter filled the gloomy waiting room.

Manya's examination was brief, and she was not required to undergo the customary "spraying" that Leila had warned her about. The doctor, a haggard man with thick glasses and a distracted air, perused her records, and when he saw that she had not been in a concentration camp or a detention center, he gave her a cursory once-over and proclaimed her healthy. Then he stamped her clinic card and with a look of relief crossed her name off the long list.

When Manya stepped back into the crowded waiting room, she was pleased to see Leila standing near the doorway, reading a leaflet. "Have you picked up your rations yet?" she asked.

"Yes. I got a box the day I arrived."

"No, I mean your weekly rations, things like cigarettes, chocolate."

"No, I haven't. Anyway, I don't smoke."

Leila laughed. "Silly girl, you have a lot to learn. Cigarettes are money. Do you have any idea what you can buy with them? And chocolate! It's like gold. You can get a pair of nylon stockings for two small bars." She slipped her arm through Manya's. "You're coming with me to the Joint office right now. We'll get your rations and go straight to Frau Heinz, my seamstress. That dress," she said pointing a finger. "You'll freeze to death this winter in that thin cotton. And to be frank, it's not the most flattering cut. Frau Heinz is making me a short jacket and I need a fitting. She'll fix you up." Leila started forward and then stopped again. "Have you got your card with you?" Manya riffled through her pockets. The newly stamped card was lying in the palm of her hand like a jewel. Leila linked her arm through Manya's and steered her toward the small building on the main street of the Landsberg camp that housed the Joint offices.

They stepped inside a room crowded with desks, each piled high with papers and folders. A woman looked up from a tall stack, nodded hello to Leila, and let them pass toward a back room that opened onto a huge warehouse. The space was so big it looked like an airplane hangar grafted onto a house. Chutes connected twelve-foot high metal shelving stacked with boxes to the counter tops where the women stood. This was the main distribution area for goods donated by the military government and all the welfare agencies that cared for the refugees.

Leila sauntered over to a woman who was unpacking toothbrushes at one end of the counter and greeted her in Hungarian. The woman took Manya's card and, reaching under the counter, pulled out two cartons of Lucky Strikes cigarettes. Then she disappeared in the back and returned with a small bag of chocolate bars wrapped in wax paper. She handed Manya one. "Keep this out of the sun," she said and stamped Manya's card.

Leila helped herself to several pieces of brown paper and some string from behind the counter and wrapped up the goods. Then she tucked them under Manya's arm. "Now we're all set," she said cheerfully. They stepped outside and began to walk toward the German neighborhood on the outskirts of the camp.

They came to a group of houses, each with its own front yard enclosed by a wrought-iron fence. Manya had heard that refugees who did not want to live in barracks rented rooms from the Germans in this area and paid for them with rations and the monthly stipend given them by the Joint. Rochel said that was what Bolek did. He needed privacy in his work, Rochel had added coyly. Manya looked at the two-story stone houses and wondered which one was his. Several days had passed since he had left Landsberg. Unbidden images of the man kept flitting across her mind: a curl of black hair carelessly falling across his forehead, a forehead that seemed too wrinkled for a man his age; the dark, half-Mongolian eyes that never left her face when she spoke. He had leaned against the door frame and listened to her in the rain. The pose made him look casual, relaxed, yet there was nothing casual about him. He seemed to probe her just with his presence, and despite his angry disapproval of her past, she sensed he understood her far too well, perhaps better than she understood herself.

"Frau Heinz is really very nice for a German," Leila said, bringing her back. "And she is a wonderful dressmaker. You should see the fabrics she has. Someone smuggles them in from France. Look at this," she said, stopping at the corner and doing a little pirouette that made her coat swing out. It was a deep rich brown and the puffed sleeves tapered to delicate cuffs at her wrist. The hem fell in soft billows just above her knees. "It's the latest," she said proudly. "Aren't you glad the short style is still in fashion so we can show off our legs with these wonderful stockings?" She stepped back for Manya's appraisal. "What do you think?"

Manya smiled. "You look like you stepped out of a magazine." And she did, compared to most of the women, a grim lot in their drab army issue.

Leila laughed. "Oh, enough about me. I talk too much. Come, let's get you something nice." She linked arms again and continued down the street.

"Frau Heinz is a widow," Leila chatted on. "Her husband and son are dead. She told me the son died during the retreat from Russia. She can't talk about it without crying. She doesn't say much about her husband. He was much older, a second marriage, I think. She was poor when she was young, that's why she sews so well. She had to make a living. But I think they had money before the war because the house is nice. Now she has to rent out the downstairs."

"How did you learn all this?" Manya asked.

"She sews all my dresses and we've become friends. We talk." Leila fell silent. "Many of the DPs go to her. She makes wonderful things." Leila turned to her with a serious face. "Look, I don't know how you feel about it."

"I haven't had much to do with the Germans yet. But I don't feel good when I'm around them, I can tell you that."

"Well, there's no way to avoid dealing with them to get the things you want. And anyway, they're not all so bad." She gave Manya an amused smile and continued walking. "Maybe I like her because she is a little like me?" Leila said. "Do you know what she did the first time I met her? 'Frau Weissberg,' she said, 'I will ask you what I ask everyone who comes to me for the first time. Do you hate Germans?' I was so surprised, I was speechless. She said she couldn't sew well for someone who hated her. Her hands would not be able to do it. I said that was an odd way to run a business and she said there would be no business if she couldn't make nice clothes. Then I asked her what if I said yes, I hate Germans. Would she send me somewhere else? She smiled and said, 'But now the question has changed. Do you hate *this* German?' I laughed and that was it. We've been friends ever since."

Leila stopped in front of one of the larger houses on the street. The front gate was broken, but the soil around the plants was well raked and the shrubs freshly clipped. Leila knocked and a few seconds later, Frau Heinz stood before them. Somehow Manya had pictured someone like Leila; instead she saw a portly, middle-aged woman with gray-streaked brown hair neatly coiled in a bun at the base of her neck. She had kind eyes that lit up when she saw Leila.

"Good afternoon, Frau Heinz," Leila chirped in broken German. "This is my friend, Manya Gerson."

"How nice to meet a friend of Frau Weissberg's." The woman extended her hand and Manya shook it. The grasp felt firm and warm.

"I thought I would bring her along since I was coming for a fitting. She just arrived and as you can see, she is in desperate need of nice clothes. She needs something warm and, of course, beautiful because she is a beautiful woman, don't you think? How many cartons do you need to make her a wool dress — something really attractive?" Frau Heinz was about to answer, but Leila cut her off. "Four cartons, isn't it? This way she could have it in two weeks."

Manya couldn't repress a small giggle. The German woman saw her and smiled back, sharing her own appreciation for their audacious friend. There was something irresistible about Leila.

Before Frau Heinz could answer, Leila took Manya by

the arm and walked her into the house. "Can we look at the fabrics? Is that all right?" The German woman nodded, and followed them up the stairs. Leila waited for her at the top of the landing, then swept into the bedroom that also served as a workroom. "How is the jacket coming?" she asked and then, turning to Manya said, "You will not believe what this woman can do with an ordinary piece of cloth." Leila stepped up to one of the many pieces of clothing hanging from a rope strung across the room. "Look at this," she said caressing a jacket of supple dark blue melton. It was half-finished and crudely pinned, but its graceful lines were already visible.

Frau Heinz slipped it off the hanger and gingerly put it on Leila's shoulders. "Let's see how this looks, shall we?" she said reaching for her pin cushion. Manya wandered around the room while the women began to make contented sounds. Frau Heinz lovingly smoothed down a lapel, then gently forced a pin through an unruly pocket flap and coaxed the satin lining into place. Her eyes never left the garment as she listened and nodded in agreement with her appreciative customer.

The bedroom, although large, was cluttered with so much furniture that scarcely an inch of wall space was visible. There was the sewing machine and various sewing implements, then dressing tables, and night stands and chests covered with intricately crocheted doilies. In the center of the room stood a majestic carved bed. Gilded mirrors hung between old paintings and clocks of various sizes. Clearly Frau Heinz had consolidated a house full of furniture into two rooms and she had not parted with any of it. Something about the clutter reminded Manya of the barracks, as if these displaced pieces were, like the refugee's shabby valises, waiting for better days.

She noticed a group of photographs clustered on one of

the dressers and drifted over to look. The largest was a silver-framed picture of a handsome young man in uniform. He looked about seventeen years old. The face was serious, but the eyes, like Frau Heinz's, had an amused glint around the edges. There were other photos of men in ancient military garb and assorted women, each laced up in severe blouses and dresses, each with a large brooch pinned to a collar beneath her chin. Then there was a young, radiant Frau Heinz in a white lawn dress, a new mother holding a chubby bundle on her lap. As Manya picked up the picture for a closer look, another, smaller snapshot slipped out from behind. It was a photo of another man in the military dress of World War II, a dark version of the young man, but austere and unsmiling. His uniform had a thin leather strap pulled taut from shoulder to waist and his chest was covered with medals. Manya immediately noticed the skull's head, the SS insignia, on his cap. She picked up the picture and brought it closer, peering into the face half hidden in shadow. It had been two years since she had seen one of these men. The last time had been in August 1944 during the siege of Warsaw when the Poles had revolted against the Germans. Manya's unit and the remnants of two other underground groups briefly held a position in a house directly across from Gestapo Headquarters. They were throwing Molotov cocktails into the building and it was on fire. German soldiers were running out in panic and one, an officer, his face blackened by smoke, spotted her in the opposite doorway. He drew his bayonet and charged past a burning jeep directly at her. Suddenly, his uniform blazed up, and he came to a halt a few feet from where she was crouching — close enough for her to see the skull's head. She remembered what had passed through her mind while she watched him try to beat out the flames: that the thin leather belt of the uniform did not slip or come undone, but remained perfectly in place around his slender waist even as he shrieked and writhed. This made her hate the dying German even more, as if he were personally responsible for the perverse and unyielding quality of his uniform. It was the only time she had taken pleasure in the sound of human pain.

The voices behind her had stopped and Frau Heinz was suddenly next to her. She was holding a tape measure and a piece of satin lining. She stood very still.

"That is my husband," she said. "He died in the war." She picked up the photo of the young man and placed it in front of the one Manya was holding. "This is my son. He's dead too." Frau Heinz watched her. "I have been alone since 1944."

"Frau Heinz," Manya whispered after a moment, her voice husky. "Your husband was an officer in the SS."

There was a pause. "I have been alone since 1944," she repeated, gently taking the photo from Manya and slipping it into the dresser drawer. Then, turning toward Leila, who was busy in front of a mirror, she said loudly, "But it is difficult to be lonely with engaging customers who keep me so busy."

Manya's heart pounded. "I have to go," she said to Leila and walked toward the landing. This woman was the first German she had had a conversation with since the war, and she had been married to an SS officer. She hated the authoritative way Frau Heinz had taken the picture from her hand and slipped it away, and the strained cheerfulness with which she spoke to Leila. She hated that this woman believed she could make Manya an accomplice in her deceit.

Leila stopped, suddenly alert. "But aren't we going to look at the fabrics?"

"I think not."

Leila looked toward Frau Heinz, who was standing with

her back to them, pretending to fuss with one of the garments. "All right, then," she said. "Will you wait for me downstairs and we'll walk back?"

Manya nodded. She was about to leave when she turned toward the German woman. "Frau Heinz," she said in a calm voice. "You did not ask me the question I am told you always ask your new customers." The woman's back stiffened, but she did not speak. Leila, who was removing her half-finished jacket, stopped and regarded them both gravely.

The woman slowly turned toward Manya and a look of disappointment passed over her face. "I'm sorry you feel this way. I would have thought a sophisticated woman like you would feel otherwise," she said in a tone reserved for school children who have failed their teacher.

Manya's heart sank. There would be no satisfaction here. Clearly, the woman felt no shame about her past or even regret at having lost a customer. She seemed, simply, to be disappointed that moral considerations would interfere with business.

Manya turned and walked down the stairs and out the door without looking back. She stopped by the broken gate and waited. The house looked more dilapidated now than it had an hour ago. The front steps were cracked, the paint on the window frames old and chipping. It occurred to her that the entire neighborhood was probably filled with former SS men and women. There was no reason to believe that any of them ever had or ever would feel remorse. Bitterness filled her. All the Allies had done was slap the Germans on the wrists as though they had broken a few minor rules, and then the Americans had pumped money into the economy to keep the Germans away from the Communists. Everywhere she looked she saw well-fed, decently clothed burghers while the DPs still looked frail and vacant. She leaned against the broken gate and took in its rusted frame. What could she blame this woman for, after all? Wanting to put the past behind her? Wanting to start a new life?

She heard muffled footsteps within the house. Leila was probably unaware that Frau Heinz had been the wife of an SS officer and Manya would not tell her. She was sure she would rather not know. And anyway, what difference did it make who made her dresses? But Manya had behaved badly and she would have to explain herself. She could say that she hadn't realized how strongly she still felt about the Germans until she was in the house — and that would be the truth. She would thank Leila for her kindness, but clothes were not that important to her. She could wait for the Joint parcels that were often donated. But she could not bear to see this woman again.

But Leila did not wait for an explanation. She came out of the house and walked toward her, her face somber and anxious. "Don't say a word," she said. "Just forgive me. I always think people feel as I do and I'm often wrong."

"There's nothing to forgive. It's not your fault. How could you know . . . how could *I* know I'd feel this way."

Leila was about to say more, but Manya took her arm, and they turned and walked west toward the last rays of pink that were fading from the wintry sky.

Chapter 8

BOLEK STOOD BY THE WINDOW in the small, bare room in the Jelen Hotel in Bratislava and waited for Celia to finish packing. The once elegant wallpaper, now brown with age and neglect, peeled like old bandages from every panel. Even the Czech folk tunes that drifted in from the radio next door couldn't enliven the atmosphere. He leaned out the window that opened onto streets overflowing with refugees and listened to the babble of foreign languages. Occasionally, he heard clanging. Whenever Bolek came to this city he was surprised to see escapees with their pots and pans tied together and dangling from their necks, and their giant bundles of bedding balanced on their backs. Pots and feather comforters — those were the most important items in life, Bolek thought. Sleeping and eating. In the end, that's what it all came down to.

The Jelen was a transit center set up by the Czech Ministry for displaced persons. It was a small hotel built to accommodate 100 people, but there were at least five times that number here now. During the previous summer as many as 1500 people a day had come through the city, fleeing pogroms in Poland, Romania and Slovakia. The flow had begun to slow down, but all the transit cities were still choking. No one could move the refugees as fast as they poured across the border. With no place to go, no place to return to, they dragged their belongings around during the day, and when they settled down at night, they heaped their sad bundles together and recreated the higgledy-piggledy landscape of their native shtetls. When Bolek had arrived that morning just before dawn, he had had to step over a sleeping family of six in order to get through the front door.

Celia, the dead Anton's girlfriend, slipped the last of her toiletries into a small suitcase. She had been planning to return to her family's village the day before, then she had been asked to wait and fill Bolek in on the details of the murder. The bed on which she had found Anton stood in the middle of the room, its mattress stripped bare to expose the stained ticking.

Celia snapped her case shut and sat down heavily on a worn arm chair. She was in her early thirties, but looked older. Her deep- set eyes were ringed with blue, her disheveled hair carelessly pinned up on the sides. A crucifix dangled from her neck. Somehow Bolek was not surprised. A number of agents he knew had gentile mistresses, a few had even married them. He wondered what it was that drew these women. Were they attracted to danger? Or was it the men who, once free from the restraints of provincial living, pursued the taboo shiksas. Whatever it was, it made him angry. But Celia was his only link to the city and he needed her.

Anton had been a code name, a rather glamorous one for a forty-year-old Jew from Pinsk who, despite having emigrated to Palestine in his youth, had remained a small-town boy with a heavy Yiddish accent and a weakness for *chulin*, the traditional Sabbath stew. But Anton, like all the members of the notorious Stern Gang, was remorseless and resolute. The gang had originally been part of the Irgun, a right-wing guerrilla movement in Jewish Palestine, but broke with them in 1943 to form a more radical group. At times members of the Stern Gang coordinated their work with the Irgun, the Haganah and the Brichah, but were prepared to go further than anyone else to get the British out of Palestine. During that summer of 1946, the Gang and the Irgun had bombed the King David Hotel in Jerusalem and inadvertently killed some Jews and Arabs along with British soldiers. Ben Gurion and other moderates in the Haganah viewed Gang members as renegade terrorists who stood in the way of negotiating with the Allies for a Jewish homeland. Some people called them extremists, but most survivors believed that after the Holocaust, nothing was too extreme. Bolek wasn't sure if he agreed with the Stern Gang's methods, but a part of him was grateful that someone had the guts to slap the British around. So polite, so civilized, yet they would rather let ships full of survivors drown off the coast of Haifa than anger the Arabs by allowing them to land.

"It was poison," Celia said, nodding in the direction of the bed. "I could tell by his swollen face. Anyone would have known that." She sat hunched over, elbows on knees, wearily puffing on a cigarette. "The welfare people who run the hotel said it was a heart attack. The place is so crowded with refugees, it would have caused a panic if word of poison got out." She threw a disdainful look toward the door. "It would have been one way to cut down on the population in this place."

"Do you know who did it?" Bolek asked impatiently. He had to call Haganah headquarters in Paris with the details of Anton's death and then get the arms to Vienna — in one day.

The contact in Vienna, who also seemed new at this, had not been of much use. He had given Bolek a Russian uniform for cover and the address of the hotel, and sent him on his way while he muttered something about Celia's connection to Czech smugglers. It seemed she was the only one left in the city who could get things moving.

"A fellow named Beneš fingered him and the British poisoned him. Beneš is an exporter. We've been using him for over a year to ship out guns. He's always paid in advance and always been reliable. But he got greedy and collected twice on this job."

"What do you mean?"

"Beneš got the usual fee from us plus ten thousand pounds from the British for Anton."

Bolek nodded. "How do you know it was Beneš who turned him in?"

"He was *seen* with a British agent," Celia said, unable to conceal her annoyance. "We tail all the hired help when a big fish like Anton is involved, someone with a price on his head. Beneš probably thought Palestine was going to open up soon and that would be the end of his business. He took the risk for the big money." She gave him a patronizing smile. "Remember that the next time you're on an assignment. People will betray you for a lot less."

"Why didn't you move Anton out if you knew Beneš had informed?" Bolek was getting nervous. Everything about this mission seemed sloppy and unprofessional.

"We knew exactly when the British planned to intercept the shipment and we changed our routes. And Anton had the best cover. We didn't think they'd act so quickly." Tears welled up in her eyes, and she reached for her bag and pulled out a handkerchief. "What did Beneš think we'd do, let him take his money and move to the South of France?"

Bolek instinctively leaned forward to take her hand, but she shook him off.

"Go to the Joint office and telephone Avigur. He's the Haganah chief in the Paris office. He'll arrange to get rid of Beneš." Bolek's heart began to pound. Suddenly Celia's face looked sharper, more defined.

"Anton would be glad if he knew his death made them retaliate," she continued. "He hated Avigur and all the moderates, hated working for them. He thought they were too particular about reprisals, so careful not to upset the British. He used to call them cowards to their faces, but they needed him, so they took it." A faint smile settled into the corners of her mouth for a moment, then faded. "The Haganah will make an example this time. If Beneš isn't eliminated and the British are allowed to get away with killing Anton, they'll be able to buy off every smuggler from here to Moscow."

Bolek sat motionless, his mind racing. He was listening intently to what Celia was saying, but at the same time he imagined calling Paris, rehearsing what he would say to Avigur. He knew they would want to get rid of Beneš before the shipment went out that night and there wasn't enough time to send someone from Paris. They would want him to do it. He suddenly felt very alert.

"Where is Beneš' office?

"Josefa Street, not far from here. He's there every day, even Sunday. He has a secretary who stays in all day. He takes his lunch at Le Train Bleu down the street. Every day at two." Celia rattled off the information in a listless voice.

Bolek walked to the window and looked out at the leaden sky. It was a thick but cloudless sweep of dirty white that

87

seemed to press down on the city. He felt himself borne toward an inevitability, a conclusion he had been preparing for all along.

"How will they do it?" he asked.

"You mean kill him? They'll probably shoot him and dump him in front of his office. Then they'll notify the Czech press and the international press and, if they're lucky, reporters will show up and take lots of pictures." Celia stood up and put out her cigarette. She glanced at the bed, then took her coat from the back of the chair, draped it over her shoulders and picked up her bag.

He turned and put his hand on her shoulder. "I'm sorry."

She shrugged. "I've been expecting this since the first day I met Anton. No one in this business could not." Her face softened. "It's a kind of relief, you know. Now I can sleep at night. Even if it's alone."

"Why don't you stay on and work for us?" He regretted the question the moment it was out of his mouth. He knew the answer.

"I'm sick of this business. It's never been that important to me. I did it for Anton, not for you people. I knew we'd never have a life together. I wish I could say it was good while it lasted, but it wasn't. He was an impossible, nasty little man." She turned to go. "I don't know why I stayed so long."

He grabbed her arm. Once she walked out the door, he knew nothing would get her to come back. "I have to get the guns to Vienna. I can't do it alone. I need you to help."

She stared at him. "You're here alone?"

"Yes."

"Oh, that's just wonderful," she said throwing up her arms. "They expected you to finish this by yourself! They couldn't wait a week for the others to come back, they gave it to a beginner. No regard, no regard. Well, I'm glad I'm out of it." She picked up her bag.

Bolek panicked. "Please," he said. It came out like a hiss.

Celia pretended to adjust her coat, then turned and studied him for a moment. Her eyes were hard. "You're taking a truck?"

Relief spread through him. "We've arranged for one with a Red Cross tarpaulin. Now all I need are some reliable people to help me load the crates. I have the uniform and papers. It should get me to the Rothschild Hospital in Vienna. We're storing the shipment in the basement until it goes to Bari."

"You are new at this, aren't you?" she said, half smiling. "I didn't need to know that."

Bolek reddened. "I assumed I could trust you."

She faced him squarely, her eyes narrow. "I'll tell you what a good worker assumes: that a woman who has just lost the only man she ever loved, whose only allegiance to your cause was through him, who now is alone and, yes, bitter, such a woman is not a safe bet." She sat down again. Several minutes passed. Then she took a few deep breaths. "All right, I'll arrange for some people to help you." She reached inside her bag and drew out a Walther PPK pistol. "Keep this," she said, handing him the gun. "You people need it more than I do."

Bolek was surprised when the operator put him through to Paris so quickly. So was the Joint official in Bratislava, a young social worker from America who spoke no Polish and very little Yiddish. He had looked confused and somewhat annoyed when Bolek barged in and tried to explain that he needed to call Haganah headquarters. But when the American heard the words "Reschash Company," the code name for the smuggling operation, he pointed solemnly to a telephone in the corner. He took up a position at the door that separated his office from the front room and Bolek began his call.

The voice on the phone spoke French with a thick Hebrew accent. Bolek identified himself and asked for Avigur, who came on immediately speaking rapid-fire Hebrew, then switching to Polish after Bolek fumbled with the few words he knew. He could hear the irritation in the chief's voice.

"There's a Belgian shipment due next week in Vienna, another big one. A number of locals are involved. We have to eliminate Beneš and we need headlines," Avigur said. Bolek remembered Celia's prediction. The voice deepened. "Paul said you've been working for the Brichah in immigration, but you were with the partisans near Vilna." There was a pause. "You have some experience in these matters, no doubt."

Bolek recalled the scrawny group of Jews and Poles who had hidden together during the last year of the war but had never managed to hook up with a real unit. Afterwards, they liked to think of themselves as partisans, but the closest he had come to the kind of experience Avigur was referring to was shooting a half-starved wolf slinking off with some of their food.

"Yes, I do," he said.

"Good. Celia will give you a weapon. After you get rid of Beneš, she'll tell you who to call at the newspapers."

Bolek stared at the numbers on the telephone.

"The shipment will leave by tonight?" Avigur asked.

"Yes. It's all arranged."

Bolek suddenly remembered Le Train Bleu café. He had

passed it on the way to the Joint offices, and it had been filling up with people taking their midday meal. It was a pretty place, with white tablecloths and real plates, so unusual in these desperate times, and something about the simplicity of people sitting down to share a meal had made him ache for Landsberg.

Avigur's voice brought him back. "The shipment has to go out tonight. What's the schedule for the other business?"

"Beneš goes to a local café at two everyday and will probably stay till three. I'll have to intercept him when he returns to his office." His mind raced, and the words fell out. "I haven't even seen the building. I haven't had time to set up anything."

"There is never enough time for this kind of thing," Avigur said in a weary voice. "Can we count on you?" Bolek knew it was not a question. It didn't matter. A certainty had already settled inside him.

"Yes."

He would go to Beneš' office building and check for a place to wait, then he would look for the informer at the café. He glanced at his watch. It was one-thirty.

He stood in the doorway of a butcher shop next to the café and looked through the French windows to where Beneš sat, by himself, at a small table. Celia had shown him a picture, yet the man was a surprise. He was younger than Bolek expected, in his late twenties like himself, but ordinary, drab really, with a pasty complexion and thin straight hair severely parted to the side. He wore rimless glasses that made him look as though he should be reading literary tracts in a dusty library, not double-dealing the Palestinian underground. It crossed his mind that Beneš was the kind of man whom, had they been friends as boys, Bolek would have had to defend against bullies. He was struck by the man's precision as he ate his omelet, slowly, punctuating each forkful with a piece of bread that he carefully tore from a roll next to his plate. He was as meticulous and repetitive as a machine. By now, he would have learned of Anton's death, yet he did not seem in the least troubled. Then Beneš turned and looked distractedly past Bolek out into the street. His face was timid and kind.

Beneš signaled for a check and stood up. He counted out his money and neatly tucked a tip under a dish. Bolek spun around and hurried toward Beneš' office. It was only three streets away, but he strained to keep from breaking into a run. By the time he arrived, he was drenched in sweat. He stopped in front of the building and glanced into the lobby. It was empty. He stepped into a recessed alcove on the side and was immediately hidden in shadow. Relieved, he took out the Walther and for the tenth time checked the pistol's magazine. He had not had time to check anything else — if there were other people in the building, if Beneš, secretary was in that day. He couldn't even be sure Beneš would return directly to his office. All he had was a pistol and bullets. He would shoot and slip out through the courtyard, even if someone came by.

Bolek reasoned that Beneš would have to pass within a foot of him before he could mount the stairs, close enough not to miss. A surge of hatred shot through Bolek. He wanted this man dead, kind face or not. He imagined anonymous smugglers reading the newspaper headlines, their faces suddenly grim. He saw the rifles he would ship to Palestine being lifted from their crates like sacred objects. Jewish hands holding weapons. Jewish fighters seeking retribution. Beneš suddenly appeared before him in his line of sight. The last thing Bolek saw before he lifted the pistol toward the soft brim of Beneš' hat was a small curl of white smoke, squiggly, like a child's drawing, rising from a brick tower in Birkenau. He pulled the trigger.

CHAPTER 9

It was growing dark earlier now and although it was barely six o'clock, the lights along the main street of the Landsberg camp were already lit. The camp was more attractive at night. The rich amber from the lamps coated the stones of the old buildings with the warmth and depth of honey. It had rained that afternoon, a drenching winter rain that soaked through the window and door frames, and the air was still pungent with the smell of damp wood. Manya walked briskly, with purpose. She was on her way to teach English to a group of refugees. Silently, she scolded herself for being nervous. She had taught before demanding students at a distinguished university, and except for the time she was being evaluated by the Party Committee, she had been confident and comfortable. And here she was, about to instruct a rag-tag group of refugees, most of them poorly educated to begin with, and she felt as insecure as though she was about to take a final examination. Would they accept her? Would they be hostile when they found out about her background?

Rochel had been the one to suggest the teaching work.

The older woman had noticed Manya lying around the barracks, withdrawn and melancholy. Then, several nights ago she had come to sit at the foot of Manya's cot, as was her habit, to watch her prepare for bed, when suddenly she asked if there was anything Manya could contribute to camp life. Manya had been so taken aback by the question that she had stopped brushing her hair, realizing she had been so self-absorbed since arriving in Landsberg that she had given no thought to the one thing that had always mattered to her the most: being useful.

"People here want to learn," Rochel had said, "and you are educated. And you'll be a better teacher than the men here, than the soldiers who only think of going home or our own survivor men who are not yet kind. You'll be better because you are a woman who has feeling for others. I can see this in your face. Surely you have something to give."

Something to give.

The words pierced Manya. All of her life had been about something to give, but the giving was always relegated to the future. Teaching nineteenth-century Polish poetry to bourgeois university students was something she had done purely for her own pleasure, not because it would help bring about a more just society. Now and then, she tried to justify her love of teaching and her passion for literature by telling herself that beauty in any form would make her students better people. But it was a ridiculous platitude. She loved to teach for personal and selfish reasons and teaching was what she did best — not writing political tracts or throwing Molotov cocktails.

Teaching was what had kept her sane during the months following Joseph's death. She would stay late at the university preparing her lessons or inventing busy work, avoiding her apartment until the last possible moment. Then she would creep home in the dark and hurl herself into bed, only to awaken, an hour later, with her heart racing. She tried to enclose herself in her beloved texts, but no heartfelt metaphor, no matter how beautifully conceived or precisely rendered, could distract her. When she heard that returning Jews were being killed by their Polish neighbors in Kielce, she began to intone fragments of her favorite verses before she went to bed, as if she could exorcise her demon fears and summon back Joseph with a phrase from Adam Mickiewicz:

> *I cannot part from you! Over the sea*
> *You follow, and on land you walk with me.*
> *I find your footsteps in the glacial ice,*
> *And, in the Alpine waterfall, your voice.*

She knew it was an absurd thing to do, but she had started doing many absurd things since Joseph was murdered. One night at the height of her desperation when she hadn't slept for days, she sat on her living room floor and talked to Joseph's picture. She alternated between screaming at him for having deserted her and replaying the scene of his death, which she had not witnessed, over and over again until there was no room left in her mind to keep him alive. Exhausted, she had wrapped herself in the feather comforter and leaned against her bedroom wall praying for a sound from her neighbors to make her feel less alone. But nothing could ward off the feverish nightmares that awaited her. Nothing made her feel better except going to teach the next day.

Manya balked when Rochel first suggested teaching. "What can I teach?" she asked. "The Polish language? The Jews here despise it. Literature? What for?"

"English," Rochel had countered. "You told me you know

English and I heard you talk to Miss Weiss. You could teach it to the refugees who want to go to the US and Australia. There are lots of them. Teach English to the ones who want to work for the Americans to get extra rations. And to the women who are looking for nice Jewish GIs to marry." She rolled her eyes. "But don't go to the Jewish Committee. They want everyone to learn Hebrew and go to Palestine. Go to UNRRA and volunteer."

And so she had presented herself at the UNRRA office. Eleanor Weiss had looked over Manya's application and pronounced that she would make an excellent teacher. Her fellow refugees needed her. Yes, there was a shortage of teachers who knew Eastern European languages and, yes, there were many DPs who wanted to learn English. Not because the British were welcoming them into Great Britain. No, Miss Weiss had begun to steam, because the British want the DPs to go back to where they came from, to places like Poland, Romania, Slovakia, where Jews were still being murdered a year and a half after the end of the war.

Miss Weiss had found some English primers, all of them dog-eared and tattered, and told Manya she would requisition pencils and writing tablets — not easy to get — and arrange for a room in which to hold classes. Maybe she could even get her hands on a blackboard and some chalk, Miss Weiss had muttered to herself, and the way she narrowed her eyes when she said this made Manya feel sure she would. Three days later, she received a note telling her she was to start teaching that night.

Now, as Manya neared the administrative building UNRRA had converted into an educational center, the pleasure of anticipation began to take over. It wouldn't matter that she didn't speak Yiddish. It didn't matter that she looked like a shiksa. They needed her or they wouldn't be in the class. She hurried up the steps of the building and saw an announcement about her course tacked to the front door. She had been assigned the back room, a large one, as she remembered, so there must have been a big enrollment. She could hear the hum of voices as she walked down the hallway and, as she drew closer, the chatter die down and then suddenly stop. When she stepped through the door, twenty-five people stood to attention. She was so startled it took her a few seconds before she could signal them to sit down. Then she looked around. Yes, she could see on their faces, in the way they sat stiffly at attention, that they already knew all about her degrees and her background and had elevated her to that most sacred of Eastern European positions, "Pani Professor."

Manya smiled, awkwardly she felt, and tried to relax. The class remained somber, waiting for her next move. The students were older than those she was accustomed to teaching, some of them middle-aged. They looked like all students on the first day of school, apprehensive, nervous, but there was a fear in the room as well, she could feel it, something left over from the ghettos and concentration camps. It struck her that many of *her* students — because that's what they had become the minute she entered the class — many of them had not held a pencil in years.

Suddenly she was alert and filled with conviction. She was about to speak, but on impulse swung around and faced the new blackboard she had glimpsed out of the corner of her eye. She picked up a fresh piece of chalk nestled on its ledge and wrote the word "Hello" across the flawless slate. The class obediently opened their books. "No," she said in Polish, "we will not be using books for quite a while." They looked puzzled, then they frowned and fussed with their texts. "Put them away," she commanded, and walked around her desk and squarely faced the sea of apprehensive faces. "I want you each to say something using the world 'hello.' It can be anything, but say it one at a time." The first few, men in their early forties, said, "Hello," and then shyly gave their names. Manya could see that this was going to be deadly and stopped the class after the fifth person.

She paced back and forth in front of the class, her mind racing to find a solution. "You're walking down the streets of Landsberg," she said as she walked down the aisles of the room. "You are going past the administration offices, past the PX, past Army headquarters. Close your eyes. What do you hear?" This caught them immediately and they seemed to lean forward as one person, more curious than confused. A few people threw each other awkward glances and strained to understand her. "Please close your eyes and try to hear in your mind what you hear on the street every day." She paused for a moment. "Can any of you tell me what English sentences you just heard?" Hands popped up and she began to point. "Hello, buddy. Going out tonight with the German dolls?" said a man in a pea green army sweater. Everyone laughed. "Let's get some smokes and head to town" another one chimed in. One man wanted to know what it meant to call a woman "stacked" and although Manya had no idea, she found it amusing when a young man, perhaps all of twenty, was able to tell them. A pretty girl with jet black hair and cupid lips blurted out, "Hello, cutie want to come with me tonight?" then stopped and blushed bright red.

The lesson sped along. The students became more and more animated as they discovered how much English they had absorbed without knowing it. Their clothing vocabulary, especially, was extensive. "Can't we get some newer coats for these poor people," one class member said he had overheard. "We must ask the Joint to send us one thousand brassieres," another refugee, also male, added. Clearly, the refugees spent a lot of time at the warehouse. There was an awkward moment when one man, a distinguished professorial type, asked what the word "kike" meant. "Sometimes I hear the GIs say this," he said, "and I know it's an insult because they say it in anger. When I asked one of the chaplains what it meant, he looked embarrassed and wouldn't tell me. He just wanted to know who had said it." Manya had never heard the expression, but the man in the green sweater who, as it turned out, worked in the PX, seemed to know all the slang expressions. "It is a curse word," he said. "Last week a Christian GI said this in front of a Jewish soldier and got punched. There was a big fight." The man paused to smile. "The Jew beat him up."

Within the hour she had stopped speaking Polish entirely and was giving directions in rudimentary English. She had guessed right. The refugees, most of whom had been living with Americans for more than a year, knew much more English than they suspected.

"We meet again on Thursday," Manya said when she saw that it was nine o'clock. "Please pay attention to all the English you hear on the street, in the offices. Keep listening and remembering." She said good night and the class stood to attention. She was about to comment on this disagreeable habit, but stopped herself. She sensed it was important for them to keep the ritual.

A few in the class — two elderly gentlemen and a rather prim looking woman in her thirties — probably wouldn't be back. She could tell by their stiff faces and down-cast eyes that they didn't like the frivolous nature of the conversations.

But several others collected around her desk as she

gathered her books and prepared to leave. "Such a good class," one young man said, "so different." "It is exactly what we need," said an older man wearing a yarmulke. "It's practical, you will help us learn quickly." Manya smiled and thanked them until one by one they had all dispersed. When she closed the door behind her she noticed the pretty girl, the one who had blushed, hanging back.

"May I walk with you, Pani Professor?" she asked. The eyes, up close, were not as young as the face.

"Certainly, but I want to go directly to the barracks. I'm sorry, but I'm exhausted."

"Of course, Pani Professor, I understand." The girl fell in stride with Manya. The streets were quiet and a thin mist had settled. "My name is Channah. It's Anna, really, but I prefer to be called by my Jewish name."

"Why?" asked Manya. Since the young woman had made a point of telling her, she wanted to know the reason.

Channah seemed unperturbed by the question. "Because that's what I am, a Jewess."

It was a peculiar word to use, Manya thought, especially for someone who looked more child than adult. Channah was very thin. Her fitted jacket fell loosely over her scrawny torso and the body beneath looked hipless, like a young boy's. A Jewess? There was nothing about her that evoked that word, nothing voluptuous or womanly. The face was beautiful, but sexless, like the faces of children during that brief and deli-cate transition from childhood to puberty. "I hope you will be many things in your life," Manya said without slowing her brisk pace, "more than just a Jewess."

Channah seemed to consider this statement for a mo-ment and answered simply, as if she were announcing the time of day. "I was in Ravensbruck for two years," she said, referring to the women's labor camp rumored to have been used by the Nazis as a brothel. "Don't you think my future has already been decided for me?"

Manya's heart twisted. This youngster couldn't be more than seventeen. "No, I don't," she said. "Just because the Germans used you doesn't mean you're a prostitute." She swung around to face her. "Whose morality is this? Are you going to let other people tell you who you are?" Manya stopped, feeling helpless and stupid. What could she say to change the girl's mind? Surely, something better than these inanities.

Channah ignored Manya's outburst and continued in the same monotone. "I had syphilis. It was too advanced when they found me. I'll live, but I can't have children. I don't want them anyway, not in this world." A look of irritation passed over her face. "But this isn't important now," she said impatiently. "That's not why I wanted to speak to you. I plan to work for the Haganah decoding messages and I need to learn British slang. Could you give me extra work to do outside of class? I want to start as soon as possible."

Manya looked at her with disbelief. The young woman was blatantly telling her she was a spy for the Jewish underground. Bolek had also hinted that he was, and that strange fellow, Paul, was probably involved as well. Was the whole camp seething with terrorist activities? Why did they broadcast this? Then it occurred to her that she was a Jew in a Jewish camp and they took it for granted that she would never betray them.

"I don't know British slang," Manya said. "I don't know American slang, either. The students were educating me as well as each other."

"Oh, what a shame," Channah replied. She looked as

though she were about to cry. "Do you know anyone who can help me?"

"I don't think so. I've only been here for a short while." They had arrived at Manya's barracks. She was about to go, but caught a glimpse of Channah's despondent face in the lamp light. "I'll see what I can do," she said and gently patted the young woman's thin arm before turning and mounting the steps.

Weizmann House was still lit even though it was past lights out. A few women had bought their own lamps and after much complicated wiring, had succeeded in connecting the fixtures to a few electrical outlets at the front of the barracks. It was a terrible fire hazard, the UNRRA people kept saying, and they threatened to take the lamps away. The women ignored these threats — as if anyone could make them follow army regulations and get into bed by ten o'clock. When Manya walked up the aisles, the barracks looked almost inviting, like a series of living rooms, each with its gathering of women sitting in a pool of light. They clustered on each other's beds and chatted softly, sometimes well into the night.

But she still had not found it easy to fit in. She knew most of the women found her marginal. They still withdrew when they learned she had been with the Polish underground while they were perishing in the camps. And they made her uneasy as well. Although none of them ever said so directly, she knew they thought her politics had been an excuse to deny her Jewishness, and as for her nationalism, what kind of fool believed she could be a Pole and a Jew at the same time?

She walked by Tovah who was sitting on her cot with a flowered coverlet draped over her feet, writing a letter. Tovah liked to sew. She pieced together scraps of fabric she collected from the sewing class she attended at ORT, the vocational training program in the camp, and made herself elaborate spreads and pillow shams. Every morning before she left the barracks, she carefully arranged her cot as though it were a fashion window. Manya nodded to her as she passed. The young woman returned her nod but made no move to engage her. Last week Tovah had approached her and shyly offered Manya an American magazine she had picked up in the PX. She had lingered by Manya's cot to tell her about the various Zionist meetings and study groups that were taking place at the clubhouse. She should stop by some night. She would find it interesting. Manya knew Tovah was trying to recruit her, but she remained quiet and let her prattle on in her girlish voice. When Manya showed little interest, the young woman leaned in and asked: "Why were you a Communist?"

Manya answered just as directly. "I believed they would build a better world."

"But you're Jewish," Tovah had added with a surprised look. "Did you really think they would include you?" The sincerity of the question hit her with the force of a blow.

"Yes," she had answered feeling her eyes fill. "I once thought so. I did."

Rochel was sitting on her own cot mending a blouse when she saw Manya approach. She smiled and set her work aside. "Well?" she asked. Manya slid next to her.

"It went well. I have a class." She kissed Rochel on the cheek. "Thank you."

Rochel grinned. "Good. I knew you would, Manyale. Now you won't be so sad." She stepped over to Manya's cot. "Come now, you must lie down and get some rest. I don't want you to get sick." She began to fuss with the covers, turning down the army blankets as though they were precious linens.

Manya started to undress. She put on her nightgown, slipped a sweater over it, and crawled under the heavy blankets. The barracks always seemed to be cold now. Rochel sat quietly and waited for her to finish.

"Now that you are settled, I have something to give you." She smiled and handed her a piece of paper. Manya took the folded note and opened it.

> I came back last night. Rochel said you wouldn't return until late so I am leaving this with her. Can I see you tomorrow? I'll be at Meyer's at noon. I think of you.
> Bolek

CHAPTER 10

THE NEXT MORNING, when Manya awoke to pure morning light filtering through the barracks windows, she felt for the first time in months a sense of accomplishment. Thoughts drifted by, fragments of last night's English class. Using slang had been a good idea. It had put the students at ease and created an intimacy they would never have found through the "Can you tell me the way to the post office?" approach. She would continue in this way, at least for a few more classes. Curious, how so much of the discussion had been about sex. It was inevitable, she guessed, being surrounded by young soldiers. Then she remembered Bolek's note.

Almost two weeks had passed since he had left her at the barracks steps with his cryptic remarks about Jewish identity. She had tried not to think about him, but decided, after some hesitation, to ask Rochel if she knew where he had gone. "He must be away on a mission again. Sometimes he disappears for weeks." The older woman had beamed. "He is a wonderful man, so brave. All our men are."

Manya hadn't succeeded in putting Bolek out of her mind, in containing the physical pull of him, and now this note had thrown her. Her attraction to him was unexpected, but what she feared most was the intensity of his convictions, his fierce love of all that was possible, his rage to tear the world apart. It was what had drawn her to Joseph, that vitality and fervor.

She lay on her bed and revelled in the quiet of the barracks. The other women were either at breakfast or filling out endless questionnaires for the Red Cross or UNRRA or the Military. Every day there was a notice for yet another form to complete or interview to hold. It was as though the world had descended on the DP camps to gather statistics. Everyone had great difficulty grasping what had happened to the Jews and they seemed to think that numbers — abstract things — could make it real. New numbers kept springing up on the front page of the newspapers like a bad dream re-writing itself: eighty thousand Polish Jews survive out of three million; 90 percent of all Jewish children exterminated in the camps; fifteen hundred Jews flee into Allied Zone from pogroms in the East.

But no numbers could compare with her own memories: going to work at the paint factory one day, she had absently turned down Ulica Novolipki and found herself in front of the ghetto. She had glanced past the German guards and through the barbed wire that surrounded the area and caught a glimpse of a little girl, no more than three years old, tugging at the disease-swollen body of her dead mother. Each time she relived the scene she was that mother and that child, dying for no other reason than because they were Jews. Cold, gray statistics were no match for the horror she had witnessed behind the barbed wire.

She burrowed deeper into the knot of linens and flannel cloth, and saw Bolek's note on the night stand. She did not want to be unbalanced by this man. He was a zealot, living the life she had left behind. She wanted no more of it. She would not live with fear again, not in any form. She had made that decision when she went with the American officer. She sat up, wrapped her sweater around her body and quickly walked to the bathroom. Her tangled, greasy hair fell over her face. She hoped there would be some warm water to wash it. She stopped. She was not going to beautify herself for this man. She would not pursue him. But by the time she had showered, she had convinced herself there was no reason not to meet him and that by avoiding him, he would take on more importance than he merited. She dressed, purposefully avoiding her rose-colored dress, the one with the bias-cut skirt that neatly draped her thighs. Her simple navy wool skirt would do. She pulled the comb through her damp hair, carelessly pushed it away from her cheeks, and left.

It was close to lunchtime and the streets were filling with people headed for the mess hall. It was one of those vivid, crisp days when sunlight seemed to beam off every surface. Even the DPs she passed in front of the Tracing Bureau looked cheered, and several of them leaned against the building, their faces momentarily softened by an unexpected breath of warm November light.

She saw Bolek through the café window, sitting at the same table as two weeks before, his leather jacket draped over the back of his chair. He was leaning over a newspaper, reading. She hadn't remembered the broad shoulders. As he picked up the paper, he turned slightly, bringing his face into profile. His nose was aquiline, almost incongruous with his probing Asiatic eyes. She saw, in the set of his mouth, a self-possession she had missed before.

The first time she saw Joseph, he had been reading a newspaper. It was in the spring of 1939 and he was sitting outside a café with some fellow students from the university. Everyone was chatting and drinking while he, turned away from the group, was absorbed in his paper. She noticed him because his face had a look of such compassion that she thought he must be reading about a tragic incident. Later, she came to know that this capacity for empathy informed all aspects of his life, and later still she realized with bitterness that it was this very quality of natural goodness that had blinded him to danger and led to his death.

Now, as she stood gazing through the café window at a man she hardly knew, she was painfully aware that this one — the force of whose passion somehow precluded compassion — this one would not have let himself be deceived by a comrade.

She was standing beside Bolek before he noticed her. He looked up and threw her the amused half-smile he had the first time they met. Then he folded the newspaper and pulled out a chair. He performed these acts smoothly, without hesitation, and as he turned and took her in, a twinge of breathlessness caught her.

"Well," he said. "How have you been since I abandoned you?" She was surprised by his arch tone. There had been so little banter between them before.

"Surviving," she retorted, using the standard camp joke. Then she hesitated. She did not want to be drawn into flippancy. She was curious about the vividness of his face, which she did not remember from their last meeting, as if all his colors had deepened. Whatever he had been doing agreed with him.

"You've been gone for a while. Where did you go?"

"To Bratislava."

"Not for the Joint, I assume."

Bolek gave her a knowing smile. "No. For my other friends."

"Rochel says you work for the Brichah. Is that what you were doing?"

"No. This was about moving rifles, not people. Sometimes we coordinate with the Haganah." He must have seen her face change because he tensed. "That upsets you," he said. "Why?"

She was thinking of Januck, a childhood friend, a member of her underground unit, shot dead while trying to steal a few rusty rifles from the Germans during the last days of the siege of Warsaw. The pity was that the rifles would have made no difference. The Soviets had lied to them, even then, and had sat on the east bank of the Vistula and waited for the Poles and Germans to annihilate each other before entering the city victorious.

"Anything dangerous upsets me these days."

He leaned toward her, and his chair, which had been precariously tilted against the wall behind him, hit the floor with a thud. "So, you think we should stop because someone might get hurt?" His eyes glittered with annoyance and she saw him assessing her. She saw, also, that she had become a challenge.

They were interrupted by Meyer who gave them both a conspiratorial smile.

"Coffee again?" he grinned, "or something to eat?"

She looked around at the steamy, smoke-filled room. She had forgotten that it was lunchtime. People were sitting in front of plates filled with sliced meat and potato salad.

"Something to eat," she said, glad for a distraction, "I'll have . . . " she paused, looked around and pointed to a nearby table " . . . that."

"Good choice," Meyer said, "because that's all we're serving today." There was no trace of sarcasm in his Polish this time, only humor. She had become Bolek's "friend" and would be treated as such. Meyer put down the salt and pepper he had been holding and disappeared into the back room.

"Rochel tells me you're teaching English," Bolek said. "People should be learning Hebrew. Do you think a Jew can be safe anywhere but in a Jewish state?"

"Is anyone ever safe from the greed and cruelty of others?"

"It's not the same thing."

"No, it's not," she said quietly, "and maybe you're right, but I'm not willing to risk my life again . . . "

" . . . and not interested in any man who is," he said, finishing her sentence for her. She stopped and looked up at him, amazed. He took her hand quickly, impulsively, and stared at it. Then he shook his head as though he were silently scolding himself.

"I came back last night and the first thing I thought of was you. I wanted to see you."

"Why?"

"You're a fighter, a survivor."

"I was. I'm a different kind of survivor now."

"I want to spend time with you. Why complicate things?"

"Because things are always complicated."

"No. People meet. Everything else is simple." She began to ease her hand out of his, but he held it fast. "Why not?"

"Because I want a normal life."

He shook his head. "I had a normal life before the war. I wanted to be an engineer and I couldn't. I wanted to go to university and I couldn't. That was normal for someone like me. I married and had a son and I went to work for my father. For the two years I worked with him, I woke up every morning knowing exactly what I could expect from the day. What was normal was not being able to change anything."

"And the Zionist groups or the Communists. Why didn't you join them?" But she suspected he had not been an idealist then, and even now she sensed that he was driven by personal suffering, not just principles.

"What did they do before the war except hold meetings and a few rallies? Did it help anything?" he asked. "Now, I can make things happen." His eyes grew somber. "And there is also revenge. It's the best feeling I've had in a long time."

Manya looked at Bolek's troubled eyes and imagined touching the black-fringed lids. No, she couldn't let that happen. She stood up. "I'd better go. I have to prepare for tonight's class." The last thing she saw as she walked towards the entrance was Meyer, holding a steaming plate in both hands, an alarmed look on his face.

Manya liked being in the mess hall and when she entered the building, her feelings of confusion and constraint loosened. She came here often, drawn by the special kind of privacy one only finds in a very large space. It was practically empty now, except for some kitchen help clearing away the lunch dishes, but even during meal time, when the hall was crammed and the din almost unbearable, she found a comforting solitude in the wall of noise between herself and others. And although the Landsberg camp was filled with foreigners — UNRRA personnel, Joint workers, soldiers — the mess hall was tacitly off limits to outsiders. It was one of the few places in the camp where no foreign eyes unwittingly reflected what they, the survivors, had become: a homeless, shabby group of people with a tragic past and a doubtful future.

She had planned to work on her lesson for that evening's class, on the verbs "to be" and "to have," and she pulled out her books, eager to crowd out thoughts of Bolek. She thought a moment and wrote "I *have* been enjoying these K rations enormously," and "I *have* more than enough blankets to keep me warm." Then she added "I do not *have* a visa because I *have* been rejected by every country in the world." These could be good examples of "to have" as a standard as well as an auxiliary verb with "to be." She paused to consider them. They might be too complicated for beginners. She scratched out the sentences and wrote "I *have* not *had* any lice for a day, a month, a year, a decade" and "I *have* not *had* a good meal since I left Auschwitz." Funnier, but still too complicated. She smiled to herself. A month ago she would have been appalled at the idea of joking in this way. By now, she had learned that the DPs loved to make fun of their situation and took every opportunity to laugh at themselves.

She looked up from her book and caught a glimpse of Leila sitting off in a corner with a man. He was hunched over a bowl of soup, which he held close to his body and sipped quickly and deliberately, as if he feared someone might take it away. Leila sat sideways in her chair, staring into space and smoking. It was the second time Manya had seen her friend with this man. The first time she had spotted them walking down main street together, and something about the preoccupied look on both their faces had stopped her from crossing to greet them. Rochel had filled her in on the details. This was Leila's husband who, thinking his wife was dead, had gone to Paris after liberation to be with a sister who had migrated there before the war. He was sick, in a hospital of some kind, and it was the sister who searched for Leila through the Joint and Red Cross. But each time they located her, Leila had just moved to another camp in search of her husband. They kept missing each other in this way for over a year until he finally caught up with her in Landsberg. As usual, Rochel was effusive. "A happy ending," she sang and clapped her hands. Watching them sitting alone at the table, the man absorbed in his soup, Leila engulfed in cigarette smoke, Manya thought they looked like they were at a funeral, not a reunion.

When Leila saw Manya, she perked up and said something to the man. He did not look up, but nodded and continued to eat until he was finished. Then they rose and walked to her table. The man was tall and gaunt and moved slowly, holding on to the backs of chairs for support. Manya stood up to greet them.

"This is my husband, Simon," Leila said. "He's just arrived from Paris. Can you imagine, he's been looking for me since the war ended! Isn't it wonderful?" She was holding him by the elbow, a strained smile on her face.

Simon bowed and extended a bony hand. It felt weightless in Manya's palm. "I'm pleased to meet you," he said. His voice was unexpectedly soft and melodic. "Leila has spoken of you."

Leila's eyes flitted nervously between them. "Now that

Simon is here he'll get better. He was sick after the war, in Paris, but they said he was cured. The truth is they didn't have enough medicine, so they discharged him from the hospital. The Americans will finish the job." She smirked. "Don't they always?" Simon stood beside his wife with a resigned look on his face, like a child waiting for a speech to end.

"Won't you join me?" Manya asked. She was curious about this much-awaited husband and anyway the man looked as though he needed to sit down. Leila had not been without male companionship during his absence. She had confided to Manya that she went out with men, even slept with them when she felt particularly lonely. But she considered that to be normal under the circumstances and thought of herself as faithful, at least in her heart, which, to Leila, was the only place that counted. Manya knew that Leila was a strong believer, if not in true love, most certainly in family. She wanted children and a home as much as she wanted pretty clothes.

"Would you like a cup of tea?" Manya asked when they were seated. "I'll get some."

Leila brightened and looked at Simon, who shook his head no. "I'm afraid I have to go to the TB clinic," he said, "but Leila can stay." His listless eyes were the color of water.

"I'll go with you," his wife chimed in.

"Don't be silly, I can go on my own. I'll see you later." He stood and turned to leave.

Leila held on to his arm. "No, I want to come. I need to know about the new X-rays."

He gently disengaged himself. "You were there yourself last week. You know the doctor said the spots were faint. They took new X-rays only because they lost the old ones." He touched her shoulder. "Stay with your friend. You haven't had any fun since I arrived." He took a breath and straightened himself. "She's a great comfort to me, my Leila," he said to no one in particular. "And I am a great burden to her."

Leila's cheeks blazed. "Simon, I told you not to say that!" He patted her arm and shuffled away down the aisle.

Leila stared after him. She lit a cigarette and fussed with the pack before tossing it onto the table in front of her.

"I don't know who that man is," she said, picking specks of loose tobacco from her lips. "It's been over a week now and he's still a stranger to me."

"Was he very different?" Manya asked. It was hard for her to imagine Leila married to a shadow.

Leila threw up her hands, her blue eyes sharp with exasperation. "You wouldn't believe it," she moaned. "For one thing, he keeps apologizing. Before the war we used to fight all the time and then make up, but he never, never, apologized. He was always too proud for that." Her face creased with pain. "And he doesn't really talk to me. When I ask him what he's thinking, he says, 'Nothing,' and he means it. He says it's a way for his mind to rest, to recover from the war, but to me it seems like a vacation from living." She gazed down the aisle toward the entrance. "The man you just saw used to laugh a lot. I used to be able to make him laugh." Tears came to her eyes, and she picked up the cigarette pack and tore at the cellophane. "I'm afraid my husband did not survive the war."

Manya didn't know what to say. The only things that came to mind were clichés: give it time, this happens often, people need to recover, etc. But she stopped herself. All this was obvious. Anyone who had been through the camps was forever changed. It was a question of how.

"You know what he told me?" Leila continued. "He said I don't have to stay with him, that he would understand if I wanted a divorce. Can you imagine?"

Manya felt she could be straightforward with Leila. She knew her friend expected it. "Perhaps he's right," she ventured gently. "It's been over a year since the war ended. What if this is what he will be like?"

But Leila looked stricken. "He's my husband," she said as though it were a holy word. "We were married for three years. We had plans, a future. He was going to take over his mother's leather business and we were going to have five children." Her face trembled. "The only thing that kept me going in Bergen Belsen was thinking of those children. During roll call, when we were made to stand naked in the freezing cold, I used to picture those children in my mind, what they would look like, what I would call them, and it helped me forget where I was. When I had typhus, I imagined them sitting around my bunk, and I talked about them so much the other inmates thought they were real." She stopped and Manya saw her struggling with the memory. "Simon will be all right, I know it. The old feelings between us will come back."

The two women sat quietly staring at the pile of cups and saucers on the table in front of them. After a while Leila stirred in her chair.

"I saw you with Bolek Holzer." She took a quick puff on her cigarette. "Be careful."

"What do you mean?"

She shook her head. "No, no, no, let's not play that

game. You can't sit in a café with someone without everyone in Landsberg knowing about it. In this camp, if a man and woman so much as smile at each other, the rabbi starts planning a wedding."

Manya had not intended to deny her relationship with Bolek. She had asked the question genuinely.

"What do you know?"

"He sleeps around a lot — with German women."

A jolt went through her. "Who told you that?"

"Paul. We're friends." Leila paused, catching herself. "No, it's not what you think. He's a distant relative. He says Bolek used to hang around the beer halls when they went to Munich on business. He liked to pick up the Fräuleins and bring them back to the hotel. Paul used to hear them in the next room." Manya waited to hear more, but Leila lit another cigarette and stared over her shoulder. "He said Bolek used to be moody all the time, get angry at everyone. He picked fights with the Germans. Paul stopped going out with him after a while. And you don't know Paul. He doesn't have enough imagination to make this up. I'm not telling you what to do, but you should know this."

As if he knew they were talking about him, Bolek suddenly appeared, walking quickly up the mess hall aisle, pushing against those who didn't move out of his way fast enough. His jacket was buttoned and he was still wearing gloves. He stopped abruptly when he reached Manya, and with one hand on the back of her chair and the other on the table, he leaned over and spoke.

"A man named Jacob Kaplan just came to file for a visa to the US. He's from Komorow, the village you said your parents came from. He listed a Sarah Reichel as a deceased sister. That's your maiden name, isn't it?"

Manya's heart began to pound so hard she felt as though it were lifting her out of her chair. "My Uncle, my Uncle Jacob . . . ," she murmured. She grabbed her coat and moved blindly toward the door. Then she stopped, turned and glanced at her papers and books. Leila waved her on, gesturing that she would take care of it all. Bolek reached the door before her and held it open. As she stepped through it, Manya felt as though a great gust of wind were depositing her into the outside world.

He was sitting in Bolek's office, twisting his cap in his hands when Manya burst in. He stood up suddenly and blinked a few times, taking her in while she searched the familiar face. Then he closed his eyes as though the sight of her was too much to bear, and opening his arms wide, stepped forward. She leaned into him. A short sob, like the sound of something small breaking, passed through him. They stood like this for a few seconds, their arms draped around each other, each trying to make solid and substantial what their eyes had seen.

"Manyale, Manyale, how can it be?" he murmured, stroking her hair. He pulled away and looked at her, his face filled with the same combination of kindness and confusion she remembered from her childhood. She pressed him to her. The form beneath the overcoat felt scant, hardly a form at all, more like a meager collection of sharp protrusions. He couldn't be more than fifty, yet he was stooped and brittle. She touched his cheek and the skin was thin, almost crinkly beneath her fingers, and then caressed his hair, also thin, not at all like the luxurious honey-colored curls she remembered. Four years. She had not seen her uncle in four years, but in that moment it seemed to her that time had collapsed like a telescope and suddenly it was night and Uncle Jacob was hugging her good-bye at the train station in Koromow. Uncle Jacob. Her mother's only brother. Her grandmother's youngest child. She buried her face in the shoulder of this old-young man and cried.

"I didn't go home afterwards," he said holding her. "When I heard that Sarah and your father had been captured in Lvov, I thought you were with them, you and Joseph, and that you all went to the camps."

She shook her head. "No, we couldn't get out of Warsaw. We joined up with other underground units during the siege."

He brushed the tears from her eyes, then put his hands on her shoulders and looked directly at her. "You know Bubbe went to Treblinka, don't you?" It was neither a question nor a declaration, but a solemn acknowledgment.

Jacob had been shipped to a Nazi labor camp with the other men of his village a year before her grandmother's disappearance. He couldn't know about the forged identity papers Joseph had miraculously located for the old woman or about Manya's plans to hide her in Warsaw; how she had put off the final trip to the village, fearing that, even in city clothing Manya would provide, even without uttering a word of her Yiddish-accented Polish, her grandmother would be found out and they would all be arrested; that just as she had procured the train pass and was about to go, Joseph had told her it was too late. The village of Komorow and its bordering district had been cleared: final deportation of all Jews from the area was under way. Why hadn't she gone for her grandmother sooner? She had found the courage to kill a German, but not to save her grandmother. She hugged Jacob tightly, bracing herself against the familiar flood of shame.

"I know about Bubbe," she murmured. Manya pulled back from her uncle and turned around, half expecting to find someone else in the room with them. But it was empty. Bolek had quietly disappeared.

"Joseph is dead," she said. The sound of her own voice uttering the words filled her with pain. She stopped to take a deep breath. "He was killed eight months ago. Someone who was with us in the underground shot him."

"He survived the war and the Poles killed him?" Jacob covered his face with his hands and burst into tears. She pulled a chair over and sat him down, then slid onto a stool beside him. He was sobbing quietly, his deep-set blue eyes rimmed with red. It hurt her how much he looked like her mother. They both had the same ruddy coloring and sharp cheek bones — and startling blue eyes. Suddenly, she longed for the vibrant woman who had swept in and out of her life, throwing her kisses from the door as she sped off to one of her endless meetings. Sarah Reichel had been more like an older sister than a mother, someone Manya both emulated and resented. She had been a contradiction — a woman of big emotions and unpredictable mood swings, yet competent, reliable and sure of herself. Now Manya longed for her just as she had throughout her childhood, wanting her reassuring presence even if she couldn't have her full attention. Had they lived, Manya was sure her parents would have left Poland. Her mother would have charged off to Moscow to accuse the Secretariat of betraying Lenin's ideals or found a way to get to America to pound their fledgling party into shape. She would not have stayed in what she called "used-up Europe," which she saw as a collection of decadent city-states without the energy or imagination to throw off its imperialist tradition. Sarah Reichel would never be paralyzed with doubt and indecision as her daughter was now. If she were here in Landsberg, she would be organizing a strike against the military for more coal to heat the barracks or demonstrating in front of UNRRA for more rations. And Manya's submissive father would be obediently trailing behind her as he always had.

Jacob withdrew a handkerchief and wiped his eyes. His resemblance to her mother was only physical. He had not been as ambitious or political as his dynamic sister. He had stayed behind, a good-natured bachelor content to care for his mother. His small hardware store gave him only a modest living, but he didn't seem to mind. He seemed never to mind anything, not his sister's constant criticism of what she called his complacent bourgeois existence nor the relentless matchmaking of the village women. His mother, of course, never reproached either of her children and was happy simply to have Jacob near her.

Manya waited silently for Jacob's crying to subside. Out the window, the Landsberg synagogue caught her attention, a shoddy wooden structure with a hand-painted sign in Hebrew and a Star of David carelessly tacked over the door. A picture floated into her mind of Jacob standing on the steps of the village shul with his friends, laughing, his head flung back, his hair golden in the twilight. As a child, her job had been to fetch him back for dinner at her grandmother's house, and she would go, always embarrassed because she and her mother did not attend services, but excited to be escorting her handsome uncle through the street. He was not religious, she knew, and went to please his mother and, she now realized, to be with his friends. She thought of the Komorow synagogue, hundreds of years old, but so stark, so completely devoid of ornamentation that it seemed to be outside history. How curious it was that the DP *shul* erected only within the last year should look just like the one in Koromow. For an instant, she imagined a trail of synagogues sprinkled like poppy seeds across a map of Europe all looking exactly the same: make-shift, humble, forlorn. And then they were gone. She shook her head. She felt exhausted.

"I thought you were dead." She squeezed his hand. "No one knew what had happened to you."

"They took us from factory to factory until there were no factories left," he said. "When the Russians started advancing and the Germans retreating, the guards took us with them. They made us walk and walk. I think they just hoped we would all die in the snow. Almost everyone did." He extended his foot absently. "I lost two toes. They waited until the last minute before they ran away, when we were already inside Germany and the Americans were close. We could hear the tanks." He turned and gave her a doleful smile. "They were very attached to us."

The smile brought her back to the time Jacob had stayed with them in Warsaw. She was about ten, she remembered, and it must have been a kind of "try out" of city life for her uncle, because unlike the previous visits, he stayed for several months, sleeping on the living room couch and sitting up late each night to listen to his sister's impassioned sermons on the joys of political activism. Away from his village he seemed uneasy and unsophisticated — and very Jewish. Yet she never felt ashamed of him. Towards the end of his visit, Manya would come home from school and find him staring out the window, stunned by the noise and the crowds. He would turn to her with this same doleful smile, and overcome with pity for him, she would throw down her books and try to make him laugh. And here he was, the only survivor of her family — and he was leaving. "Bolek said you want to go to America. Don't. Stay here."

"Here? In Germany?"

"Yes — no. I mean in Europe."

"Europe? Who will take me?"

"Someone will. Just wait. The French are opening up quotas, so are the English." Manya clasped his hand. "This is familiar. At least we're all Europeans."

He raised his eyebrows in surprise. "You still have such faith in people? You think a Catholic Frenchman will love a Jewish refugee more than the Poles did? No, no. In America everyone is a refugee." She shook her head, dismayed that Uncle Jacob was one of those survivors who believed no place was better than mythic America. That Europe had little to offer. That life in these war-ravaged countries was going to be hard for a long time.

"I don't know if you remember, but Bubbe had a brother who went to the US when he was young," Jacob said. "He never wrote and Bubbe didn't talk about it because she was hurt. You know she never said a bad word about anyone. So, I filed papers with the main Tracing Bureau in Munich and they found him. Not him — he died in the 30's — but his son, my cousin. Imagine, he wrote back to me in Yiddish, and he's sponsoring me! He lives in Chicago with his family, two grown children, he wrote, but no other relatives." He grabbed her by the shoulders, his face bright with excitement. "You'll come. We can go together. He has money, some kind of printing business. He wants to help. You can study, Manyale. There are big universities there, and then you'll teach, just like you always wanted to." Manya looked away. She didn't want to point out it was unlikely Chicago had a burning need for teachers of Polish literature nor that whenever she thought of America her heart filled with a hollowness.

"I don't know if I want to go to America."

"Why? It's the best place for us."

"For an ex-Communist? I don't think they'll take me. The newspapers say they want to put us in jail."

"Oh no! With a sponsor, you'll get a visa," he continued, "and we can both get a place on a ship."

She put her arm around him. "Tell me where you've been? Bolek said you don't live in Landsberg."

He hesitated for a moment. "In Peiting, a small town about eighty kilometers from here. I work for a German woman and her brother who have a hardware store. Hardware is hardware no matter where. They needed someone to speak Polish with the refugees. I've been there since the war ended." He took a breath. "But I'll explain later. You'll see for yourself. I have a room in the house, the same house I went to right after liberation. We were near there when the guards ran away, and I went with a group of inmates into the first house we came across. We needed food and clothing and, well, I've been there ever since." He seemed to be searching for words. "I live there. You'll come and meet Frau Weber — she's the owner. She was understanding — I mean, she helped us when she saw how bad we looked. We were starving, half dead. She rents to me — her brother has the store." Jacob shifted in his chair. He looked uncomfortable. "And you, how long have you been here?" he asked.

"Two months."

"Well, Manyale, now you're the one living with Jews and I'm with the goyim." He gave her a sad smile. "Have you converted yet?"

A silence fell between them. The afternoon sun streamed in, warming the air in the room. She looked out the window again. The synagogue was empty. It was not prayer time, she supposed. She took Jacob's hand and clasped it in hers.

CHAPTER
II

MANYA HURRIED down the hall to her class, pulling off her scarf and unbuttoning her coat along the way. She liked to get there early, before the students arrived. It put her at ease to be alone in the room. No, it was more than that. It was a way to take possession of the space and make it her own. This was a habit she had acquired during her last year in Warsaw when the university classroom became her only refuge. The more threatened she had felt, the more often she found herself roaming the halls on the third floor of the bomb-scarred main building of the university. Then, as now, her room was one of the few places in which she did not feel displaced. She put her papers on the desk, draped her coat over her chair, and began to pace along the perimeter of the room, letting her hand trail along the desks as though they were objects to be greeted. It was only when she had come fully round and was facing her desk again that she noticed a stack of books on the floor beneath the blackboard.

She untied the bundle. More textbooks. This was the third time that Miss Weiss had left these packets for her, fresh off the boat from America, and although she was flattered to be getting so much when she knew supplies were scarce, the books were invariably out of date and of no real value. She leafed through them. In fact, they looked just like the ones she had used when she had studied English in gymnasium. She smiled at the familiar drawings of women in long dresses with bustles and mustached men in top hats. They must have been donated by private schools, she thought, perusing the chapters, because the lessons varied from the proper way to serve tea to how to graciously accept (or decline) an invitation to dance at a ball. Her students certainly didn't need to learn the English words for parasol and horse buggy. "May I call a carriage for you, Madam?" she said bowing theatrically to the empty room. Then she chuckled and shut the books.

Miss Weiss, who knew about Manya's somewhat unconventional teaching methods, trusted her judgment and didn't pressure her to change them. Manya thought back to her year at the university in Warsaw when she and all of the Polish teachers had been under suspicion by the Soviets because they had been brought up in a capitalist society. From the day the Communists opened the school, they had held endless meetings. The last one she had attended, just weeks before she left Poland, had been particularly painful.

She had sat with her friend, Helena, in the Great Hall that evening, freezing as usual. Fuel was still scarce and it was impossible to heat the old, bomb-damaged building. The teachers, most of them Polish Communists who had worked with the underground, sat in neat rows, their heads bowed like frightened children while the president of the university, a small, balding man, stood on the podium flanked by his Russian overseers and accused them, again, of being too "soft-hearted toward bourgeois values," and not being dedicated to "expurgating anti-revolutionary sentiments."

"Stalin would be ashamed," he had shouted. "The victorious Russian Army sacrificed its men to liberate you not only from the Germans, but from the evils of capitalism as well." The man was so nervous that despite the cold, sweat poured down his face, and each time he wiped his forehead his rimless spectacles slid down his nose. Manya remembered him from her undergraduate days as a soft-spoken, genteel man, easily flustered by bad manners, and she knew that this uncharacteristic performance was a measure of the fear he felt under his Communist superiors.

Throughout the meeting, Helena chewed on her lower lip. Manya watched her gaze reverently at the spectacle on the podium and knew that tomorrow her friend would redouble her efforts in the classroom, not out of fear, but out of the purity of her allegiance. She was suddenly overcome by the distance between them, she who had lost heart, and her dear Helena whose faith in the Communist Party was only surpassed by her loyalty to her friends. Tears sprang into her eyes, and Helena, sensing her distress, had turned and slipped her small hand into hers. "Don't be afraid, Manuska," she had whispered like a school girl sharing a secret. "I'll help you. We'll go over all the books together."

Now, the clock on the classroom wall read four-forty-five. Manya lifted her arms over her head, arched her back and took a long stretch. She still had a little time before her students began piling in. She rubbed her forehead and closed her eyes. When she opened them there was a man standing in the doorway.

He straightened up abruptly when she looked at him and stepped back, as if he had been caught at some impropriety.

He was very tall and slender, and wore steel-rimmed glasses. She recognized him from the line of interviewees her first night in Landsberg. She remembered his name, Emmanuel something, his Czech accent, his easy manner.

"Excuse me, Pani Professor," he said quickly. "I didn't mean to startle you. The UNRRA people told me I could join your class if you have a place for me."

She did not. Word had circulated throughout the camp that her course was good, and by the second session the class was full up. She was about to say that she regretted there was no room, but hesitated. There was a gentility about this man she liked. Unlike most of the refugees, he seemed reluctant to impose himself.

"I can wait," he said when he saw her hesitate. "I know it's difficult to teach with too many students. I was a teacher myself." His Polish was still stiff.

"Oh," she said. "Where?"

"The University of Prague. Microbiology." He leaned in tentatively and spoke in those soft, melodic tones that had caught her attention that first night. "I was more of a researcher, really, but I taught advanced courses. I was not very good at it — teaching I mean." He stopped. "Unlike you, from what I hear."

There was something endearing about his awkward flattery. "Why do you want to learn English? Are you going to America?"

He came over to her desk. "I'm not sure. When I was at the university I worked on the development of antibiotics. Some people at the Joint think an American research center will want to sponsor me. If not, they tell me I could get something at an English university or maybe the Pasteur Institute in Paris." His face clouded for a moment. "It's been a long time since I did any work," he said. "I don't know if I will be of any use to anyone." He shoved his hands into his pockets and forced a smile. "But English would be good to know."

Antibiotics. The word was familiar. It was a new kind of medicine she had read about in the newspapers, like penicillin. Everybody wanted it and complained about how hard it was to get any, except on the black market. Last week she had overheard two doctors at the clinic say that the Americans had developed "a miracle drug" that could cure TB. The real miracle, it struck her, was that somewhere normal life had gone on despite the war and that people had found the time and peace of mind to write books, invent machines, even cure diseases. She took Emmanuel in for a moment, silent and waiting. They both had a lot to catch up on.

"There is always room for one more, isn't there?" she said.

He extended his arm and bowed like a cavalier. "Thank you."

She could hear her students coming down the corridor and in a moment they began to straggle in. The older men, always the first to arrive, entered and gave her a little bow before drifting toward the back to sit. Then the younger women strolled in and commandeered the front row where they continued to talk till the last minute. Except for Channah. She always came alone and sat removed from the rest of the class. The young woman had stayed on even though it was clear that the course work would not help her chances with the Haganah. Manya had avoided her after their talk. There was some shadow that hovered around the girl that kept Manya away. She seemed to lurk even while she was sitting still.

The class was almost full when she noticed the man still standing in the doorway. She had forgotten his name.

"What's your name?"

"Kozak. Emmanuel Kozak."

"Why don't you take a seat?" He walked to a seat near the window and sat down. Several students looked toward Manya, hoping for an introduction. But she decided it would embarrass him, that he would prefer to find his way slowly into the class.

"Tonight, before we begin, I would like each of you to write down your ideal menu, in any language you like." There was a rustle of interest from the students. Emmanuel was impassive. "Breakfast, lunch and dinner." Several students looked at each other, confused. "I mean list your favorite foods. Then we'll rearrange the chairs and pretend this is a restaurant and you can each take turns ordering your menu in English."

An older man who had been a law clerk, spoke up. "Excuse me, Pani Professor," he said with disdain. "I don't plan on spending much time in restaurants." This man tried her patience. He always sounded a dissenting note not, as he would have everyone believe, because he loved the art of debating, but because he was cranky and didn't like female teachers.

"Food is important to people. This is a good way to learn the English words for the foods you like best, don't you think?" She tossed a piece of paper onto his desk and raised an eyebrow. "Or do you have a better idea?"

Channah raised her hand. "I've never been in a restaurant," she said defiantly. "My family was too poor, and I was only twelve when the war broke out."

132

Manya was quiet for a moment. This was the first time Channah had spoken spontaneously. "Can you remember a favorite dish from home?" she asked.

"I can't remember anything about my life before," Channah blurted out and stared at the top of her desk. Everyone in the room stopped to listen.

"You don't have to participate in this, Channah. It's all right."

The young woman continued to stare as if she hadn't heard. "The only dishes I remember are the ones the women in Ravensbruck talked about. They used to describe them to each other before we went to sleep at night. It helped with the hunger."

"Will it make you sad to recall them?"

Channah bit her lip, thinking. The people nearby her sat staring stiffly in front of them, as if nothing would happen as long as they didn't look at her. A few seconds passed before she relaxed and lifted her head. Her face was composed. "No, I don't think it will make me sad," she said, softly. "Those were the only happy times." A rustle of relief ran through the class.

Manya handed Channah a sheet of paper. "Then write it."

She stepped onto the street and shivered. The temperature had been dropping slowly during the last few days and the bitterness of this night caught her by surprise. There would be no more reprieves. It was December and winter had set in. She rubbed her hands together. The woolen gloves she had received when she arrived almost two months ago were worn at the tips, and she felt her fingers poke through. She needed new ones and a scarf as well. She pictured rummaging through the mildewed cartons at the Joint warehouse and grimaced. Most of the donations were shabby, especially the woolen things that pilled so easily. She remembered passing a shop last week in the German sector. The window had been decorated for Christmas — small items of clothing were attractively arranged on pieces of tinsel. She had stood staring at a pair of brown fur-lined gloves carefully displayed on a bed of pine needles. They were made of smooth, exceptionally fine-looking leather, and she had longed to feel the soft fur between her fingers. She sighed. Now she wished she had bought them. She could go back and offer the shopkeeper several packs of cigarettes, she thought, tightening her scarf against the night wind. All the women in her barracks did it. Even Rochel had finally thrown out her tattered black shawl and bought a new hand-knit one in pale cream for a carton of cigarettes and two bars of chocolates. Manya pictured herself entering the shop and facing the owner, and her heart began to pound. The other women had been living with Germans for over a year and were used to them. She, on the other hand, had murdered one. Every few nights the soldier's face floated up out of her dreams, then faded before she could sense who it was. Only when she awoke did she recognize the young face that she had fled from, half-hidden among the dirt and broken boxes in the field behind the munitions factory. Since the incident with Frau Heinz, Manya couldn't bear the thought of giving the Germans anything — especially after Rochel told her that Jews from a nearby network of concentration camps had frequently been marched through town. The townspeople would have seen the living skeletons pass under their very windows. Had they felt guilt as she did or satisfaction?

She wrapped her coat tightly around her and waited at the bottom of the steps until her students dispersed into the night. Tiny crystals glittered under the light from the street lamps. It had started to snow.

"May I walk with you?" It was Emmanuel.

"Certainly." She turned toward her barracks, and he fell in beside her.

He had been attentive but quiet during class. After the incident with Channah, the students had become animated. They played out their restaurant scenes with great enthusiasm — too much, Manya thought, as though they were celebrating having averted a disaster. When it was Emmanuel's turn to order a meal, he tried to describe a potted beef dish that no one had heard of, something his grandmother had prepared for him when he was a child. But his English was too poor, and a Czech woman whose mother had come from the same area of Slovakia and who knew exactly what dish he was talking about, jumped in with glee to translate. Manya made a mental note to copy out the basic work for him so he could catch up.

"I liked your class," he said. "You're a fine teacher."

"Thank you."

"Your English is so good. Where did you learn it?"

"In school."

"Really? In school? It sounds so authentic."

"Languages have always been easy for me, I don't know why."

"You're lucky. I've never been good at anything except science. I'll probably be a poor English student, even though

I study hard." He smiled to himself. "Actually, studying is all I did when I was a child. I have no other talents. I never even learned to kick a ball. When my sons started playing soccer I had to ask my brother-in-law to explain the game to me."

There was a slight change in his voice, just enough to tell her these children were no longer living.

"I'm sorry to be talking so much," he said. "You must be tired."

"No, it's all right." She slowed her pace. "Where were you?" She didn't need to elaborate. The refugees had their own verbal short-hand.

"In labor camps. Near the end, in Bergen Belsen. I came to Landsberg two months ago because someone told me my brother had survived and was living here. It wasn't true, but I stayed anyway. It's much better than the camps in the British Zone."

"Oh, are the British bad landlords?"

"It's hard to say. There's not as much food and what there is is awful. I guess they're just poor." He turned up the collar of his coat and held the lapels closed. "Do I sound as though I'm defending them? I don't mean to. They're no friend to the Jews, but they don't have much to give away." They walked past a street light, and she noticed his hair was thinning on top. He was probably in his forties, although he had a boyish look about him. His glasses made him seem like an eager student. "I remember you from the night we were processed. You came with the Brichah group. I arrived earlier that day by train, but they put us all together anyway." He turned and smiled. "So. Are you going to America with your wonderful English?"

"No!" she said, too loudly, and stopped. The force of the word surprised her.

"Why such a big no?"

"There's nothing old in America," she retorted. She was conscious of the glibness of her tone, but she didn't care. She felt light, almost exuberant. Something was unfolding inside her, some understanding of herself that had been trying to work its way out since her talk with Uncle Jacob. Finally, she was able to speak the truth.

"So you only like old things?" he asked with a wry smile.

"Yes. They remind us of what we belong to." She took a deep breath, letting the icy air fill her lungs. She needed to reduce her feelings to one simple childlike statement that felt right.

"Why not belong to the future? There's only the future for people like us now that everything we had is gone."

That was not what she had meant, but she wasn't sure how to explain herself, only surprised that she wanted to.

"I don't mean that I want to live in the past," she said straining to regain her clarity. "But I want to live in a place where people carry their past around inside them. It gives them an emotional depth I understand."

"I know what you mean. America seems so naive sometimes. I saw that film the UNRRA people showed last week — that comedy, "Bringing Up Baby" — only I didn't understand what was so funny."

"I saw it too," Manya agreed. "Wasn't it ridiculous?" Leila had persuaded her to go to the Cultural Center to see a new American movie, but there was nothing cultural about it. It was a farce about two silly people and a leopard. The actors, both of whom spoke with affected British accents, kept falling off ladders and bumping into each other. Everyone lived in lavish homes and wore expensive clothes. Even the gardeners looked rich.

"I can't remember an American film I liked," she said. "They're all fluff and slapstick. Except for Chaplin, and he's European to the core." She loved his poignant, bittersweet movies, sentimental, of course, but with something to say. She had read somewhere that Chaplin was Jewish, but that Hitler had such a weakness for the little tramp that he watched Chaplin's movies on the sly even though he had banned them.

"Ah, yes, Chaplin. He was my favorite," Emmanuel said.

"And what about you," she teased. "Don't you want to live in the land of gold-paved streets?"

"Me?" he asked with surprise. "Oh, no. The thought of America terrifies me. It will be a difficult adjustment for a man my age, but I'll go if it's the only place that will take me." He paused. "Although I don't think I could ever understand people who chew gum."

"Don't all scientists speak the same language?"

"Only when they are sharing a test tube."

They stopped in front of Weizmann House and stood under the lights mounted over the front door. She could hear the women moving about inside. It was nine o'clock, and some of them would be preparing to go out for the evening. The young ones liked to go dancing at the social club.

She put out her hand. Emmanuel took it and looked at it thoughtfully for a moment. Then he kissed it. "Thank you," he said. "I enjoyed our conversation."

The wind had picked up and snow began to swirl around them. The flakes fell and coated them with a thin film of cold. He nodded again and she watched him weave his way into the night. He was oddly elegant in his long army coat. But she suspected he was the kind of man who didn't pay special attention to his appearance. And he didn't have to. His charm came from his intelligence and gentle humor. She was intrigued. Manya took in a last breath of fresh air and mounted the steps to her barracks.

CHAPTER 12

THE SNOW THAT STARTED that December night turned into a heavy storm, leaving the camp and the village of Landsberg locked in a deep and solemn cold. Since then, the mornings had been hectic, the barracks transformed into a comic scene of shivering women frantically flinging on their clothes. Washing became torture. The sink water turned to ice and the first half hour of the morning was punctuated with the gasps of women trying to wash. Everyone had taken to wearing most of their clothing at once. It was so cold that one night Tovah had brought in a pile of twigs she had gathered during an outing with her boyfriend in the woods. No one paid attention while she stuffed the stove with the still green branches, but within ten minutes the barracks was filled with smoke. All the women ran out coughing and stood in the snow until a soldier came and hosed down the smoldering wood. No one blamed Tovah, though the barracks stank like a wet chimney for days afterwards.

"I need tea," Rochel said one morning as she sat up in her cot and groped for her shawl. "Quick. Let's go for breakfast before my legs cramp up." Rochel always woke abruptly and grim-faced, a habit left over from the concentration camps when inmates were severely beaten if they didn't jump out of their bunks immediately. It took her a few seconds to grasp where she was before her face softened. Manya, who was going over her notes, nodded without looking up. She was already dressed in her two sweaters and an extra pair of socks over her cotton stockings, but Rochel liked to play this little game of "Let's Hurry Up," and Manya indulged her. Once out of bed the older woman was slow and deliberate, and tended to wander around before she mobilized herself for the day. And Rochel misplaced things, but refused to let anyone help her. The previous week Manya had tried to help her search for her comb. "If I can't find it myself, let it stay lost," Rochel had said, her voice full of anger.

This morning the two bundled women sat on the edge of their adjoining cots and slipped on the rabbit-trimmed boots they had received from the Joint. All the women had oohed and aahed at this unexpected bit of luxury, but when they put on the stylish boots, they saw that the buckles were missing. The young Hungarian who worked for the office supplies section at UNRRA Headquarters had given them rubber bands to keep the boots closed. Luxury had turned into a bit of a joke, but Manya was grateful for anything warm to put on her feet. She turned up Rochel's collar and, linking arms, they half-slid down the snow-banked streets to the mess hall.

They had been eating breakfast together for a few weeks. Manya had let herself be appropriated by the older woman because, for all her bossiness, Rochel was a cheerful presence. She told endless stories of life in Feilda, interspersed with good-natured gossip about the other women in the barracks. She seemed to have a gift for finding things to be happy about. "You know, Tovah got herself a GI," she whispered to Manya this morning, "a Jewish fellow from California. They're going to be married before he gets shipped back." Then she stopped and gazed wistfully into the air. "I've heard about California. They say the sun shines all year round, and oranges and apricots grow everywhere. Can you imagine such a place? What a lucky girl!" Rochel's chatter was, in reality, a monologue, and although she took genuine interest in Manya, she rarely asked her opinion or solicited her advice. Manya could sit back and let the melodic shifts of the woman's voice soothe her. Rochel liked all of the young women in Weizmann House, but most of them tended to ignore her. Manya had noticed how they smiled indulgently when Rochel chatted at them, then quickly turned to find something else to do.

When they first started sharing their morning meal, Rochel had tried to bring up Bolek. Bolek had entrusted her with his note for Manya and she felt a certain possessiveness towards the couple. But when Manya shrugged her shoulders and changed the subject, Rochel stopped. She even refrained from pointing him out in the mess hall. Manya saw him anyway. Earlier in the week she spotted him sitting with Paul on the other side of the room, and when he glanced up, their eyes met and he nodded. She nodded back and turned away to let the jolt of the contact subside. She expected him to make the first move and when he didn't, she avoided looking at his corner of the room for the remainder of the meal. Now, as she was finishing her scrambled eggs and about to go for a second helping, there was Bolek standing next to her, his hands thrust deep in the pockets of his winter overcoat. They hadn't spoken in two weeks.

"Bolek, sit," Rochel said, her face filling with delight. She pushed out a chair for him.

"Thanks," he said, but remained standing. He looked down at Manya. "A theater group's here, doing Shakespeare in Yiddish. You should go and see what our people can do. They tour all the DP camps. Professional actors, all of them. Some from the Vilna Troupe. And they're all survivors."

"Which play is it?" she asked, trying to match his casual air.

"*King Lear.*"

She hesitated. It was not one of her favorites. "Oh my. That's a serious undertaking. And a long one."

"Don't worry, it's been shortened. It usually is. I saw the great Wegrzyn play *Julius Caesar* in Warsaw before the war, and even then it wasn't a full version."

What a strange man, she thought. A carpenter and a theater lover! "Yes. I'd like to see it," she said. "Only I don't understand Yiddish."

"It doesn't matter. It's the acting that you'll find interesting. Now, you notice I didn't say 'enjoy' because I can't promise that. But I'll translate if you need help."

"You're very persuasive."

Rochel interjected. "Go, my darlings, go to the theater. What could be better? When I was a girl, troupes passed through Feilda all the time. My friends and I would wait on the road to watch them enter our village. They were like wandering minstrels in those days. How we cried at those plays! And the music!"

"Then why not come with us?" Bolek asked.

"Oh, no! I'm an old woman. I go to bed early."

"Stop acting like an old woman and you won't be one. There's a full orchestra playing. They even had music composed especially for this production."

Rochel seemed to consider this for a moment. "I don't know this *King Lear*. What's it about?"

"It's a typical Jewish family drama," he replied winking at Manya. He slid onto the chair next to Rochel. "Lear is a rich man who divides his fortune among his three grown children, all girls. But first he wants them to tell him how much they love him. The two oldest make a big show of this, but the youngest refuses to play the hypocrite and says little, although she really loves him best . . ."

"A father would sense this," Rochel said with conviction.

" . . . but he disinherits her and banishes her."

"No!"

"Then he goes to live with the older daughters who find him an annoying old man and take everything away from him."

"How terrible! No father deserves such treatment, no matter how bad."

"He gets so angry at them that he becomes crazy. Then one night, during a storm, he leaves their home and roams around from place to place. Now, he is completely *meshuge*. When his youngest daughter hears about it, she finds him, takes him to her home and nurses him back to health."

Rochel's face filled with relief. "What a wonderful ending."

"No. In the end, everyone dies."

"What? Even the good daughter?"

"Everyone. One bad daughter poisons herself. The other stabs herself. The good daughter and father are thrown into jail by a traitor and although the father is rescued, it is too late to save his daughter. He dies broken-hearted."

Rochel was silent. Her eyes grew wide. "This is not a happy story."

"No, it isn't, but neither is the story of the Jews," he said, and seeing Rochel's sad face quickly added, "I'm teasing you." Then he laughed and quickly kissed her on the cheek. "Rochel, Rochel, there's more to it than that. I know you'll like it."

"Oh, you!" Rochel pushed him away with mock annoyance. "I think I'll skip the play, though." She sighed. "I don't want to see all those deaths."

"That's the idea," Bolek said. "You have a good cry and go to bed feeling better."

Manya watched their exchange with curiosity. These two seemed to understand each other in a special way and it warmed her to see their playfulness and affection for each other. It was clear that Rochel encouraged these games. She glimpsed what Rochel must have been like as a young woman — high spirited, flirtatious. It struck her that she knew nothing about Rochel's family or what had become of them. The Feilda stories were all about her shtetl childhood, filled with idyllic descriptions of peaceful Sabbath evenings, perfect challah and loving parents gathered around a humble table. She never talked about her married life or children, and the husband had come up only once, when Rochel had told her about the notions store they owned before the war. Since then nothing.

Tovah walked by carrying a tray of bread and donuts. She nodded toward them and sat down with a group at a nearby table. Suddenly, Manya remembered an incident during her first week in camp when Tovah got the news that the one brother who might have survived had, in fact, perished in Buchenwald. The young woman had stood in the middle of the barracks holding the official notice of his death and begun to moan. The women had rushed to her side and encircled her as though they could form a human moat to contain her grief. But Rochel had remained seated on her cot, her head buried in a blouse she was mending. This had seemed curious and Manya wondered why Rochel was avoiding Tovah, someone she had lived with for some time.

Bolek, having given up on Rochel, stood up and began to button his coat. "I'll see you tonight at the Cultural Center," he said to Manya. "Eight o'clock."

"Tonight?" she replied surprised. "That's not much notice. My class doesn't end till eight."

"Finish a few minutes early. You won't have many students anyway. I'm sure most of them already have tickets." She bristled at the authority in his voice, then brushed it aside. She wanted to go.

"It sounds like an interesting evening," she said, looking into Bolek's eyes with a show of command. "I'll meet you in front." She picked up her tray and moved toward the urns to get a another cup of ersatz coffee which, bad as it was, she preferred to the omnipresent Ovaltine. As she glanced back for a moment, she caught him looking at her. Their eyes met and he tipped his cap to her. She managed to turn away before he could see her smiling to herself.

Bolek was right. By five-thirty only five students had shown up for class. During that afternoon she had noticed posters and bulletins announcing the play all over camp. The troupe was scheduled for three performances — not enough for a camp with five thousand people. There would be big crowds. Last week she had wanted to hear a Beethoven concert performed by visiting musicians from Palestine, but when she arrived at the box office a half hour before the performance, she was told the performance had been sold out for weeks. She wondered if Bolek had gotten these tickets in advance with her in mind.

She turned to the five students who sat glumly watching the door for their classmates to appear. They did not look enthusiastic. "Shall we break early?" she asked after they began shifting in their seats with premature boredom. They nodded and she dismissed them. She headed back to the barracks to change.

Emmanuel followed her outside. He had been to every class since joining and usually walked her back to the barracks. She liked him more each time they talked, but was grateful that he hadn't imposed any further. Tonight, he seemed particularly lively. She bent her head into the wind. She was in a hurry.

"I'll be lost without my class. You're sentencing me to an evening with the men in my barracks. There's usually a poker game going on, and I'll have to listen to a lot of grumbling. My fellow refugees don't like to lose. Sometimes they throw things." He looked over at her. "You're putting me in mortal danger by sending me back early." He tilted his head when he spoke as though he were preparing to hear her say something amusing.

Manya remained silent. She knew what was coming.

"Why don't you join me for dinner? I hear there are some very good restaurants in town."

"I'm going to the theater."

"I see."

"It was a last-minute invitation." She was annoyed with herself for apologizing.

"Some other time perhaps."

"I'd like that very much."

He left her at the corner with a nod and turned down the street towards his own barracks. It struck her she was always watching him walk away.

The sidewalks of the camps were bordered with piles of encrusted snow tinged blue by the failing daylight. It was a beautiful time, dusk, neither day nor night, but with a dovetailing of colors that illuminated the world like stage lights. She stopped and took in the silence of the air, her eyes sweeping the deepening mauve of the sky, so hushed and intimate.

As she passed the Immigration building, she saw a light in the office she knew to be Bolek's. On impulse, she crossed the street and glanced in the window. He was there, sitting at a desk examining a map so large it overflowed onto the floor. Paul was next to him hunched over the table. She was about to withdraw when Bolek reached over toward his backpack and saw her. He waved for her to come in. She shook her head. He motioned again, this time more insistently, and stepped toward the door.

"Come in, come in," he said, running his hand through his rumpled hair. "We're just finished." He turned to Paul, who had not lifted his head. "We are finished, aren't we Paul?"

The other man looked up and stiffened when he saw her. "It seems so," he said sharply and quickly folded his map.

"You don't have to do that. She knows."

Paul stopped, the crinkled paper filling his hands. "Knows what?" he asked frowning.

"Nothing, nothing," Bolek replied, shrugging his shoulders. Then he took Manya by the arm and pulled her into the room.

"I was on my way to change," she said. His hands felt strong, even through the coat. "You were right. Almost all my students were absent. I had to cancel class." She knew it would give him satisfaction to know this and instantly regretted flattering him. He was confident enough without her encouragement.

"Don't you know Jews love the theater?" He took her books and placed them on top of a desk cluttered with papers. "Stay for a minute. Paul was just leaving. We've been working since I saw you this morning. It's time to quit, but I can't tell that to this man." He slapped Paul playfully on the back. "He'd make me work in my sleep."

"What do you mean 'she knows'?" Paul asked again.

The two men stared at each other for a moment, then Bolek threw up his hands in irritation. "Oh, come on. She knows what everyone else in this camp knows." He folded his arms across his chest. "What is the matter with you? We leave a trail everywhere — you and me and the dozen other agents here. And why not? Who will inform on us? The Joint people, who are all American Jews? UNRRA, who doesn't care and has no power? The American Army, who want us out of here as much as we do so they can go home? She's a Jewish refugee just like the rest of us. She isn't going to tell anybody anything."

Paul turned back to the desk and finished folding his map before he spoke. "You should think about this more carefully. This is not like smuggling canned peaches to Marseilles." He swung around and glared at Bolek.

"You're overworked and underloved. You need a break. I keep telling you that."

"Don't you read the papers?" Paul continued. "You're in a position now to endanger other people." He turned to Manya with the same impassive face she remembered from the café. "You seem to be in this now, so I'll give you some advice. Your friend needs to keep a low profile. Don't let him beat up any Germans or he'll end up in a military prison again, and this time they won't let him out." He scrutinized her face, as if he could decipher how much she knew, then turned away. "I guess he spends too much time with you to get into trouble with the Fräuleins."

Bolek paled. "You've got a big mouth," he said in a strained voice. "Just stick to your truck routes."

"And you stick with your nice Jewish girlfriend, and nobody will have to worry about you." Then Paul slid his papers into a rucksack, flung it over his shoulder and, without turning around, walked into the cold January night.

Bolek leaned against the desk and rubbed his forehead in a gesture of exasperation.

"Ignore Paul. He gets angry whenever he thinks I'm involved with a woman. It used to mean trouble."

Manya moved toward the door. "You don't have to explain anything," she said. "We'll meet in an hour."

He blocked her way. "No, please sit down. I can't let you leave without explaining." He pulled out a chair and waited until she sat down. Then he reached for a cigarette, absently offered her one, and when she shook her head no, lit his and inhaled.

"I don't want you to get the wrong idea."

She was silent. It would be silly to deny the tinge of jealousy. Even now, confused and angry, she felt an urge to touch him. She had a fleeting image of him in bed with a beautiful, pink-skinned woman, and it annoyed her.

"So why do you beat up Germans?" she asked. The question sounded more belligerent than she had intended.

He stopped, his cigarette in mid-air, and was quiet for a while. Then he came and sat down beside her.

"When I first came here last year, I was angry." He shook his head. "No. That's a stupid word. I was sick with rage and there was no way to get away from it. It was like being nauseated and knowing you couldn't vomit." His voice was steady with effort. "I had a wife and a baby, a boy. Abraham. They didn't survive. When I found out, I couldn't stand it. If someone had asked me then to blow up the world, I would have done it.

"During the day I behaved like a normal person. I worked for Immigration and for the Brichah. But at night . . ." He turned toward the window. "I've never been afraid of anything before, but my dreams made me afraid, so I put off going to sleep. I went drinking instead. It took three beers and I was ready to look for a German to hurt. I'd purposely bump into one on the street or in a bar and if he gave me a hard time, I'd punch him. They were usually too surprised to fight back right away so I had my chance to hurt them, even the big ones, before someone pulled me off. Then I could go home and sleep. A few times someone called the MPs and they put me in jail overnight for disorderly conduct. But they always let me go in the morning."

He stopped and watched her, but she remained quiet. "Paul's afraid that the next time I go to jail they'll trace me to the Haganah." He was silent again. "I don't fight anymore. It was getting too dangerous."

She shifted in her chair. "What about the women?

He raised his eyebrows and smiled. "Are you jealous?"

"No."

"Then why do you want to know?"

"You said you wanted to explain."

"Does that need explaining? Why do men sleep with women?"

"To help them sleep better, of course." She felt herself color. She stood up and reached for her books.

"Manya, Manya, every time I see you we end up arguing," he said. "Let's stop this. You're too good at it." She was about to protest that she was not arguing when he caught her eye and they both laughed. He took hold of her arms and pulled her to him.

She gently pushed him away. "We'll meet in front of the theater at eight, okay?" He studied her for a moment, then released her, watching while she adjusted her coat and pulled on her hat. She didn't remember where she had put her books and looked around distractedly. Arguing like this was assuming too much. They had met only a few times and the meetings had been brief, yet she already knew more about him than she wanted to. No. More than she knew what to do with. Now, as she saw Bolek casually leaning against the desk, his hands in his pockets, his face bemused, she knew that her confusion fired him. She spotted her books and gathered them from the desk behind him.

"All right," he said. "I'll see you in an hour."

There was a huge crowd milling around in front of the Cultural Center. People clutched their tickets and paced to keep warm while they waited for the lobby doors to open. Many of the refugees had made an effort to dress up for the event, and the effect was a strange mixture of shabbiness and unexpected glamour. Some women had tied brightly colored silk scarfs around the collars of their worn coats. A few held dainty black and white fur muffs that made them look like little girls at a skating party. Manya spotted Tovah and Leila near the entrance, both in new felt hats coquettishly balanced on their upswept hair. They looked vivid with excitement. When Leila saw her, she waved gaily, but made no attempt to approach her through the crowd.

Manya too had been caught up in the promise of a night out. She had put on a dress that was much too flimsy for the weather, but the only one that seemed special. It was a dove-gray jersey made just before the war with some extra money she had earned tutoring. The bodice hugged her breasts and flared around her small hips. There were no full-length mirrors in the barracks, and she had been unable to see how she looked in the small shards the women had propped against the beams. But when she smoothed down the fabric across her stomach, she could tell that the dress still fit. She had decided to pin up her hair, piling it up in soft curls on top of her head and clipping it with an old tortoise-shell barrette she had gotten for her eighteenth birthday. She rarely wore make-up, but decided to try the peach lipstick she had received in a Joint parcel. The effect was startling. The color brought out the creamy cast of her complexion and highlighted her amber eyes. She stopped to stare at herself for a long moment. She felt she was looking at a stranger, someone young and full of hope she had met briefly a long time ago.

The doors opened and people began to move inside. It was just eight o'clock, and Manya, who had arrived early, was getting nervous. As the crowd thinned, she noticed Channah standing by herself a few yards away. She was wearing a cordovan-colored leather coat cinched tightly at the waist. It was very long on her, hanging almost to her ankles. Channah's beret was pulled down over her forehead half-hiding her cheerless face. The young woman stared out at the street, nervously puffing on a cigarette. An American soldier pushed his way towards her and when Channah saw him, she broke into a strained smile. He seemed delighted to see her, and taking her familiarly by the elbow, he steered her into the lobby. One of her many boy friends, no doubt. Too many. Over the weeks she had seen Channah with a variety of men, none of them DPs. She must be visa shopping, Manya thought. Then she remembered Channah worked for the Haganah and planned to go to Palestine. She must be spying then — or else she had acquired an appetite for men. Manya sighed and turned toward the street again.

A bell sounded from within as she saw Bolek rushing towards her, out of breath, his cheeks flushed with the cold. He had not changed his clothes. He seemed always to be in a hurry and she suspected that he had a hard time dragging himself away from his work.

"I'm glad you're here," he said, taking her arm. "I was afraid you might not come and I'd have to go on a search mission."

She opened her mouth in surprise at his cockiness, but before she could say anything he led her through the crowd that was pushing its way into the auditorium. Inside a woman with a flashlight looked at their tickets and hurried them to their seats just as the lights began to dim and the orchestra began a slow, plaintive melody. The music swelled into a wail and the velvet curtains parted.

The stage was bare except for a long wooden table and chairs that looked as though they had been hammered together and painted bright green ten minutes before curtain time. Lear, wearing a crown and robe, sat facing his daughters who stood in long dresses with their backs to the audience. There was a moment of silence while Lear glared at his children, then he hit the table with his fist demanding that they declare their love for him. Manya forgot about the shabby costumes, the too-bright lights, the tacky scenery, and gave herself to the passionate theatrics. When Cordelia declined to express her love, Lear threw back his head and clutched his chest as though he had been shot. The audience gasped, shivering at the thought of so ungrateful a child. "Shame on you," someone up front shouted directly at the stage. "No respect," the people around her muttered. Manya understood enough Yiddish to make out most of the comments, but Bolek seemed to enjoy whispering the translations in her ear. Throughout the play people yelled advice to the actors as though they believed they could change the course of events. Nothing she had ever seen came close to the hysterical enthusiasm before her.

By the time the play was over, Manya was dazed. The lights came up, and they walked toward the lobby with the rest of the audience.

"You liked it," Bolek said over the din in the lobby. Everyone was loudly voicing enthusiasm and opinions. She was aware that several people had started to argue about the director's interpretation even before the curtain had closed.

"Yes, I did. But I don't know what I saw!" she said shaking her head in disbelief. Just then someone jostled her from behind and she fell against Bolek. This time she did not move away.

There was a pause. "We should be together," he said. Manya remained silent, her face filling with heat. He took her hand and put it against his chest. She could feel the warmth beneath his shirt. Then he brushed his lips against her forehead and slipped his hand inside her coat. He waited again, and still she did not move. He pulled her closer until she was leaning against him with her whole body.

"Let's go," he whispered into her hair. She looked out at the lobby, and everything became a glaze of color and noise. There was only his hand, like a brand, on her waist.

"Yes," she replied and let him pull her through the door and into the night.

It was a simple room, the one Bolek rented from a German widow on the outskirts of the camp. It had a bed, a dresser, a curtained window. The spread was pulled taut and neat across the bed. She caught a glimpse of a corner bookcase piled with papers and a rucksack carefully propped against the closet door. The room felt as austere and still as a monk's cell. He turned on a small lamp and gold light fell across the muslin curtains. When she took off her shoes, she felt a small warm rug beneath her feet.

He was undressed first and standing next to her, gently smoothing back her hair from her forehead. She unbuttoned her dress slowly, not out of modesty, but because she could not tear her eyes away from the unabashed look of pleasure on his face. When her slip fell noiselessly to the floor, he took her hands and guided her onto the bed.

He was beautiful. She had never thought of men in that way, but this man, stretched out beside her, was beautiful. Everything about him was defined, molded, hard. In the dusky light of the room his skin looked burnished, as if he had lived outdoors all his life. Her eyes took in his body and she wanted to touch everything she saw—the smooth muscles of his thighs, the solid curve of his neck. But instead she lay back and let herself feel his hands on her. His fingers caressed her breasts and the line of her hips to where they curved and yielded to the loop of her stomach. Her hands flew to his shoulders and grasping them, she lifted herself to him. He began, gently at first, to move within her, then more and more, until he found that place inside her that was deepest. Suddenly, she needed to touch his face. She held his head between her hands and kissed his eyes, his cheeks, his wet mouth, all the while moving for him, for herself, for all of sad and lonely humanity.

It had begun to snow again. They pulled the blanket up to their shoulders and listened to the gentle crackling of the flakes against the panes.

"The refugees were everywhere in Bratislava. Thousands of them pour in every day with their bundles and torn valises. They're crammed into the transit centers. They sleep on the streets. I saw wild children, orphans, roaming in bands, looking for food. Every afternoon on the main street a group of them sang strange songs and juggled. The youngest passed the hat. He was six years old." He stared at the shadows on the ceiling. "He looked like a forest creature."

"Will they go to Palestine?"

"Who else will take them?"

"I came home from work one afternoon, it was sometime during the winter of 1943 when Joseph was away. Before I could enter the building, I sensed that something was wrong. My Polish neighbor was sitting by her window waiting for me. She pointed with her eyes to a German in civilian clothes on the other side of the street. I pretended to adjust my stocking for a moment and continued walking."

"A good Pole?"

"There were a few."

"Where did you go?"

"To my friend Helena's house until Joseph came with the forged papers."

"Did you love him?"

She lifted her head from his shoulder. "Very much."

"There was a man in Bratislava who betrayed one of our agents. I had to get rid of him."

"You killed him?"

"Yes."

"Does it bother you?"

"No."

"I killed a German during the war."

"Lucky."

"No. He was just a boy. I remember his face."

"Do you think he would have remembered yours?"

She lay on her side with her back pressed against him. His body was warm and hard. It had stopped snowing and she could hear the silence of the white streets. She spoke into the darkness.

"In my dream I see a woman and a girl in a cart racing ahead of me. The horses speed up in the moonlight and I run. I want to catch up with them, but I can't. The girl turns and smiles at me. 'Hurry up. You're missing all the fun,' she says, and the wind rips the skin from her face. The old woman motions to something in the distance, then lifts her shawl to the wind, and it starts to unfold over and over again and rolls down the road towards me. I reach for it, but the woman yanks it higher, like a banner, and with one sweep of her arm, she turns the night into white ash."

The room was still. Bolek listened to her hoarse breathing for a moment and then took her damp hand in his. He smoothed the scars on her palms with his fingers, then kissed them.

"How often?"

A breath, a soft catch in her throat. "Every night."

He bent over her, slowly, and she clutched his shoulders to steady herself.

CHAPTER 13

SHE BEGAN to drop by his office in the afternoon when she knew Bolek had less work to do. She would come in, sit on a chair next to his desk and turn to him only to find she had nothing to say. Instead, she just sat quietly and watched him move around the room. He avoided direct contact with her as well, chatting with Yankl, his Joint co-worker, and occasionally including her with a nod. It was Yankl who filled the gaps with a running commentary on camp life. "Pani Gerson," he would say folding the *Landsberg Zeitung* to the humor section and swinging round to face her, "Of course we all know that Yiddish is impossible to translate, but you might appreciate this anyway." Then he would read to her from a column called "The Happy Pessimist," a title that, Manya decided, suited him exactly. "Today we have some interesting definitions." He began gravely, as though he were about to relay a new medical discovery. "The Committee of Landsberg has redefined the term president as a person who travels everywhere by automobile, but only arrives at banquets." He would clear his throat while she chuckled, then go on. "And by their behavior the Camp Committee has also redefined politician as a person who has a permit to do what is forbidden to others." Yankl himself never laughed, but his eyes sparkled whenever she did.

The first time she saw Yankl, she had been repelled by him. He was an ugly man with a straggly beard and dirty fingernails who always wore the same black vest and greasy yarmulke. He reminded her of the stooped and ageless Orthodox Jews who had lived in the Warsaw ghetto before the war. But Yankl was friendly, spoke wonderful Polish and was fond of quoting Adam Mickiewicz, the nineteenth-century Polish poet. When she asked him how he had developed a taste for Poland's greatest nationalist poet, he launched into a lecture.

"*Konrad Wallenrod* is read even by the Haganah," he said seriously. "It's a justification for using violence in the cause of national liberation."

Manya was impressed. She had taught Mickiewicz in her class and had understood the exile's passion for liberty. But she had never connected the romantic Pole with Jewish causes. Then Yankl put his hand over his heart and recited:

> *Out of the moist dark*
> *Dawn without glow brings*
> *Day without brightness.*

Delighted, Manya finished:

> *Sunrise, a whiteness*
> *In a thatch of mist,*
> *Shows late to eastward.*

"Or shows not at all," she amended sadly.
Yankl said, "With beauty, all is forgiven," and continued

to recite Mickiewicz's "Pan Tadeusz". From then on their friendship grew.

But when Paul began to stop by to discuss "business," Manya found reasons to stay away. It was disconcerting how freely he now spoke in front of her, as though his outburst on the day of the play had given him license to implicate her in their intrigues. He and Bolek would retreat to a corner of the office and the all-too-familiar conversation about rifles and ammunition, smuggling routes and bribed sentries filled her with an unbearable heaviness. The last time Paul had come in, she slipped out, leaving the two of them huddled over their maps.

But she and Bolek still saw each other at night. They had fallen into a habit of meeting at the mess hall after dinner, if she didn't have class, and returning to his room. Or on nights that she taught, she would find him leaning against a lamp-post outside the Club House patiently waiting for her in the bitter cold. She would step up to him, ready with some clever greeting she had rehearsed in her mind, then fall silent as he took her hand and led her toward his section of town. Some-times they didn't make it back without first making love in some unlikely place. Once, Bolek began to rub her palm, and she knew he would be unable to walk the remaining streets to his room without being inside her. He guided her to Paul's truck parked in its usual spot near the kitchen entrance of the mess hall, pulled back the flap and helped her in. Then they took each other among the coarse Army blankets and surplus K rations.

After these episodes, they would return to his room, fling themselves on the bed and doze, then wake and make love again before slipping into the nourishing sleep of late night. Toward morning, if they awoke together, she would lie with her head on his shoulder and listen to him murmur bits and pieces of his life into her hair.

Most often, though, she was up first, waiting for dawn. Then she would slip down the hallway to the bathroom and quickly wash. There was always the moment when she feared he would wake up and they would be faced with the awkwardness of speaking of ordinary things like tooth aches or new shoes that would jolt them out of the silent allegiance they had formed. She would hold her breath as she tiptoed around the bed, but Bolek always slept an unmoving, weighty sleep. She would dress rapidly and leave, carefully pulling the door closed and listening for the catch of the lock as it slid shut behind her. It was a reassuring sound. Once outside, she walked the empty streets back to the barracks in a state of exultation and panic. She couldn't be falling in love with this man when it seemed they had no future together. She did not want to struggle. She wanted simply to live. For him, there was no difference between the two.

One morning in January of the new year, Manya slipped out of Bolek's room before daybreak. Before returning to camp, she walked the dark streets to the old bridge to watch the Lech glide like strips of black satin toward Garmisch and the mountains in the southeast. The thinnest line of pale rose glowed on the horizon. The air was sweet and pungent. She felt a surge of happiness, then astonishment at how reckless Bolek made her feel.

There had been no time for reckless feelings with Joseph. They had been married only a few months before the Germans invaded Poland, and their life had quickly become about fear and hiding and getting through the day. She had been in love with him, but what they came to understand and appreciate about each other had been circumscribed by the war. He had the potential for so much — an accomplished theoretician as well as an activist; a lover of poetry, a lover of people — but she was only 21, he 24. She would never know what Joseph might have become.

She leaned against the stone railing and looked out at the turbulent winter sky. She had left her country like a criminal, turning her back on the party that had betrayed her and its principles. Joseph would not have left. He had been an optimist who believed in his power to change things, even tyrannical bureaucrats, even party policy. He took risks because he was not afraid to die. She was. She had never been good enough, she saw that. Even now, she shamed herself. Not yet a year since his death and she was obsessed with another man, one who was wrong and impossible. It didn't matter that Joseph would have given her his blessing. She had expected greater loyalty of herself. It didn't matter that he would have appreciated Bolek's passion and commitment, regardless of his motives. Joseph had been wary of noble motives. They blind people to suffering, he always said. Manya shivered in the damp morning mist. It wasn't Bolek's motives *she* questioned; it was the life they led to.

Chapter
14

Manya ran into Tovah at the barracks door. They had become friendly, if not friends, mostly because of Tovah's boundless cheerfulness which descended on everyone, regardless of their mood.

"Your uncle came by last night looking for you," the young woman said. She slipped several broken Hershey bars into her purse and snapped it shut. She was the only woman in the barracks who did not save her chocolate for barter, but actually ate it all. "He asked me to tell you."

Manya had met with Jacob several times since their reunion, usually in the mess hall where they sat over cups of coffee. He only came to Landsberg to see her.

"Is something wrong, did he say?" asked Manya.

"Not that I know. He looked disappointed when I told him you weren't here." Tovah stopped buttoning her coat. "I couldn't very well send him looking for you, could I?" Tovah understood these things. She had a fleshy prettiness that drew men and an appetite for enjoying them. This was their strongest bond — young women having affairs.

"What did he say?"

"He's coming back this morning, to do some business. Something about buying fabric." Tovah pulled on her gloves, then adjusted her felt hat. "He was with a woman, a German, I think. She waited for him outside, but I saw her when he opened the door to leave." She grinned. "I think your uncle has a girlfriend," she sang over her shoulder and walked out the door.

Later that day Manya was returning from the UNRRA office with a Polish newspaper Miss Weiss had put aside for her, when Jacob came rushing toward her. Perhaps it was the cold that gave his high coloring an added depth, but he looked vibrant and surprisingly animated. He stopped beside her. He was out of breath.

"Manyale, I was just coming for you." He hooked his arm through hers and steered her toward the mess hall. "I have good news."

Her heart stopped. "Your visa came through?"

Jacob looked confused for a moment, then flustered. "No, no. I've had a change of plans." He pulled her forward. "Come. It's too cold out here. Let's get something warm to drink and I'll tell you all about it."

"So Saul let me have three hundred yards of French silk and wool in exchange for the Retina cameras and all the sugar and coffee we've saved from our rations for the last six months." Jacob took quick gulps of coffee. "You know I never had a sweet tooth," he laughed. "Well, it's paid off." He explained to Manya that the hardware store was failing because it was impossible to get supplies. The Allies were pouring money into rebuilding Germany and construction companies gobbled up every bolt and nail in the country. But cloth — suit and dress material especially — was in great demand. Jacob's friend, Saul, a survivor he had met in the labor camps, traveled regularly to France and brought back merchandise to sell. "He's been generous with me, very generous," Jacob had confided. "We helped each other in the camps, and he hasn't forgotten." Manya listened and caught herself smiling. "Why Uncle Jacob," she teased, "you've become a black marketeer!"

He laughed when she called him that. "Imagine! It's like winning a lottery. I know people who will pay tops for this fabric — in American dollars." He sighed. "But it was a real hardship for Helga to be without sugar. She loves to bake . . ." He stopped and looked down at his napkin.

"She's the owner of the store?"

"She and her brother."

Manya was silent. Jacob was uncomfortable and she knew he would retreat if she probed too directly. She sipped her coffee and waited.

"Her husband was a soldier. He died at the beginning of the war." Jacob stared at the doughnut crumbs that had accumulated on his plate. "They're simple people and they were very kind to me from the beginning, even though they didn't have much themselves." He searched her face. "Her brother wasn't in the war. He had bad asthma. He still does, so they rely on me." He paused again, but still she remained silent. "In any case, I'm useful to them because of the Polish and my connection with the DP camps."

"I'm sure they appreciate the rations you get from the Joint."

He shifted uncomfortably in his chair and took off his cap. He began to turn it over in his hands as he spoke. "I've become an old man. I'm only fifty, but the war . . . I don't want to be alone." He held up his hand. "Don't protest. I can see what I've become. It's too much for me to go to another country and learn a new language. You should hear my German after a year. And I don't have the heart to start again. I'm comfortable where I am. I never wanted much, you know, and now things seem to be happening." He turned to her with shining eyes. "This woman loves me."

Manya was touched by the longing in his face. As a child she had adored and idealized Jacob, and only now could she see that he had, in truth, been a timid, bashful man with no life outside his family. She could not remember any girlfriends or talk of marriage. Looking back, she felt there had always been something asexual about him despite his good looks. She had never heard him talk like this.

He grabbed her hand and squeezed it. "Say you'll meet them," he said eagerly. "They are my family now, too."

Jacob was visibly relieved when she agreed to meet Helga and see the house and store. On the walk back to his trolley stop, he told her about his plans to add a bakery when sugar and butter were easier to come by, and perhaps even a small leather goods shop, since Saul was bringing in a truckload of skins from the east. They would set up a stall in Munich to sell any merchandise they couldn't unload privately. She had never seen him so happy and although a bitterness began to rise within her, she fought it. She had no right to stand in his way — even if she could. His life had taken root in this country, in a small town much like the one in which he was born. Except this one was filled with Germans.

The Starnberger Trolley that ran from the gates of the DP camp over the old bridge into Landsberg was almost empty on Sunday. Manya sat alone in the back and stared out the window as the ancient town slid past. In the center of modern

Landsberg was a medieval city surrounded by gothic battlements, impressive half-timbered houses and narrow stone passageways. The streets shone beautiful and serene under the white-blue Bavarian sky. As the streetcar turned a corner, Manya caught a glimpse of a group descending the steps of a church, turning up their collars, and hunching their shoulders against the cold. Everyone was probably heading home for a typical Sunday dinner, just as she was.

The trolley passed through the fortified walls of the city's southern gate, crossed another bridge to the south, and stopped. She descended and watched it make a U turn to repeat its run. Before her stretched a meadow and miles of unbroken fields. At first glance, the landscape looked bleak, but she could tell by the regularity of the plots and the neatness of the hedgerows that every inch was cultivated. In the distance, a horse-drawn covered wagon slowly made its way toward town and then, from another direction, she heard the sound of an engine. A rusted truck came careening down the road towards her. As it neared, she saw Jacob clutching the wheel, his face strained with concentration. The truck rattled to a stop and she slid in next to him. He was sweating.

"I learned to drive two months ago," he apologized, his lips pale. "Thank God the roads are empty." He fumbled with the gears. There was a terrible scraping sound and then a backfiring before he turned the truck around and headed in the direction of Peiting.

The hour trip from Landsberg was harrowing. Although the road was practically empty, Jacob had trouble controlling the truck and kept veering across the road and into ditches. By the second disaster, Manya decided to take over the driving. She slid into first, fumbled with the clutch for a moment, then felt the engine glide them forward. The truck hugged the road nicely for an old heap, and she began to enjoy the ride. She liked driving so much she made Joseph give her the wheel whenever they had access to a car. He never objected because she drove with style, he said, and he liked to watch her. The memory sank into her like a stone.

Helga was buffing a porcelain plate when Manya and Jacob came into the dining room. She jumped when she saw them and ran into another room, returning in a few seconds without her apron. She extended a small hand to Manya. "Jandubrei," she said, and then, as though the Polish word had startled her, she turned to the table and straightened the perfectly laid-out silverware. She was slight with thin, fair hair and a pointed chin. She looked very young. Jacob took Manya's coat and muffler and signaled to Helga, and they both disappeared into the sitting room where Manya heard whispering. When he returned, Jacob was carrying glasses and a bottle.

"Come inside and have a little schnapps. Helga wants to finish preparing the table."

She followed Jacob into the sitting room and sat down on an elaborately carved chair. All the furniture looked dark, heavy and over-polished. Manya sipped her schnapps. The room's teutonic formality did not help her mood. Helga returned and hopped into the chair next to Jacob. Her cheeks were garnished with two pink spots, and she had hastily combed her straight hair into a bun that was already coming undone.

"This is Erik," Jacob said motioning to a small, thin man who was standing in the entrance way. When he heard his name, Erik bowed slightly in her direction and sat down on a settee. Manya was surprised at how young Erik and Helga were. She wasn't sure why she had expected them to be older, but this brother and sister seemed scarcely out of their teens. They were probably orphans, like herself, she thought, and had inherited the house and store from their parents.

There was a silence while they all sipped their drinks. Helga glanced at Jacob several times, mutely appealing to him with her pale eyes. Then there was some small talk which Jacob translated. Manya learned that Helga had been married at eighteen and widowed at twenty, that her parents had both been killed in Berlin during the bombing. She and Erik, who was two years her senior, lived alone. She glanced nervously at Jacob who gently took her hand and held it while she continued to address Manya.

"Helga says she heard about the terrible bombing of Warsaw. She wants to know if you suffered badly during the war?"

"Tell her I was lucky. I suffered like a Pole, not like a Jew."

Jacob turned red. Helga, sensing something was wrong, looked first at Manya, then at Jacob to translate. After a moment he told her what Manya had said. The young woman looked thoughtful for a moment.

"I know," Helga said while Jacob translated. "Many people suffered much more than I did. I think about this often. Even though I lost my husband and parents, Erik and I were lucky. There were food shortages, but no bombing here. And now we live with the Americans who are very kind." She looked at Jacob. "I have a lot to be grateful for."

Erik sat quietly through this and watched his sister with impassive eyes, his long face a mask of control. Manya noticed the other two scarcely looked at him.

"Tell me, do you think my uncle can have a life here as a Jew?" Manya asked.

Helga seemed to weigh the question seriously. "That depends on the other Jews in the vicinity. There is a small community nearby and I think they will be more offended than the Germans." She gave Manya a small smile. "You know, the Germans have to be on their best behavior now."

Manya put down her drink and looked at Erik, who was staring out the window. "But will that be good enough?" she asked in halting German. Erik stood up abruptly, knocking over his glass, and strode out of the room. Manya waited, unmoving, while Helga and Jacob exchanged looks.

"Your brother seems reluctant to be a brother-in-law. Is that because my uncle is too old or because he is a Jew?"

Jacob stood up. "Manya, please . . . " Helga reached for his arm, alarmed, but he shook her off.

"As long as you know the answer, Jacob, I don't need one. Just tell me how you expect to live among these people? He despises you."

"Erik couldn't join the army because of his asthma. He was ashamed and now . . . well, he's afraid people will think he didn't join on purpose because . . .

"Because he was sympathetic to the Jews."

Jacob was silent.

"It's still a crime in this rotten country, isn't it?"

"Try to understand."

"Understand what?"

"It takes time for people to change. And Helga's not like that."

"You believe people can change? After what you said about the French, you think the Germans are better candidates for neighbors?"

"Maybe it's more a wish than a belief," he said sadly.

She stood up and walked into the hallway. Her temples

throbbed. Jacob was behind her immediately. He was pale, and his hand shook as he took hold of her shoulder. He stood a long time before he spoke.

"Please don't do this," he said with finality. "Try to understand. Even when you were small you understood so much, Manyale, more than I did or even your mother or father. Don't ask me to choose between you. You have so much of Bubbe in you."

His voice had a soft, entreating quality, but his face was resolute. She looked over his shoulder into the dining room at the lovingly prepared table with its shining silverware and starched white linen that smelled slightly of moth balls. The cloth caught her eye, and she noticed a fringe hastily mended in large, clumsy stitches of the wrong color thread, like a child's first sampler. Jacob was waiting for her to speak. Jacob was waiting to start a new life. She looked into his anxious eyes, then touched his elbow and nodded toward the other room. He smiled with relief and took her by the arm, and they both walked into the sitting room, where Helga was already rising to greet them.

CHAPTER
15

Paul placed the wad of bills on Bolek's night table. "The money for Italy," he said and sat down on the bed. Then he leaned back and swung his legs up.

Bolek looked through the money, all fifties and hundreds in American bills, and shoved them into his jacket pocket. Later, he would carefully spread them into a special zippered belt Paul had given him. He returned to the small suitcase he was stuffing with toiletries and waited. He was anxious for details, but he knew Paul would enjoy meting them out in his own oblique way. It occurred to Bolek that it was one of the few things Paul *did* enjoy. He glanced up for a moment at the dour-faced young man stretched out on his bed and thought, not for the first time, that had there been no war, no concentration camps, no need for a Palestine, Paul would have lived out an ordinary, uneventful life in his backward village somewhere in eastern Poland. He would have gone through the motions of marriage, since he needed some minimal human contact, and grown bitter with the struggle to keep food on his table. His work for the Brichah and Haganah had awakened in him a passion he would never have known and one he could no longer do without. Bolek had long ago surmised that the source of Paul's zeal was not so much a commitment to a Jewish State or even the need for revenge — he did not have enough imagination or empathy for either — but his addiction to danger.

Bolek snapped the suitcase shut, placed it against the wall and sat down on a chair.

"Our arms dealer in Rome has a delivery for us," Paul finally said. "We want it on a ship that's leaving Spezia next week." Another silence. "Contact Rome headquarters and Ben-Levi will give you instructions."

"How much money am I carrying?

"Twenty-five thousand dollars."

Bolek leaned forward in a rush of excitement. In the two months since Bratislava, his only assignments had been some paper work and a few document deliveries to Munich. He was getting restless — and now he finally had something important to do.

"I have to stay here and wait for Yehuda," Paul continued. "I'm helping him set up a training camp near Kaufering." The Haganah had taken over the Joint-sponsored sports clubs and secretly used them as paramilitary training centers for DPs on their way to Palestine and the war with the Arabs. This was Paul's new project and he wasn't happy about it, Bolek could tell. There was too little risk involved.

"You can go to Rome without me," Paul threw in. "We know we can trust you."

Bolek understood. Now that he had killed a man, no one worried that he would skip out with the money. They had too much on him.

"Where's the ship headed?" he asked.

"Palestine, of course."

"People aboard?"

"Yes."

"A crossing in winter? I thought it was policy to try and avoid the rough weather."

"They want to start off 1947 with a bang. There's a lot going to happen during the first half of this year and they want press." Paul always said "they" when he talked about the politicians, whom he hated. "We" was reserved for the people like himself and Bolek who didn't get involved in a lot of talk, but carried out the actual work.

"How many people on this ship?"

"Almost one thousand."

Bolek let out a long whistle. "A big enough ship?

"It's supposed to look big enough to get to Argentina. That's the cover story. All the refugees have nice visas from our 'art department,' but the Italians will have to be bribed anyway. It should go smoothly." He reached into his pocket and withdrew a document. "I have a train pass for you." He slipped it onto the night table.

Bolek got up and walked toward the window. The afternoon sun was fading and a bleak chill had descended on the street. This was his first time away from Manya since they began their affair a month ago.

"How long will this take, do you think?"

"That depends. I'm giving you two weeks to get the money to Rome and arrange for transporting the shipment. Contact the Haganah people in Rome." Paul pulled out another paper. "Here. I've written down the address. And don't worry. This time you'll have help."

He lay behind her with his arm around her waist, his face in her hair. Her body was like warm silk where it touched his. It was late, almost midnight, he guessed. He knew she was not sleeping. He couldn't see her face, but he felt her alertness. He usually fell asleep before she did and when he awoke in the morning she was gone. But not tomorrow. He would have to get up early and they would have to talk.

He buried his face deeper into her hair. He liked the smell of her after they made love, to drift off with her odor still on his face. He took a deep breath. She stirred.

"Why are your bags packed?"

He opened his eyes, alert, and glanced in the direction of the window. He had forgotten that the bags were there. He rolled over onto his back.

"I'm leaving for Rome tomorrow," he said into the darkness. "I'll be gone about three weeks." He could feel her stiffen. She lifted herself up and sat on the edge of the bed. "It's not dangerous," he added.

He reached for her in the darkness, but she stood up and crossed noiselessly to the chair where he could hear her slipping on her robe. Then she was at the window, a willowy form against the curtains. He began to talk, quickly, about his assignment, about the shipment, about the refugees. He described the training Paul was setting up, right in their own back yard, and how hopeful everyone was that a resolution was near. But his voice sounded strained. He was trying too hard. There would be no killing this time, he said. He had not become an assassin. Each time he paused he could feel her receding from him, as though she were fading from the room. Suddenly he was angry. "You know this is what I do."

She was silent.

"I've gone away before. What do you think I do when I'm in Munich?"

"This is different."

"How? Just because it will take longer? That's because Rome is further away." He paused. "I told you it's not dangerous. Don't you believe me?"

"That's not the only problem." He heard her move away from the window. "It will be harder for me to lie to myself when you're gone that long."

"Lie about what?"

"About what's possible between us."

He was up and holding her before she could say more. "What are you telling me?" he whispered.

"Nothing you don't already know."

"I know what we have. Tell me that's not important."

"It doesn't matter how important it is. It can't last. We've both known all these months. Why is it we never talk about the future? Why don't you tell me where you go or why you go there?"

"You never ask."

"And why is that?"

He fell silent. Then he tightened his grip around her and pulled her towards him. She slid her arms around his neck and lay her head on his shoulder. Then she let her arms drop to her sides and leaned on him with her cheek against his chest.

"I love you," he blurted out. The words hung in the air between them, inadequate, silly at that moment.

"Does that matter?" she said.

"It matters."

Everything seemed to go smoothly in Rome. On the day of the arms transaction Bolek accompanied Ben-Levi, a Vilna-born Jew who was Brichah chief in Rome, to a warehouse in Ostia where the goods were to be inspected. The person waiting outside the warehouse was an elderly Italian gentleman with refined manners and old-fashioned but expensive clothing. He was with his assistant, a younger version of himself, and a chauffeur who sat nearby in a pre-war Bentley. Bolek and Ben-Levi followed him quietly into the basement of the building, and the Italians respectfully stepped aside while Bolek pried open a corner of each crate so Ben-Levi could look inside. There were five crates filled with Browning automatic rifles, grenades and rounds of ammunition. When Ben-Levi had satisfied himself that all was as promised, he handed the money over to the gentleman who slipped it into a bag, then passed it to his assistant.

"I'm a business man," the Italian said, offering his hand to Ben-Levi "but you have my sympathies."

Ben-Levi looked at the man's hand for a long time. "Where were your sympathies during the war? In the bank?" The Italian pressed his lips together and stood motionless while Ben turned on his heels and left.

After that Ben-Levi was nervous about leaving the guns in the ship overnight. He told Bolek to wait until the morning of departure before loading them onto the vessel. That was cutting it very close, but he insisted. And Ben-Levi worried about the Italian Officials, if the right people in the right places had been properly bribed. It seemed the Rome Bureau Chief worried about everything, but Bolek didn't know him well enough to tell if it was the man's natural state or if it was this particular operation that made him uneasy. Bolek finished making his truck arrangements and caught a train to Spezia where he would stow the arms onto the Brichah ship, glad to be away from Ben-Levi and his group.

The train pulled into Spezia station with a loud hiss. Bolek pulled down his rucksack and small suitcase, and instinctively ran his hands across the belt beneath his shirt. He had been alone in this compartment since boarding the train in Rome, and for the first time in two weeks he had been able to relax.

He descended onto the crowded platform. The second and third-class compartments were so jammed that passengers seemed to be falling out of the cars, then stopping to pull their bundles through the half-open windows behind them. Within seconds, the entire length of the station was filled with people and baggage and crates, and Italian porters sang for customers above the din of the still-steaming engine.

Bolek had been to Italy before. Once he had helped smuggle a truck-load of refugees out of a DP camp in the British Zone to a town at the foot of the Austrian Alps. There he handed the refugees over to a hired Italian guide, a mountain shepherd really, and three Brichah people who knew the terrain. The group was going over the Alps on foot into Italy, where a ship waited to take them to Palestine. Afterwards, he heard that it had started to snow halfway up the mountain and that one of the older survivors had had a heart attack. The guides carried him down on their backs, sliding most of the way, but he died before they could reach the weigh station on the Italian side. The shepherd, who would not have attempted a winter crossing had he not been well paid, disappeared back up the mountain, and no one had been able to find a new guide for the group scheduled the following month. The Brichah agents had to delay the next convoy until early spring.

Another time Bolek had gone with Paul to arrange safe passage for a group of refugees travelling from the Brichah station in Merano to a steamer moored in Bari. The ship never made it to Palestine. It was intercepted by the British and everyone ended up on Cyprus. At the time Bolek was furious, but by now he had learned that there was no such thing as a failed mission. Even if a ship never reached Palestine, it could always be salvaged with newspaper headlines.

But these trips to Italy had depressed him. In Germany, the weather kept people and poverty indoors, but in warm Italy, misery stayed outside and visible all year round. He had passed through DP camps that were nothing more than a cluster of rotted Quonset huts and decrepit shanty towns on the edges of cities. He remembered seeing a skinny, barefoot woman in a tattered dress who stared at him as he walked through a refugee camp in Brindisi. She was clutching a screaming infant and he wondered how someone so emaciated had been able to give birth. It made him think of the camps and he turned away, momentarily filled with a nauseating wave of despair. Even driving through the countryside added to his gloom. Italy had been devastated by the Allies' slow, agonizing drive against the Germans, and tanks and artillery, now picked clean of all moveable parts, littered the landscape and lay baking in the sun like the skeletons of dead animals.

He hoisted up his bags and quickly wove his way through the crowded train platform to the street. A taxi pulled up beside him, and he handed the driver a slip of paper with the address of the Hotel Terminus, a seedy hotel near the dock often used by Haganah agents.

A half hour later he was standing in front of his open hotel window, scanning the harbor below. In the distance the Mediterranean spread out before him, sparkling in the afternoon sun. Then he spotted the mast of the Haganah steamer silently moored between two fishing vessels. Paul had exaggerated. It looked too small for a thousand people. It would be an uncomfortable trip to Haifa, but the refugees had known worse. He checked his watch. Three o'clock. Everything looked peaceful. The only activity on this mild January afternoon was a few bicyclists riding past on their way up the coast. Later, Bolek would look for a café with a view of the waterfront and check out the area while he had something to eat. After that, he would have nothing to do but rest until morning, when he had to oversee the loading of the weapons. He knew he wouldn't sleep.

He took off his coat and shoes and, sinking onto the bed, stretched his arms over his head and thought of Manya. With half-closed eyes he summoned up the feel of her against him as they lay curled together, and as her image deepened, his heart suddenly raced. He opened his eyes. During the past two weeks he had not been able to think of her without feeling uneasy. It had started shortly after he arrived in Rome. He was working late with Ben-Levi and his unit, and every night he returned to his pensione exhausted. Then, just as he was drifting off, Manya's face would swim up before him and jolt him awake. She had an elusive quality that troubled him. He wondered what she would be once she had recovered from the trauma of being transplanted. Even if she recovered, a fighter temporarily out of commission, he worried he would never sway her to his side.

He had sensed from the beginning that this would happen, from the very first time that he saw her sitting in the mess hall with Rochel on the morning after her arrival in Landsberg. Something about her had caught his eye and he had stopped to watch her from a distance. He saw her bend forward and reach for her coffee cup with gestures so languid and supple, he thought she must have once been a ballet dancer. Then, when he approached her table and she looked up, he was startled by her calm hazel eyes. In the weeks that followed, he saw glints of what she must have been when she worked for the underground, and it angered him. She was a Jew and she had wasted herself on a false ideology. She understood her mistake by now, he knew, and it pained her. But he would heal her. They would make a life together and she would be happy.

He shifted on the bed, suddenly uncomfortable. A breeze ruffled the curtains carrying in the smell of the sea. He sat up and began to lace his boots. He had an urge to see the soothing sweep of an unbroken horizon. The last time he had been to the sea — a large lake really — was when he and Manya had gone to Lake Ammer some twenty kilometers from Landsberg. Weeks had passed without an assignment and he had grown tense and morose. The weather was still cold, but he thought it would calm him to walk with her along the banks. And it had. On the trolley ride home they were approached by one of her students, a tall, older man whom she introduced as Emmanuel Kozak. The man shook Bolek's hand long and hard, then turned to chat with Manya. A few days later, just before he left for Rome, he saw this Kozak talking to Manya after class. The familiarity between them made him uneasy. He stepped up to them and took her by the arm. There was an awkward pause; then the man nodded abruptly and slipped away. She didn't speak of him and he never asked, but Bolek put a tracer on him. A friend at the Joint told him Kozak had been a scientist in Czechoslovakia before the war, and higher-ups in the agency were trying to place him in a prestigious laboratory in Europe or America. He had not applied for immigration to Palestine. Bolek was not surprised. The people who were most needed, who had the most to give, were leaving the fastest — usually for the States. He felt a rush of anger. The hotel room was stuffy, and the sunlight coming through the shutters exposed the grimy spots on the walls. Tomorrow, this would all be over and he would be on his way back to Landsberg. He grabbed his coat and rucksack, and ran down the stairs and out into the empty sun-baked streets.

Chapter 16

The Golden Stag Restaurant was tucked away on the Alte Bergstrasse, a narrow, winding alley in the old section of Landsberg. An ancient free-standing stone fireplace stood in the middle of the dining room. The owners did little otherwise to make the restaurant appealing. They didn't have to. A row of windows faced the street, and anyone passing was immediately drawn to the blazing hearth. There were always a few people standing outside gazing in at the fire which, during this exceptionally cold February was lit all day long. The plain wooden chairs and simple cloth-covered tables were bathed in its golden warmth.

It was early, only six o'clock, and Manya was seated at her usual table. Since Emmanuel had first brought her here two weeks ago, they had come several times, always sitting in the same place near the fire. A few customers, holdovers from the tea-drinking crowd, lingered over their empty cups and stared dreamily at the flames. Manya, too, let the flames pull her into a pleasant stupor. How good it was to be in a warm, quiet place away from the camp. It was the time she thought of as the awkward hour: that empty stretch in the late afternoon when it was too early to prepare for the evening's events and too late for the business of the day. This was the hour when a sadness descended on the women of Weizmann House and the muffled weeping began. At first, it had distressed her to hear them crying, especially Tovah, whom she had grown to like, but even after she realized that the crying was a necessary, almost ritualistic part of their daily lives, Manya felt compelled to leave. The women's pain roused an old need to comfort and, at the same time, a feeling of helplessness. She longed to help, but knew this was neither possible nor wanted.

This part of the afternoon used to be her favorite time to read and had she been able to do so, she would have found a place to curl up with a book and let a story or a verse carry her away from the grimness of the Landsberg Camp. The books were there — there was an extensive library in all languages at the Education Center — but she wasn't ready. Since Joseph's death, it seemed as though her mind had become a smooth steel wall that nothing could penetrate or cling to. She wondered if it was because she was dreaming too much. Perhaps she was using up her imagination to create her own nocturnal stories and had nothing left over for other people's tales. Last week over dinner, she had mentioned her problem to Emmanuel. He nodded and told her how when he was in Bergen Belsen, he had dreamed of sitting in an enormous room filled with six-years worth of scientific journals and a huge pot of tea. But a few weeks after liberation, when he opened a book for the first time, the words came swimming up to him as foreign as hieroglyphics. He was so shaken, he hadn't tried to read again for several months. He could read now, he said, but only for short periods before his mind began to wander and his eyes burned. And the UNRRA and Joint people kept sending him journals that were piling up, just like in his dreams. There were so many, he added laughing, that the men in his barracks started calling his cot "University Corner."

Manya felt a rush of air at her back and turned to see Emmanuel walk into the restaurant. He said something to the waiter, then took off his hat and hurried toward her. She could see his fair cheeks turn rosy with the heat of the room. There was something jaunty about him as he moved with his scarf flying behind him. When he reached the table, he sat down unceremoniously and faced her.

"The Pasteur Institute wants me to join their research team," he blurted out. "They've offered me a full position. I've always loved Paris. Have you ever been?"

"No."

"Oh, it's beautiful. I'm sure you'd like it." He paused, then gave her an impish smile. "Lots of old things."

She smiled back. She had never seen him so vibrant.

"It's a good opportunity. They have a strong microbiology department." He stared at her for a long moment and she looked away toward the fireplace. She did not want to spoil his happiness, but something about the conversation made her uncomfortable.

"You don't teach French by any chance?" he asked with forced humor.

"No, and now you needn't come to my English classes any longer."

"Oh, no, I want to come. I love to watch you teach."

She picked up a spoon and turned it over in her hand, searching for something to say. "You must be a good catch if the French are being generous."

"Oh, I don't know. My work was of some interest before

the war." He laughed when he saw her scolding look. "All right. I'll admit it. I'm a good catch." He took her hand and kissed it. Behind his glasses, his eyes glistened with emotion.

"I worked with some Frenchmen briefly in 1935. They seemed nice enough and there are so many Poles and Czechs living in Paris it won't be difficult to adjust, especially if we went . . . "

Manya slipped her hand from his and picked up the linen napkin from the table. She shook it out and placed it on her lap. "I'm so happy for you. It's just what you wanted, isn't it?"

He fell quiet and she saw the joy drain from his face. It pained her to see it, but she was not ready to encourage him. Two weeks had gone by since Bolek had left for Italy and even though it was a relief to be away from the turmoil of his presence, she still smarted with missing him. Emmanuel must have known Bolek was gone because suddenly he was asking her to dinner, to a Chaplin film, to the camp orchestra's concert. This was their third rendezvous at The Golden Stag. They always lingered late, talking, and he always left her with a kiss on the cheek. She sensed that he wasn't judging her past as Bolek did. Blame was not a category for Emmanuel. He knew life was too complicated for simple solutions.

Emmanuel signaled the waiter and when he turned back, she saw he had rallied, determined to make the evening a success. A waiter appeared pushing a cart with a silver bucket on it. He lifted a large bottle wrapped in a linen napkin and began to open it. "When I came in, I told him to find the best champagne in the house," Emmanuel whispered. The waiter placed two fluted glasses in front of them and Manya and Emmanuel sat in silence while he struggled with the cork. After a tense moment, there was a hollow pop, then a spiral of vapor escaped from the top and the waiter quickly filled their glasses. Emmanuel took off his spectacles, then leaned forward. He held up his glass toward the fire.

"It's beautiful, isn't it?" he said, peering at the tiny bubbles. His light brown eyes reflected the tawny glow of the champagne. He lifted his glass.

"To Paris." He took a long sip, then looked her straight in the eyes. "Come with me."

Manya took a gulp from her glass, and the bubbly liquid floated straight to her head. She stared at the silverware next to her plate, unsure what to say.

"Do you love this man Bolek?"

"I don't know."

He winced. "Thank you for being honest." He waited a moment. "How will you decide if you love him?"

"I don't have to decide," she replied instantly. "I won't go to Palestine and he will."

"And if he didn't go, what would you do?"

"Break with him, anyway."

"Why?"

"I don't want the life he wants and he can't live any other."

Emmanuel considered this, then lifted the champagne from the bucket and refilled both their glasses. "You're sad. Don't be," he said. She was about to protest when he interrupted her. "I love you. That's more than I thought would be possible for me. Let's leave it at that." She touched his hand and nodded. Emmanuel would take care of her, if she let him. With Bolek, she would have to take care of herself and *him*.

By the time the food arrived, Manya was tipsy enough to pretend the conversation had never taken place, and when they walked out onto the cold night, her only thought was to get back to camp as soon as possible. They headed toward the bridge, their heads bent against the harsh wind that blew off the river. Suddenly they found themselves in an unfamiliar part of town. Emmanuel took her hand. "Let's go this way. It's a short cut," he said and steered her up a winding, cobblestoned street. The moon was high and silvery, and the old stone houses looked bathed in milk. They stopped at the top of a flight of stairs leading to an arched alleyway and silently took in the moon-filled scene. Then Manya heard a familiar voice. She turned and saw Channah and a man standing in front of the entrance to a small building. Channah was flirting, Manya could tell, trying to appear carefree with her broken German. She was leaning against a lamppost and as she lifted her face to be kissed, Manya saw her smile and slip her hand under her companion's coat. The man, who looked scarcely older than she, registered alarm, then surprised pleasure as he let himself be pulled through the door.

Manya stood frozen. "What is she doing here?" she whispered.

They both stared at the house into which Channah had disappeared as though they could will it to reveal its secrets.

CHAPTER 17

THE LINE OF REFUGEES at the Spezia harbor had been slowly moving up the gangplank since seven that morning. They stood clutching their bags and waited to inch their way toward the two carabinieri who were carefully examining their papers. Bolek wondered why it was taking so long. The Italians knew the visas were forged. They had all been bribed. He had even helped distribute these "donations" to various Roman officials in charge of this district. Now, it was almost nine A.M. and not even half the group had been allowed to board. He stopped pacing and leaned against a pile of crates to watch. Everyone seemed tense. The refugees looked frightened and they had a right to be. The odds of their reaching Palestine without being intercepted by the British were slim. That meant Cyprus and detention camps.

Bolek watched the crane carefully lower a crate marked "Fragile-Furniture" that concealed the rifles and grenades. Next to him was a legitimate pile of boxes filled with personal items that would go into the ship's hold last. Suddenly, there was the screeching of brakes, then car doors slamming. He turned and saw British soldiers running toward the dock from opposite ends of the waterfront. They stopped and knelt to take up positions. A shot was fired. For a second the refugees seemed to freeze with their heads lifted toward the cloudless sky, as though they had been given a sign. Then someone screamed and everyone hit the ground. Another shot rang out and then a short round of fire. Bolek felt a jolt in his right shoulder and leapt behind the crates. Before him was a low expanse of grass, then the road, then rows of small bleached-out houses. The soldiers were flanking the dock area and had left this approach to the harbor unguarded. Still crouching, he ran across the street toward the cluster of buildings. He ran, not daring to turn around until he spotted an alley. He ducked into it, dropped his rucksack and pressed himself against the side of the building, straining to hear above the pounding of his heart. There was scuffling and shouting in the distance, then the sound of more vehicles pulling up. The British would throw the refugees into prison vans and take them to a camp on the outskirts of town. They had been tipped off. That's why the Italians had taken their time examining papers. He surveyed the narrow alley. It opened onto the street at one end. He listened again. No footsteps. No one had seen him.

He slumped to the ground and took in deep breaths. There was a burning sensation in his right arm and then a sharp pain rippled across his shoulder. He reached for it and felt a hole in his coat. He eased his injured arm out of the sleeve and examined the fabric. The lining was stained, but the blood had not yet soaked through. Quickly, he undid his shirt with his left hand, pulled off his undershirt, and, using his teeth, tore the undergarment into strips. Then he carefully wrapped his shoulder with the pieces of fabric and tucked the ends under each other. He rummaged through his rucksack, found his handkerchiefs and placed them against his shoulder before putting his shirt back on. He checked his coat again. Two holes marked the spot where the bullet had entered and exited. Relieved, he settled back and waited.

He thought back to his hotel room and mentally scanned it. His suitcase contained clothing and toiletries, but nothing that would give him away. He had his train pass, money and UNRRA papers in his rucksack. But he would have to wait out the night in the alley. It was too dangerous to go back to the hotel and the train station would be watched. A pain made him catch his breath. He automatically reached for his shoulder. At least the bullet was out. If he didn't lose too much blood, he could make it back to Landsberg.

The night was cold. The on-shore breeze blew through the dark alley, jolting him awake each time he dozed. Bolek curled up against the wall and hugged his rucksack. When the first pale light stained the sky, he stood up slowly and stretched his legs. He was stiff and filled with pain, but he managed to hobble through the dim morning to the train station almost a mile away. He felt remarkably clear-headed despite the agonizing throb in his shoulder. He casually draped his coat and secured his scarf to cover the bullet holes. He even thought to pinch color into his cheeks before stepping up to the ticket window.

He stopped to buy a roll and coffee from a station vendor before boarding the train. He was not hungry, but forced himself to swallow it. Whenever he felt weak, it triggered a panic for food. Something left over from the camps, where sickness meant imminent death and food — in any form — was the only possibility of survival. No matter how you felt, you ate.

An hour later he was staggering to the bathroom. He hunched over the sink, gripped the wall handle to steady himself and vomited. He was getting feverish and Landsberg was still far away. It would take ten hours to reach Munich, where he would change trains, and then another hour to get back to the camp.

In the corridor, he opened a window and paused to let the crisp air of the Italian Alps wash over his face. The sun was shining on the snowcapped peaks in the distance and the glare made him wince. He headed toward his compartment, remembering the elderly German couple waiting there. They had been watching him with growing concern since they boarded the train in Milan and now they were silent with suspicion. When he returned, they stopped talking and became stone-faced. A feeling of fatigue swept over him, and he fell into his seat and closed his eyes. The pain in his shoulder was constant now. He began to squirm in his seat. Each time he shifted, he opened his eyes a bit and saw the couple peering at him. He wondered if they could smell the blood. Alarm passed through him. He sat up quickly and looked directly at the woman.

"Bitte, excuse me," he said in broken German, "*Ich bin krank*. I had malaria during the war. I get relapse." He mopped his forehead. "It's unpleasant, but it passes. Not contagious."

The woman's face broke with relief and she nodded sympathetically. Her husband, who had been hiding behind his newspaper, looked up and gave her a reassuring pat on the arm.

"Isn't there medicine that will help?" she asked with motherly concern.

"Yes, but I don't bring pills with me. I am with UNRRA.

I will get more." This made an impression on them, as he knew it would, and they relaxed back into their seats.

The man went back to his newspaper, and the woman reached into a basket on the seat next to her and withdrew a thermos. She poured something into a small glass. "Won't you have some tea? It will make you feel better."

"So kind, so kind." He leaned forward, then stopped midway. "Another glass, bitte. I don't drink from this if it's your only one."

She smiled at him, then looked through her basket for a moment and pulled out a small mug. "We'll use this one. The glass will be yours for the rest of the trip," she declared with satisfaction as she filled it.

"Danke, danke." He sipped the strong hot tea for a moment, then he held out his mug in a toast. "Delicious."

Paul appeared out of nowhere. Suddenly he was standing beside Bolek at the Landsberg station, clasping his arm. Bolek looked up, but the glare from the street lamps hurt his eyes. Everything seemed to glow. He had a fever, he was sure. The pain in his shoulder had changed into a deep, dull ache and his neck was starting to hurt. He spoke to Paul, but his voice sounded strange, as though he were talking through a defective microphone. Paul didn't answer, just steered him to his car and helped him in. He wondered how Paul knew he was injured, but he was too tired to ask. How light he felt! He closed his eyes and leaned back into the car seat. It felt good to be in the dark. He fell asleep for a moment, then groaned awake in pain. He could no longer move his arm.

"Rome called. They told me what happened." Paul sounded blurred. "When you didn't call they thought you had been taken, but the Spezia contact said no one had seen you get in the trucks. I guessed you were on your way back." Paul shifted into first and the car lurched forward. "You look terrible."

Bolek half-opened his eyes, but he felt too dreamy to talk.

"Ben-Levi said there was shooting. He thought no one got hurt." Paul paused. "Where were you hit?"

Bolek pointed to his shoulder.

"Is the bullet still in?"

He started to shake his head and stopped. It made him feel sick.

"I'm taking you to Blum's house. I want him to look at you."

The next thing Bolek knew someone was tugging on his sleeve. He groaned.

"It's bad," he heard. He opened his eyes a bit and then quickly shut them. Someone was shining a light on him.

"It's infected. We can't take any chances. He has to go to the hospital." He heard the back door open and a rush of cold air chilled him. There was a movement in the seat behind him.

"I'll admit him as a typhus case so he'll stay in quarantine. No one will report it."

Bolek saw Blum's round face float over him. He smiled, picturing fat Blum in one of those tight suits that made him look like a sausage. He was a serious little man with a bald head so shiny Bolek thought he must polish it with Vaseline every morning. He was one of the camp doctors and he liked to scold people, liked to throw around his expertise. He pictured Blum shaking his finger at him, angry at having been disobeyed, saying, "I *told* you not to get shot." Bolek giggled softly and began to drift off until he felt himself swallowed up by the darkness somewhere beyond the speeding car.

CHAPTER
18

MISS WEISS ENTERED the barracks and scanned the room until she saw Manya. She looked irritated, her face stiff with authority.

"I've had a report from the US Commander's adjutant," Miss Weiss began abruptly. "It's about one of your students, Channah Lobel. She moved out of her barracks several weeks ago and took a room in the German sector. She's taken up prostitution." Miss Weiss spit out the word. "She is in your class. I thought you might be friendly with her, although she didn't strike me as the kind who had many friends." She looked hard into Manya's face. "Do what you can. I don't like the Army complaining to me about my people."

Manya thought of Channah's sly smile under the lamp post. No one was going to tell her what to do. "She's just a student. What makes you think I can do anything?"

"I've checked her background and I know all about Ravensbruck," Miss Weiss continued, ignoring her. "If she needs help, we'll get it for her, but she can't be allowed to do this."

"Isn't she of age to live on her own?"

Miss Weiss raised her eyebrows. "Living alone is not against the law. Prostitution is. Do something before the MPs get involved. Does she still come to class?"

"Yes."

"Talk to her after class then."

Manya deliberated for a moment. "No. I'll go to her quarters. I saw her last night."

Channah did not seem in the least surprised to see Manya. "I've seen you several times with Emmanuel in the restaurant down the street. It was just a question of time before you saw me." Her voice was light and friendly in a way Manya had never heard before.

Her room near The Golden Stag was small and bright, a garret with a slanted ceiling and a window overlooking a courtyard. An old chest of drawers stood against one wall and a narrow, neatly made bed against another. A few articles of clothing were draped over the headboard as though Channah had been deliberating over what to wear. She gathered them up and tucked them back into a drawer.

"Let me take your coat," she said, and motioned Manya to an upholstered chair.

"You have to stop this," Manya said, not moving. "The army will arrest you."

Channah blinked. "For what?"

"For selling yourself. The military is strict about that ."

The young woman smiled wearily. "Who told you?"

"Eleanor Weiss came to see me this morning. Someone from the army complained."

Channah's face twisted into a smirk. "I don't take money. I'm giving it away — free," she said and threw up her hands like a delighted child.

Manya stared at her. "Good for you. Good for the lucky Germans. I'm impressed."

"Did you come here to scold me?"

"Yes."

Channah flopped down on the bed. "The Haganah didn't want me," she said. "They kept telling me I was too young. One of them told me to go to school in Palestine to become a teacher. Imagine! Me, a teacher. No one should let me near children." She pulled a pillow onto her lap and hugged it as she spoke. "Now you might say I'm working for them anyway, informally, even though they said I shouldn't."

Manya waited.

"When my syphilis became active again, I thought, why not give it back? The Germans gave it to me, why not share it with their brothers? Now I can do some useful work."

Manya slowly lowered herself into the chair. "Is revenge part of the Haganah's work?"

Channah's face flashed with anger. "Punishment should be, don't you think?" She propped her pillow against the wall and leaned on it. "I like you," she said. "I watch you in class so closely I can see you think. You are very sure of yourself. I like the way you weigh your answers and listen to the people behind their questions. Oh, I know you're not comfortable with me. No one is. No woman will talk to me — except the social workers, of course. People blame me for what happened in the camps. They think it's my fault, that I let it happen. In their hearts, they think I should have killed myself before I let the Germans fuck me and become a disgrace to the Jewish people." Channah leaned forward as though she were sharing a secret.

"I told you about Ravensbrück that first night in class because it's a kind of test, you know, to see how people will react. I liked it when you said not to let anyone tell me who I was." She smiled. "You see, I took your advice."

Manya was about to protest, to say this was not what she had meant, but she knew it was useless. The sweet-faced young woman sat cross-legged on her bed like a child.

"You remind me of a woman I loved in Ravensbrück," Channah continued. "She saved my life. I had a bad case of measles. I was very sick and all the women were sure I would die. The Germans would have killed me if they found out, but this woman protected me. She told the commandant that I had gotten my period, which was strange because none of us had it — we thought they had put something in the food to stop it. But they left me alone for a while. I was too sick to eat so she hid my bread so no one would steal it. She saved it for me because she knew I would need to get my strength back when I recovered. And I did. Somehow one of the Germans found out that she had lied about me and they shot her. In the barracks. In front of me. I had recovered by then and maybe because I was the youngest, the only child, they didn't kill me. There were a few SS who had a taste for that, and they could still use me." Channah paused. "You have her eyes."

The late morning sun streamed in through the window near the bed. Channah stretched out toward the light and yawned as though she were tired of the conversation. Manya could see the faint blue veins on her forehead snake their way into her black hair. Her coloring was pale and creamy, like one of the porcelain figurines the Germans are so fond of.

"Don't waste your time," Channah said calmly. "I won't stop."

"Are you getting any treatment?"

"Not yet. I have a few weeks left before it becomes dangerous. I'm taking advantage of it." She smiled to herself. "I quite like this, you know. I don't have to talk much because my German is poor, so the men think I'm sweet. That makes them gentle. When my time is up, I'll take my medicine." She leaned toward Manya again and patted her hand.

"I survived Ravensbrück. I promise you I'll survive liberation."

CHAPTER
19

Voices rose dimly from the background. Bolek opened his eyes and let the room come into focus. The men were huddled in the doorway with their backs to him, a light falling on their hair and shoulders. He thought it was night, but he couldn't be sure. The blanket under his chin felt scratchy and when he moved his head, he flooded with pain.

"It's inflamed around the entrance wound, but it's just an abscess," he heard Blum say. "We've started him on penicillin. Let's wait and see how he does."

"Wait? The infection may have already spread to the muscle. If you wait any longer you'll jeopardize his life as well as his arm." Bolek didn't recognize the voice.

There was a long pause and Blum grumbled something. Then, "All right. When?"

"Do we know when he last ate?"

"No. Olesky met him at the station. He was coming from Italy."

"Then not till the morning. I can't take any chances. I'll clear the operating room for eight A.M."

"Blum," Bolek called, and the pain surged.

Blum stepped to his bed side and stood over him. The doctor's hand on his forehead felt cool and smooth. "I'll have the nurse give you something," he said. The other doctor with Blum was short and stocky, not unlike Blum, only younger. They could be brothers. Bolek closed his burning eyes and pictured an endless line of identical little men lined up next to his bed, stethoscopes dangling, ready to listen to his heart. He waited to feel the cold instrument against his chest, but there was a sting on his arm, then no more.

He awoke to the sound of metal being dragged across the floor. He opened his eyes and Paul was sitting in a chair next to him in a glaze of light. He felt strangely refreshed. When he moved to speak, the pain was still wrenching, but distant.

"How long?"

"It's morning. Blum and I brought you here last night."

"They gave me something."

"You were in a lot of pain, but you slept."

"It was just one bullet, wasn't it? Shoulder?"

"Yes, but it's infected. They have to operate."

"But the bullet is out."

Paul folded his arms across his chest and leaned back. "Blum wants to operate right away. He thinks you may lose the arm. If the infection has spread, it could mean your life. He says he won't know until he goes in."

Bolek instinctively reached for his shoulder. He saw the dock and the refugees falling on their children to protect them from the gun fire. "Anyone hurt?"

"The British got everything. No one else was hurt." Paul's voice was dry and measured. "We don't know who tipped off the Brits, but the shooting was a freak thing. Some hot-

203

headed officer wanted to scare everyone, so he ordered his troops to shoot in the air. You happened to be in the wrong place." His face twisted into a sneer. "Too bad we can't tell the press. The British shooting a Jew in Italy would make nice headlines."

"What about the refugees?"

"Carted off to the local prison camp."

"And the guns . . . "

"There'll be more. The Jews are raising lots of money in America. They're good at that."

Bolek turned away. Next time he would — what? Not be so stupid as to get shot? Tear the British apart with his own hands? If there was a next time.

"Tell Manya I'm here," he said.

Paul was quiet. "She can't come here. You're in quarantine with a typhus cover. The other staff might get suspicious. I don't want the Americans at our throats."

"Just tell her."

Leila pushed her way past the crowded noontime tables in the mess hall. Since her husband's return she had lost most of her easy gaiety, but Manya had not seen her this distressed before. She stood up, suddenly tense, and waited for Leila as she squeezed down the narrow aisles toward her.

"I just met Paul in the street," Leila said, out of breath. "Bolek's been shot. He's in the hospital. He came back on the train last night from Italy."

Manya felt her heart drop. "Where is he?"

"In the hospital in town. Paul said they put him in quarantine so no one would alert the police. One of our doctors is taking care of him."

"How bad is it?"

"I don't know."

"Where's Paul."

"He looked like he was on his way to the office. Wait, I'm coming with you."

The nurse had a Slavic face with a broad jaw and pale blue eyes, and each time she bent over him her head seemed to expand like a cartoon figure's. She wasn't wearing a surgical mask, so she had to be working with Blum. Bolek wanted to talk. He wanted to fill the frantic spaces in his head, but each time he moved, his shoulder fired with pain.

"Where are you from?" he mumbled, trying to keep his head still.

The nurse smiled. "Palestine." She spoke with an odd Polish accent, one he couldn't place. He must have looked surprised because she continued. "We went there in 1936 when I was nine years old. My father was a Zionist. I came here last year to work with the refugees."

Twenty years old and she looked as though she had been handling these instruments all her life. She had gone to school, not a concentration camp.

"Do you despise us like all the Palestinian Jews?"

Her smile continued as if the question did not surprise her. "Would I be here if I did?"

"One of your countryman, a sabra who worked with the Brichah, came to help, too, but he hated us. He told me that only the worst people could have survived the death camps." The nurse's face remained composed while she pulled a tray next to the bed. "He informed me that survivors gave all Jews a bad name because they didn't fight back. Even Ben Gurion doesn't want us. He's only using us for sympathy to force England to give us a Jewish State." Bolek remembered the arrogant young man who had stupidly thought to confide in him, and for the hundredth time he regretted not having punched him in the face.

"Stop talking nonsense." She wrapped his arm firmly in the blood pressure band. The blue eyes, now earnest and professional, ignored him.

"You look like a shiksa."

"Don't I know it," she said in Yiddish. "Now be quiet." She put the stethoscope on his arm and stared at the gauge. In profile she looked prettier than she had when she was facing him, and he suddenly wanted her close to him. Then he saw himself caressing her with one arm while an empty sleeve lay pinned on the side of his shirt. He turned away.

"I'll lose the arm, won't I?"

She undid the blood pressure, then gathered up the equipment and scrutinized him for a moment. Her face softened and she leaned over and gave his injured arm a gentle pat. "The doctor is good. He'll do what he can."

Manya marched into the Joint office. Paul and Yankl swung around when they heard the door slam. In a second she was standing over Paul with her hands on his desk. Leila stood behind her near the door.

"What happened!" she demanded to Paul, who turned back to his papers and carefully folded them before answering.

"He was shot three days ago and has an infection. Blum and I brought him to the hospital last night. That's all I can tell you."

"Don't be ridiculous," Leila said. "You know she's safe."

He glared at her.

"What does that mean, 'He has an infection?'"

"I saw him just before they operated this morning. I haven't been back yet."

"You're not telling me something."

"He could lose the arm," said Paul. "If the infection's spread too far, he might die."

"Why didn't you tell me this?" Yankl interrupted, pushing away from his desk. "You've been sitting here for an hour and said nothing."

Paul looked at the three of them and his face went red. "What would you like me to do?" he shouted. "Inform the Military Government? Telegraph the international press?" He returned to his desk, slammed his files shut and jammed them into his brief case. "Don't think about going to see him. They won't let you in." He grabbed his coat from a peg on the wall and pushed past them. "Blum can give you the medical details, but that's all," he said and bolted out the door.

"We'll go," Leila said, holding her by the shoulders. "I'll take you."

"No," Yankl interrupted. "Blum doesn't know either of you and you're not family. I'll take an UNRRA jeep. We'll go tonight."

Yankl was waiting for her at ten P.M., wearing a broad brimmed hat and an overcoat instead of the standard army issue he had worn earlier. Seeing him on the darkened street silhouetted against the old buildings, she had a vision of the Jewish Quarter of Warsaw on Friday night with men like him returning home from Sabbath services. Conspicuous orthodox Jews in their black clothes and side curls had been the first to disappear from the ghetto. Post-war Poland no longer had a Jewish Quarter. All the Yankls were gone.

Yankl was pacing with his hands behind his back. When he saw her, he stopped abruptly, then silently ushered her into the jeep. Manya could see Landsberg's towers illuminated. The ramparts and spires were delicate silhouettes against the violet of the night sky, but the sight always irked her. The Germans *would* spend money to light up their monuments while their people were still hungry.

Yankl stared at the road in front of him, his profile stern with worry. She knew he was fond of Bolek, perhaps even admired him as older men will admire younger ones in whom they see a future they once wanted for themselves. But she knew he wouldn't talk about this friendship. She turned to watch the darkness whiz by. Dread spilled over her. She was desperate for Yankl to talk, to reassure her, and say all the things she knew neither of them could, by nature, believe.

They were crossing the bridge into town when he did speak, "If you read this in a book, it would sound romantic. A young woman running to her wounded love in the middle of the night. But it doesn't feel romantic, does it? Fear is not a romantic feeling, but no one remembers that when they read books. They only want to know if the boy gets the girl."

"Did all this come from reading European literature instead of the Talmud?" she asked.

"It came from watching the two of you. You think religious Jews don't know about love. We do, but our love affair is with our family. A different kind of love between husband and wife comes later."

"What are you saying?"

"People are marrying in haste," he continued, a disembodied voice in the darkness, "and they're not suited to each other. They're lonely, they want children, they want to replace the ones that were lost. They don't know who they're marrying. That will make unhappy families. That's not good."

"How do you know what's good for me?" Manya bristled back. "I'm not one of your Orthodox women."

Yankl kept a steady gaze on the road. "I know who you are. I know you're intelligent and I know that even now you understand me."

"What do you mean 'who I am'?"

"You're not settled in yourself. Someone who has been through what you have should know better than to get on another roller coaster. You're tired of living with fear. Bolek isn't. He's just discovering his own strength. And he likes the feeling."

She turned her weary face from him. How right he was, but the anger twisted inside her anyway. They were riding through the empty town square. The shutters were drawn on the shops and cafés. "We don't even know if he'll live."

"You'll survive even if he doesn't," Yankl intoned in the dark. "You should be prepared if he does."

The back of the hospital was deserted and dimly lit by a single light over the door. Yankl and Manya stepped into a corridor, also dimly lit, also deserted, and moved cautiously toward the nearest staircase. She could hear voices coming from the front office, but the rest of the building felt as though it were asleep. Doors to the wards and individual rooms were closed and she sensed no movement behind them. She crept up the stairs to the second floor landing and spotted a door marked "Quarantine."

Bolek was alone in the room. A soft triangle of light fell on a table cluttered with bottles and metal pans next to his bed. He lay in shadow with his face turned away from her, but even before she was near him, she sensed the rhythmic rise and fall of his breathing. His blanket was tightly tucked under the mattress and covered him up to the waist. She saw his right shoulder and arm wrapped in white bandages and moved closer. The dressing stopped at his elbow, but the rest of his muscular arm lay naked and intact on top of the cover. She touched it, and everything that had been suffocating her since the morning surged into one overriding desire: that he would not die; that he would open his eyes and propel her into the next moment of her life.

Then, to spite herself, as though she did not deserve even this modicum of joy, as though she still must be punished for betraying the dead, she imagined that he stopped breathing and his body was transformed into a shell, not just empty, but bloated with emptiness, like the body of the German she had killed, like her grandmother must have looked as she was thrown into a blazing furnace, like Joseph after they brought him home ripped by bullets.

But Bolek stirred and the image vanished. She pulled a chair over to the bed and sat down and watched the delicate, almost imperceptible movement of his breathing until her own returned to normal. There was a murmur behind her and she remembered Yankl. He was standing near the light, swaying over his open prayer book. She wanted to tell him to stop, that she knew this life before her could subdue any force that tried to diminish it, but she checked herself. She took Bolek's hand and waited.

He looked pale and slack in the dim light. His moist black curls lay strewn against his brow. He stirred again, opened his eyes and blinked. Then he reached for his bandaged arm and relief filled his face. He gazed at her for a long minute before he spoke.

"Fancy meeting you here," he murmured with a weak smile. His gaze moved to Yankl, who was swaying in the corner. "Thank Him for me, will you."

Yankl kissed the book and closed it, then came to the side of the bed. "If I didn't take such pity on your irreligious soul, I'd be insulted by that," he said.

"Everyone knows it's impossible to insult you," Bolek whispered in a hoarse voice.

"I'm happy to see they left your sense of humor intact."

"That's because they knew I'd have to share an office with you." Bolek paused and closed his eyes for a moment. "What did the doctor say?"

"We haven't spoken to him. We sneaked in here like criminals because Olesky said we had to stay away for security reasons."

"Then maybe I shouldn't be thanking Him so soon." There was a lull while Bolek stared at Manya. "I missed you."

"Then don't leave me again," she blurted out and gripped his hand.

He lay still and watched her. His eyes turned sad.

She released his hand and let the moment ebb. She

had hoped that these weeks apart would make it easier to say good-bye, but almost losing him — instead of fortifying her to end the relationship — had only made her weaker.

They heard footsteps in the hall. The door swung open and the blonde nurse stood in the entrance.

"Who are you? How did you get in here?"

"Meet my wife and my friend," Bolek said softly. Manya stood up, embarrassed, and made way for the other woman while Yankl retreated to a shadowy corner of the room. The nurse raised her eyebrows, then quickly walked to the bed. She examined the bandages, picked up Bolek's wrist and pulled out a pocket watch.

"Miss Goldilocks," he said, "will I live to see you a doctor?"

"You will live to plow the fields in Palestine with both arms," she replied. "The muscle was all right. The infection hadn't spread. The doctor cleaned it out and now it's draining." She slipped the watch back into the pocket of her blue uniform and wrote something on a piece of paper. "I don't know how Dr. Blum gets penicillin, but it saved your life." Then she felt his forehead and neck. "You're a healthy horse, you know that. Most people would be too sick and groggy to host a party after surgery." She turned to Manya and Yankl. "Don't make me scold you. I'm too young to act like a mother. You know what you should do." She walked briskly to the door and held it open.

Bolek closed his eyes and seemed to drift, then opened them and beckoned Manya to come to him. She took his hand again and he pulled her closer until she was leaning over him. She smelled iodine and bandage adhesive and the unmistakable scent of his skin.

"Ignore her." He clenched her hand. Manya stood suspended over him until his grip loosened and she felt him fall asleep.

CHAPTER 20

MANYA VISITED Bolek in the hospital every night. He was out of danger and recovering, but she was not. Each night before she went to see him, she resolved to end their affair that evening. But with the first touch of his hand, her determination crumbled. Tension was exhausting her. When Emmanuel asked her to come to Munich to help him pick out new clothes for Paris, she accepted eagerly.

Emmanuel confided that he didn't have the courage to buy clothing, not important clothing like a suit, on his own. He needed her help, her "eye," he said — she, who gave little attention to fashion. And she would make sure he didn't get cheated, he added. She doubted he needed help for that. Emmanuel was an avid poker player and a very good one, with an excellent memory and a talent for bluffing. It was at the gambling tables that he had accumulated his American dollars, the only currency of any value in inflation-riddled Germany.

The hour-long train ride to Munich was unexpectedly pleasant. They found a compartment with an unoccupied window seat and like school children on an outing, watched the landscape roll by. Emmanuel told her about Mohlestrasse, Munich's black market area, and the hundreds of stalls that had sprung up after the war. He described how refugees flocked there from all the DP camps in the surrounding area — from Foehrenwald, Deggendorf and Leipheim, even from as far away as Stuttgart. Germans, too, came from nearby villages and towns to trade and buy. It was like an open-air Mediterranean souk, bustling with commerce. He was excited to have captured her for an entire day, and his eagerness infused him with a feverish glow. Every once in a while she stole glances at him while he gazed out the window and wondered what else she didn't know about this gentle-faced gambler.

They arrived at ten A.M. and made their way through Munich's crowded streets toward the market. It was April, but there was little sense of spring in the city. Most of the buildings were still half-missing, the top floors gutted and exposed by bomb damage. Piles of rubble lined the sidewalk in front of empty lots where homes had stood before the Allied bombing raids. They walked down Maria Theresastrasse past the large white building Emmanuel said was the headquarters of US Army Counter-Intelligence, then past a series of decrepit brownstones now occupied by the countless organizations that oversaw every aspect of refugee life. The American Jewish groups and the Jewish underground were so active in this part of town that the Germans had dubbed the trolley that ran past the administrative buildings "The Palestine Express."

The first stalls of the market lined a street closed to traffic. Shoppers were already milling about with their string bags and satchels. A few yards down they spotted a stand that had men's clothing suspended from hangers on a rope. Emmanuel reached up to touch a blue suit jacket with thin stripes and stylish narrow lapels.

"This is nice," he said turning the jacket over to get a better look.

"Here, here, let me help you." A young man in a leather coat and cap scooted over and quickly took down the jacket. As he lifted his hands toward the garment, his sleeve slid down, exposing the number tattooed on his arm. When he turned back to them, he noticed Manya staring at it. "Dachau," he said perfunctorily while removing the hanger. "How about you?"

"I hid in Warsaw."

"You're lucky — or smart." He smiled at Emmanuel and held up the jacket. "Not bad, eh?"

Emmanuel slipped into the jacket, then stood in front of a mirror propped against the stand. "I don't know," he said, turning from side to side to get a better look. He tilted his head toward Manya. "What do you think?"

She smiled. The body of the suit fit well, but the sleeves hung down to his knuckles.

"You like it? Now be honest. Do I look like a man of science or a maitre d'?"

"You look handsome. Really." He did. When he buttoned the front, the jacket hugged his slender torso, making him look graceful and reedy. "But the sleeves . . . "

"I'll have them shortened. Or should I leave them like this to make people feel sorry for me?" His eyes twinkled as he inspected himself in the mirror.

The vendor jumped in, holding up the suit trousers. "And look here. It has pleats and the legs are the latest style, nice and narrow." He anxiously watched Emmanuel check the lining and the seams. The pants seemed to be all right.

"How much for the suit?"

"Fifty-five dollars. American."

"The lady thinks I look handsome, so I'll take it." Emmanuel seemed unperturbed by the price and withdrew a wad of bills, peeled off a few and handed them to the vendor, who slipped the suit into a large paper bag.

"No box?" Emmanuel asked.

The merchant pointed to the buildings across the street. Many of the empty windows had cardboard inserts instead of glass panes. "That's where the boxes go."

Further on into the market they came to a book stall and Emmanuel ran his hand lovingly over the spines of some old texts. He leafed through one and glanced at the copyright page. "I should buy this just out of curiosity," he said, holding it up for her to see. "Physics. Printed during the war. Hitler banned Einstein, along with all the other Jewish scientists. I wonder who he had left." He glanced over the pages briefly, but his face turned somber and he let the book drop back on the pile.

Not everyone had a stall. Some merchants spread out their goods on blankets on the sidewalk, and Manya and Emmanuel had to be careful not to bump into kneeling shoppers. One blanket was covered entirely with watches arranged in rows like silver sardines. There were tables where linens and cameras were mixed in with American canned coffee and boxes of sugar. The merchants seemed to work in pairs, one dealing with customers, the other keeping an eye on the goods.

Emmanuel stopped to buy a brown felt hat and black

leather gloves, then paused to look at two rather splashy American ties of yellow silk accented with tiny blue saxophones. He touched them cautiously and eyed her. "What do you think? Too loud?"

Manya didn't know what to make of them. "That's one way to get attention."

"Maybe not the kind a scientist should get," he said.

Just before the market area ended, they came to a display of women's nylon stockings pulled over plastic legs that had been propped up, like strange weather vanes, toes pointing toward the sky. Some of the stockings had tiny roses embroidered up the back seam; some had zigzags like lightning bolts. Manya examined a pair that seemed particularly sheer. She had not seen such a fine mesh before. She ran her hand over the glossy material.

"You like hose, don't you? Won't you let me buy you those?"

Manya did like hose. They felt wonderfully smooth and luxurious on her legs whenever she wore them, which was rare. They were very expensive these days. "Yes, but . . . "

"But what?" he interrupted. "Do I seem like the kind of man who will force you into bondage if you accept a gift? Do I?"

She smiled. "I'd love a pair."

"Pick one. I can assure you I'm not going to be of any use to you on this one."

Manya reached for a buff-colored pair with a simple black seam. From the front they seem almost invisible, tinted just enough to make her legs look elegant. She held them up gingerly. "These are nice."

Emmanuel turned discreetly toward the woman behind the table, muttered something, and slipped her some bills.

She wrapped the hose in paper and handed them to Manya. Then she leaned in confidentially. "Silk," she whispered holding up a sage and rust colored scarf. "It came in yesterday. From Paris." She spread it out on the table and it fluttered open on top of the packages. Emmanuel stepped up to the woman before Manya could speak. "How much?"

"Ten American dollars."

Manya was horrified. This was more than a new pair of leather shoes. She was about to protest, but Emmanuel was already handing the woman money.

"Why not wear it now?" He stood and waited.

She took the scarf, wrapped it around her neck and tied it loosely in front. When she moved her head, the fabric glided across her cheeks. She had never owned such an exquisite thing. No one in her family had earned that kind of money. No one in Poland did now, except perhaps the Russian bureaucrats.

Emmanuel and Manya walked in silence to the end of Mohlestrasse. Later, in a crowded, smoky beer hall, they had a lunch of bratwurst with potato salad and good beer, then strolled the city before boarding the train back to Landsberg. It was only five when they dropped, exhausted, into their seats, and within a few minutes the train's motion had lulled them both to sleep. Manya awoke with a start just before they reached their station, confused for a moment by the weight pressing against her shoulder. When she tried to straighten up, Emmanuel murmured and shifted sleepily, burying his face deeper into the silk scarf that was still wound around her neck.

CHAPTER 21

THE DOCTOR OFFERED her his arm. She gripped it and swung her legs over the side of the examining table. He seemed solemn; he must be overworked, she thought, trying to stem the alarm spreading through her. He motioned to the small room across the corridor that served as his clinic office. "When you're dressed, come talk to me inside."

Manya dressed slowly, fumbling with the buttons of her sweater. When she stepped into the corridor, he was waiting for her at the door. They entered the office and sat down facing each other across the small desk. There was a long pause while he scanned a file she knew was hers.

"You're pregnant," he said. "About eight weeks. But you probably knew that."

She had suspected it. She had noticed the changes in her body, but had decided to ignore them. She had made her clinic appointment blindly, without telling herself why, sensing that it was something she should do. Now she felt relieved, as she always did when uncertainty resolved itself. But the doctor was waiting for her to speak.

"Yes. I thought so."

"You're married?"

"No."

"Do you know who the father is?"

"Yes."

"Do you plan to marry?" The doctor glared at her, his eyes sharp behind the steel-rimmed glasses. He leaned forward with his elbows on the desk, his face close to hers.

"We lost a lot of Jewish children in the camps, but I can't tell you what to do. Society is very harsh about certain things. I can tell you we've had forty-five births here in the last two weeks. The journals say survivors have the highest birth rate in the world. Think carefully before you make any decision. Many unmarried women *are* having babies."

She was aware that he was waiting for her to say something, but she wasn't really listening. She saw Bolek sitting up in his hospital bed trying to exercise his arm even though it was much too soon; and Emmanuel, leaning against her on the train; and Channah's face — the face of a child who would never have children.

"You could have the baby and give it up for adoption."

She sat up. Give the baby away?

"There are many Jewish couples in America who would want a Jewish child."

Couples? A Jewish child? The words made sense, but she seemed unable to string them together. She stood up. Her coat slipped from her lap to the floor and she bent over to pick it up. When she looked again, the doctor's face had softened.

"All right then," he said and hurriedly wrote something down on a piece of paper. "The other women will tell you to go to the midwives for an abortion. Don't. I've had to patch up too many mistakes." He put the paper in her hand. "If you must, go to this German doctor. He knows what he's doing and *his* office is clean."

The room filled with dead air. She turned brusquely and the doctor opened the door.

"Stop by the nurse's station." He stared at her over the rim of his glasses. "That is, if you decide you want another appointment."

When Manya stepped out of the clinic, the sharp morning light stabbed her eyes so that she squinted. It was spring at last, May. Everything seemed clean and newly made. The few spindly trees planted along the camp's main thoroughfare were covered with a thin haze of green, even though winter hovered beneath the spring breeze. The confluence of soft air and light and fragrance that rushed up at her filled her with melancholy. Suddenly she ached for childhood, the dusty roads of the shtetl, and her grandmother, standing in her narrow doorway, smiling as Manya ran toward her from the deepening dusk. Manya yearned for that warm round face and generous arms. She yearned to sit again on a wooden stool at the kitchen table, her hands flying, telling her grandmother the day's school tales. Her grandmother would surely have advised her to keep the child, even if she didn't marry. She would smile and touch Manya's cheek and say, "Nothing in life can be so bad if you have a child to love." She would be ready to defy the pontificating neighbors, but be too shy to ask about the father. If Manya had told her about Bolek, about her agonizing doubts, she would have understood immediately, cutting away all the obfuscating details of the relationship to what was most simple and direct: her granddaughter was unhappy. But she would have liked Bolek, Manya knew. Bubbe liked people with dedication. Even though her own daughter had forsaken religion, she was proud of her commitment to helping people. It was a good deed, a mitzvah, to dedicate one's life to the oppressed. It was what God wanted us to do, even if we didn't use His name. She had adored Joseph, the least Jewish member of the family, for this reason: his goodness, she said, was like a religious devotion. A simple, uneducated woman, Bubbe always found something to like in others and with unerring precision, it was always what was best in them.

Manya stood in the clinic entranceway and watched the people hurrying around her. These refugees looked, outwardly, as they had on the streets of Warsaw and in her grandmother's village. But something was different. There was a brusqueness in the way they moved, a determination in their stance that she had not seen before. Life around her had movement and purpose. In the past, *she* had always been moving: toward a future of peace and equality; toward a man who would share her dreams and whose wisdom would endow her with more courage; and when she found that man, she matched his stride and they both moved side by side, this time out of necessity, away from the tyranny of the Nazis, together trying to side-step death. Since leaving Poland, she had felt weighted with the enormity of nothingness. But now she thought of her child and her heart quickened. She moved away from the doorway against which she had been leaning and stepped into the street.

A gust of wind came up from the east and Manya shivered. She looked up the roadway toward the mess hall where Leila was waiting to meet her after the clinic appointment. Suddenly she couldn't face her friend whose forced cheerfulness these days did not disguise her unhappiness with her husband Simon. He remained remote and silent, she confided, but she believed in a future Simon who would resemble the man she had married. And that seemed sufficient. Any day they were expecting a visa to America. An uncle of Leila's was sponsoring them and they would start their lives again. Manya turned toward the barracks. Sometimes Leila's simplistic optimism irritated her.

Rochel was sitting alone when she entered, her lap filled with sewing. She was busy these days mending clothes the women picked out of the Joint shipments. When they found something they liked, regardless of its condition, they brought it to Rochel, who happily repaired it. Last week she had surprised Manya with a gift, a taupe gabardine skirt and a white cotton blouse she had altered. Manya had tried it on under Rochel's admiring gaze and was wearing it now.

Rochel looked up from her sewing. "You left so early this morning." Her eyes filled with pleasure at the young woman wearing her creations.

"I've come to take you for a walk," Manya said gazing down at the kind face. They would enjoy the beautiful day. They would walk side by side and Rochel's chatter would soothe her like a protective balm. She beamed with relief at the diminutive woman. It always surprised her how small Rochel was. Hunched over her work, her small lap filled with garments, she looked like a half-buried doll.

"Come outside," Manya insisted. "It's good for you to be in the sun."

"Is it?" Rochel glanced toward the windows. "But Tovah needs this finished by tomorrow." She held up a black dress trimmed with a band of white satin around the shoulders. Small, half-crushed feathers stuck like old gum to the collar. Manya burst out laughing. It was amazing the things the Americans sent and even more amazing that Tovah would have some place to wear such a thing.

"It's so peaceful in here," Rochel continued, looking around. "I like sitting." The barracks did, indeed, look serene. Someone had washed the grimy windows and shafts of sunlight streamed in, warming the bare wooden floors.

"I never told you that right after the war I was afraid to be alone," Rochel said. "Sometimes I would even follow strangers and sit next to them, like a stray kitten. Now I don't mind. Isn't that good? It's a kind of healing, isn't it?"

Manya sat down and took her hand. "Yes, that *is* good," she said, "and if you want to stay here and enjoy the quiet, I won't disturb you."

"No, no. I'm almost finished, and you're right. It's important for the health to be outside." She carefully placed Tovah's dress on top of the clothing pile. "You're such a smart girl, so educated. You know what's best." She reached for her coat, and slipped it on. "Did you go to the clinic this morning? Is everything all right?"

Manya was startled. She hadn't mentioned where she was going.

"I saw you take your clinic card from the drawer before you left." Rochel stopped. "Oh, I'm doing it again, aren't I. I'm being snoopy."

Rochel was guileless. "Everything is all right," Manya replied. Before Rochel could ask more, she stepped toward her, finished tying her scarf and ushered the older woman out the door.

Rochel peered up at her as they walked. "Something is the matter. Is Bolek all right?"

Bolek. He would always be all right. "Yes, but the doctor says he isn't healing well. He won't rest his arm."

"What can you do," Rochel sighed, "It's his nature."

His nature. Rochel had no idea how right she was. It was Bolek's nature to ignore his body, to ignore the advice of the people around him, to move through the day with reckless impatience. She had been there this past week when Blum had scolded him because all his activity had reopened the wound. "I'll toss you out and let the Americans deal with you if you don't stop this," the usually well-mannered doctor had threatened. Bolek was dismissive. He pointed to the stack of newspapers that had accumulated around his bed. "The UN is about to vote on Partition. We can't win the war without guns." Blum waited until Bolek finished shouting, then added coldly, "I was unaware that the fate of the Jewish people rested on your shoulders." Bolek had smiled then like a mischievous child accustomed to having his transgressions indulged. He let the conversation drop while Blum gave the nurse instructions in terse, angry tones. Manya had been embarrassed by Bolek's silly performance, but the moment they were alone and Bolek took her hand, she wanted to kiss him — and did.

"Where should we go, Manya?" Rochel's voice snapped her back to the street.

"I don't know." She touched her stomach. She wanted to walk along the river bank and catch the play of light on the rushing water. She wanted the cool breeze on her face. She was about to turn down a side street when Rochel stopped abruptly. She drained of color, and terror spread across her ashen face. Manya grabbed her by the elbow, but Rochel shook her off and pointed across the street.

"My God, it's her," Rochel whispered and ran headlong across the road. "Stop her. She's a murderer!" Rochel began to scream, flailing her arms. Manya saw a portly, middle-aged woman in a small black hat and tight winter coat come to a halt on the sidewalk. The woman stepped back and flattened herself against the building as Rochel closed in on her.

"Get her," Rochel screamed, although the woman wasn't going anywhere. "Kapo!" she screeched again, her face a fist of hate.

Manya reached them just as Rochel started to pummel the cowering woman about the head. A young man in a cap and overalls who was walking by stopped. He took hold of Rochel's arms.

"Wait a minute! What's going on?"

"She's a kapo! She killed my daughter!" Rochel squirmed, trying to get at the woman. "It's you, you devil, you murderer. I thought you were dead." She dislodged an arm and slapped the woman sharply across the face before the man could stop her. He wedged himself between the two of them.

"Stop this," the man said. "We don't behave this way toward Jews. File charges if you think she's a kapo. Go to the Camp Committee to hold a trial."

"She killed my daughter, my only child, and my cousin," Rochel yelled to a group of passers-by that had gathered around them.

The woman shielded her head with her arms. "This is

a mistake." She pleaded with the crowd. "I don't know this person."

"Don't know me?" Rochel fell silent for a moment, her lips a thin line of white rage, then bent back her head, took a deep breath and spit into the woman's face. "*Muser*! Jewish traitor! Worse than the Germans!" she screamed.

The crowd grew silent and stared at the bespattered woman. "I've done nothing," she pleaded, her mouth trembling. She turned to Rochel. "I was in Auschwitz, just like you."

"How did you know where I was? You see! She knows me. She does remember!" Then she lunged at her again.

The man held her back. "Calm yourself! If you want justice, go to the Courts of Honor."

"Justice? Where is justice?" Rochel grabbed at Manya to steady herself.

The other woman frantically searched in her purse for a handkerchief. She pulled one out and wiped her face with shaking hands, then tried to push her way through the crowd. An older man came forward and grabbed her, but she shook him off with an indignant look. "What are you doing? I'm not a criminal," she shouted.

"This woman might need to get in touch with you. Where do you live?"

"Let go of me. I'm a survivor just like all of you."

"Let her go," someone yelled. "I know where to find her. Herzl Barracks. She won't go far." A hum went through the crowd and Manya heard the word "kapo" again. The woman glared back at them, straightened her hat and stalked away.

Rochel had grown quiet, but Manya could feel her heart hammering. As the crowd drifted apart, a few women moved toward Rochel. "Don't worry," one said patting her on the back. "My friend lives with that woman. She'll keep an eye on her."

"Go to the committee," another woman advised. "I have a friend who did last month. They had a trial."

Rochel gave Manya a look of despair. "What's the difference? Nothing will happen to her. It never does."

"File papers."

Rochel mopped her forehead with her hand and nodded. "All right, all right," she muttered. "I want to go back now," she whispered to Manya. "Can you take me, please?"

Manya was glad the barracks were still empty. She helped Rochel to her cot, then she pulled the covers over her. She took a glass from a nearby table and filled it with cold water from the bathroom. When she sat down, Rochel was twisting and untwisting a handkerchief. She reached for the glass Manya offered her and when she had finished drinking, the old woman sighed heavily and lay back.

"You're lucky you weren't in a camp. You don't know, you don't know . . ."

Manya smoothed her hand. She felt weak with helplessness. "The woman is Jewish, isn't she?"

Rochel nodded.

"What did she do?"

"She helped the Germans. She was like a guard. She got special privileges for beating us."

Survivors considered kapos traitors, Manya knew, but many had had no choice. Accusations of collaboration flew around all the DP camps, and the Camp Committee, a political body elected by the DPs, had set up secret courts to settle matters peaceably. The Jewish leadership adamantly forbade revenge, much to Bolek's chagrin, so what else does a Jew do?

He turns to the Law. Trials were held in Landsberg, much like those taking place in Nuremburg at the same time and for the same reason: to try individuals convicted of crimes against the Jewish people. "We would never let anyone else judge us," she remembered Bolek telling her. "Only survivors can judge survivors, no matter what the rest of the world thinks."

"What did she do?" Manya asked.

Rochel stared into space for a moment. "I was with my daughter, Luba, and Esther, my cousin. We had all been deported together . . . I didn't know where my husband had been sent. It was our second day in Auschwitz. We were still in our clothes from home. We had just been assigned bunks, and that woman . . . " Rochel looked in the direction of the street. "Her name is Borenstein, Malke Borenstein . . . The other women told me she pulled Luba out and told her she had to go to the quarry right away to break stones. Luba was so beautiful, everyone said so. Twenty-two years old. She was too beautiful. People noticed her. That's why this woman must have picked on her. People told me Luba ignored the woman, didn't know she was a kapo. The woman grabbed her and pulled her out of line. Luba was so surprised that she pushed her back. She didn't know . . . we didn't know yet. It was only our second day. My child was gentle, she was, but it's instinct to push back, isn't it? The woman hit her with her club and Luba screamed for her to stop. After all, they were both Jews. An SS guard saw them and he came over and shot my Luba on the spot. No questions. I heard the noise and ran out of the barracks and saw her on the ground. There was no more face. The guard smiled at the people around us and said very calmly, 'This is your first lesson. Never hit. Never scream. It disturbs the other inmates.' After that I couldn't cry anymore. I cried in my heart, but my body became silent. I would lie awake at night and want to cry for all the times I couldn't, then after a while even that stopped." Rochel looked up with hollow eyes. "From the minute I got up until I went to sleep, I was a stone."

Manya stroked her thin hand.

"I would like to put a knife in her," Rochel said, waving her fist, "but I know it wouldn't help. All they'll do is put her name in the newspapers to shame her, if they find her guilty. They'll tell the Joint to stop giving her rations. Maybe they'll make her leave the camp. Maybe. That's all." She lay back, her eyes filled with grim resignation. "But it's not important. It doesn't matter."

Manya's face went warm. "It does matter. Some things must matter."

"Some of us live out of habit."

They sat, silent, in the empty barracks and Manya heard the murmur of women's voices floating in from the street. The sound filled their corner like a brief flight of birds and was gone.

"You know, Luba's always with me. I can feel her on my skin. She's always close by."

Then Manya heard herself ask, "If she could speak to you now, what would she say?"

Rochel blinked. A small red blotch appeared on the tip of her nose and slowly spread across her face. She groped for Manya's hand and opened her mouth to speak, but her eyes filled with confusion, as though she heard something from a distant room. She sat up, and after a moment of hesitation when it looked as if she were about to say something, she slumped into Manya's arms and wept.

■   ■   ■

It was five o'clock and Rochel, who had fallen into an exhausted sleep, still lay curled on her side with her mouth pressed against her pillow, gently snoring. Even the chatter of the women coming in and out of the barracks had not disturbed her, although it had awakened Manya, who had been dozing with her arms around Rochel. Now she lay staring at the ceiling and rubbing the spot on her cheek where the old woman's head had lain.

She had another half hour before it was time to leave for the hospital. Blum wanted to keep up the pretense of Bolek's quarantine and still insisted she come in the evening after most of the "uninformed" hospital staff had left for the day. Except for the two nights she taught her class, she had taken to slipping into Bolek's room just after he finished his dinner and staying until the nurse signalled her it was time for lights out.

She pulled her suitcase from under her cot, snapped it open, and found the blue cotton dress she had packed away because it was too flimsy for winter. She slipped it over her head and felt the fabric strain across her chest. Then she pulled it down and hooked the side closed. It was snug. Stepping up to the fragment of mirror on a near wall, she got up on her tiptoes and turned sideways. Her stomach looked rounder. She leaned in to peer at her face. It too seemed fuller, and her eyelids had a glossy, slightly puffy look. She was starting to show. In another month everyone would know. She took off the dress and put on her skirt and blouse. She would not tell Bolek about the baby. If she told him he would want his child and would overpower her with the sheer force of his need. He had lost a son and regardless of his love for her, he would go wild if he knew she was even considering an abortion. She tried to imagine life in Palestine and saw herself sitting on a cot just like this one listening for the footsteps that would bring her the news of his death. And she would be alone again.

The nurse was removing the tray from a sullen Bolek when Manya entered. Since his operation, she had watched his initial elation dissolve — first into irritability, then into simmering rage. He was counting the days till he left, he had said, but no one had told him how many there were.

"Blum says next week," he said to Manya without looking up. "It's ridiculous."

She stepped up to his bed hesitantly, her hands still in her pockets. "Does the doctor want you to heal properly or is he just smitten with your company?"

"How does he know whether I'm ready to go?"

The nurse carried the tray to the door, pushed it open with her hip and rolled her eyes at Manya before disappearing into the corridor.

"Well, most doctors *can* tell by looking at a wound, don't you think?" She sighed and touched his hand. "I know it's unpleasant, but it's necessary."

"Don't patronize me. I told him I'm leaving."

She sat down and stared at the night table next to his bed. Medicine bottles were laid out like surgical instruments on an operating table. "What difference could a few days make?"

He averted his eyes. He was planning to leave again. How long would her child have a father like this? Her child. The thought rose up as if it had always been inside her.

"Even Paul wouldn't let you go in this condition." Her voice sounded small and far away.

"If he needed a job done, he would."

The nurse came back in with a stack of newspapers under her arm. She handed him one.

"Paul's bringing me home the day after tomorrow. In the morning." His eyes were already roaming the headlines. "Will you meet me?" Manya hesitated, then nodded. She pulled the door shut behind her and walked the dim hall toward the exit sign, her heels sounding clipped and desolate as they echoed down the corridor.

The next morning Emmanuel stopped by the barracks to say he had "interesting news, just for her," and would she come with him to dinner that evening at The Golden Stag. Having decided she would not visit Bolek in the hospital again, she consented.

As Manya sat in the cozy restaurant waiting for Emmanuel, she looked forward to a quiet dinner, a slow stroll back to camp and an easy exchange on the bridge where they liked to stop. In his gentle, humorous way, he always got her to talk about herself. He did not offer much information about his own past, only that he had been to labor camps, then deported to Mauthausen, but that his wife and sons, along with a brother and two sisters, had perished. He told her this one night as they stood and watched the Lech flow past them. He told it simply, in that neutral tone most survivors used when recounting their concentration camp experiences. She had not probed. There was nothing more she needed to know. He was a good friend and she felt she could always trust his motives. Once, he had even suggested she consider Palestine because it was a socialist state and she might find a sense of purpose, something he gathered had always been important to her.

As for his own beliefs, Emmanuel was a non-observant

Jew with no intention of emigrating to Palestine. He had been brought up in what he called a "provisionally Jewish" home by parents whose commitment to Judaism varied with their monetary fortunes, and by the time he had disappeared into university life, their importing business had become so successful they could generously endow a seat in Prague's most exclusive synagogue without feeling obliged to attend. He had had a brief flirtation with Communism like most Jewish intellectuals, then settled down to his studies. The last time Emmanuel had been in a shul was for his Bar Mitzvah.

The door slammed in the half-empty restaurant and Emmanuel rushed in. It had grown quite warm during the past few days, but he still wore his gray wool muffler, and Manya believed it would hang around his neck into summer unless someone reminded him. She noticed he was wearing his new felt hat. His spectacles gleamed.

"This time I've good news for you," he beamed, "and I wanted to tell you here so we could celebrate." He slipped into the chair across from her. "I mean, if you want to celebrate." He looked confused for a moment. "That is, I assume it's good news. Oh, I hope I'm not being presumptuous in thinking . . . " He stopped and threw up his hands in mock exasperation. "Will I ever learn to finish my sentences?"

Manya laughed.

He leaned forward. "I have a friend," he said, "a microbiologist from Prague, someone I knew before the war. He's at the Pasteur Institute now, has been for over a year. He was very big in the field, very big. It was because of him that I was considered for the position. I've been writing to him and I told him about you — that is, about your background . . . " He pulled an envelope out of his pocket and held it up. "I just got a letter. He wrote that the Institute offers language courses for their scientists and English is a favorite. He could get you a job teaching, only part-time, but who knows? It's a beginning. The important thing is it would get you a visa out of here." He paused to take a breath and, seeing the uneasy look on her face, fell silent for a moment.

"It would be enough to make you independent," he ventured, correctly guessing her fears. "And you're very beautiful. I don't doubt you will marry again."

"I'm pregnant," she blurted out, wondering why she had chosen this moment.

He glanced down at the table, then cleared his throat. "Oh. I see." He paused. "So you will be marrying."

"No."

"Oh." He looked confused for a moment, then his face softened with sympathy. "You're young. You'll have other children."

"I'm keeping the baby."

"Oh. Does the father know?"

"I haven't told him."

He shook his head. "I don't understand any of this, Manya. Will you tell him?"

"I'm not sure."

"Why? I would want to know."

"He's not you."

He sat silent for a moment, then took a deep breath. "You're very brave."

Tears sprang into her eyes. She had not thought of herself as brave. It seemed as though she had not made a decision at all, rather that her body had made it for her. Now Emmanuel's words had unleashed the full weight of her want. A child. A new life.

"This doesn't really change anything," Emmanuel said, "except that you'll need more money."

"How can I go to Paris, a pregnant woman without a husband?"

"You're a widow, aren't you? Who will know when your husband died? And you could get help from the Joint in Paris. They have an office there. And I would help you, of course." She was about to protest, but he lifted his hands as if to fend her off. "All right. I'm sorry I said that, but I couldn't let you starve, you know."

Emmanuel turned and signaled the waiter. The young man lifted a bucket with a champagne bottle and came towards them.

"You don't have to give me an answer right now," Emmanuel said. "Let's drink to the baby."

"Mr. Olesky is waiting out back," the nurse said to Bolek, "to drive you to the camp." She held up a paper bag. "Your medicine. They're all labelled. Be sure you take them or you'll be back in this bed in a week." She put them into his backpack. "Try to stay sane," she smiled, threw him a kiss and left. Blum had avoided Bolek during the last two days of his stay, preferring to communicate through the nurse. He had antagonized the doctor, but he didn't care. It was his badgering that had forced Blum to release him earlier than planned and that was all that mattered. He had stopped the doctor in the corridor last night and tried to thank him, but Blum had stiffened and turned away before Bolek could speak.

Bolek knew he was a bad patient, always had been. Even as a child he had been unable to stay in bed, no matter how sick, and had driven his gentle mother to such extremes that she once barricaded his sick room door with their dining table until the doctor could examine him. It turned out he had scarlet fever and had to be put to bed for a month. From then on doctors meant trouble to Bolek, and he retained something of the childish belief that if he eluded them, he would never be ill.

The past week had irritated him beyond his limits. The newspapers said the English had called for the UN to create a Special Commission on Palestine. That meant the Brits had finally been pushed to the wall. And then he read that the brave and audacious Irgun terrorists had stepped up their attacks on British soldiers. Yesterday, he saw the best article of all: An English battalion in northern Palestine hadn't left their campsite in over a month because the surrounding roads had been mined. It was the beginning of the end of the British occupation and he was lying in a hospital bed in Germany.

Excitement gripped him as he gathered his clothes into his duffle bag and strode out into the corridor. Halfway down the hall he became dizzy and was surprised to find himself slumped against a wall. It took a few sobering minutes for his head to clear. Then, trembling with weakness, he walked into the morning sunlight. A warm breeze carried the scent of the linden trees toward him. He took a deep restorative breath and stepped up to Paul, who was standing by the hospital entrance.

"All right," Bolek said and clapped him on his back. "Another week and I'll be ready for anything."

Paul took the duffle bag from him. "You don't look well," he said and began to walk toward his truck. Bolek followed. He would not let Paul spoil his mood, he decided. He slid gingerly into the seat beside him and adjusted his arm sling.

He rubbed his eyes, then gazed with pleasure at the passing crowd. It was good to be outside.

"I've been working the hand every day." He lifted his arm out of the sling and wiggled his fingers. Paul drove on in silence. "What's the news from Avigur? He must be planning something since the British started making retreat noises."

"He's getting arms shipped, don't worry."

"What about the job you mentioned?"

Paul's face remained impassive.

"Spezia was not my fault," Bolek said angrily.

"I know."

"You mean you've got nothing for me?"

"As a matter of fact, I do."

Bolek stared at Paul's sharp immobile profile, then turned back to the road. No use asking directly. They were passing the marketplace near the cathedral and about to cross the bridge into the DP sector. Bolek looked upstream, in the direction of the lake where he and Manya had walked one Sunday not too long ago — perhaps it was a few weeks, perhaps a few months. Everything seemed so long in the past.

"I spoke with Avigur this week," Paul announced. "He's gathering Brichah commanders to organize escape routes for Romanian Jews."

"Romanians?"

"A famine is driving them out."

This was not what Bolek had in mind. The British were on the run! Guns would keep them running.

"And there have been anti-Semitic demonstrations in Bucharest." Paul's face tensed. "The bastards! We've gotten reports of Jews murdered by locals in the mountain villages. Avigur asked for you especially. He was impressed with your handling of the Bratislava job on such short notice."

Bolek knew Paul was flattering him, but said nothing.

"He wants to get the Romanians out. People hired so-called guides to take them across the border into Hungary and were left stranded. We're going to bring them into Germany."

"Why Germany? Why not directly into Italy and onto ships?"

"What's the matter with you? You want to send half-starved people over the Alps and let them sit in the middle of the Mediterranean until the British throw them into cages on Cypress?"

Bolek looked up, surprised. Paul usually kept his voice a monotone and remote. If he raised it, it must mean he had lost some men on a recent assignment. But he would never talk about that and Bolek would never ask.

Paul turned down Bolek's street and stopped in front of his house with the motor running. Manya was standing by the gate with her arms folded across her chest. A strong morning breeze whipped her skirt across her legs. He noticed she looked fuller and smoother; she had finally lost the gauntness that stamped most of the refugees.

"I'll speak with you later," Paul shifted into first. Bolek reached for his duffle bag in the back seat, but Paul grabbed it. "If you think you can handle the Romanian job, let me know." He handed him the bag. "You'll need to be on your way to Bucharest by the end of next week."

Bolek tightened his lips. He knew this was an ultimatum. "I'll be ready," he said and got out of the car. He turned to Manya and opened the latch with his good arm.

In the corner of his room a table had been laid with a fresh white cloth. Crusty peasant bread and a brick of raisin-studded farmer's cheese rested on a platter next to a bowl of sour cream and scallions. A small glazed applecake sat in the center. Manya spread out her hands toward the table. "Compliments of your landlady."

The widow who owned the house had a crush on him, although she was too old to entertain hopes of more than a friendship. Bolek sat down. He was starving.

Manya picked at her bread while he ate, moving the pieces around her plate, looking more dejected than usual. Then she turned and wrapped herself into a position she favored: legs twisted around each other, elbows propped on her knees, her face resting on the heel of her open hand. It made her look sulky and alluring.

"You don't seem very happy to see me."

She swung around and reached out to touch his cheek. "I've been worried."

He intercepted her hand and kissed the palm. "No need to worry now."

"Does it still hurt?"

"No."

"Would you tell me if it did?"

"Why? What could you do?"

She pushed her plate away and sat back. "That's just it. I can't change anything about you."

He watched her while he ate, too hungry to question her further. When he stood up, he felt the heaviness of fatigue overtake him and, slipping off his sling, lay down on the bed. She followed and untied his shoes and belt. He closed his eyes and felt her hands graze his cheeks while she adjusted the pillow beneath his head.

"Come," he said. He touched her breast, soft and full in his hand.

"Your shoulder."

"I can love you like this," he murmured and brought her close to him. She resisted for a moment, then slid next to him and rested her hand lightly on his chest. He ignored the throb in his shoulder and pulled her to him.

Afterwards, she watched the curtains flutter at the half-open window. They billowed rhythmically in the gentle breeze. She turned on her side and spoke: "I've applied for a French visa."

He tensed, suddenly cold beneath the sheets.

"I've had an offer of a teaching post. I'm going to Paris."

Still he did not move, as though his silence could change what he had heard.

"At The Pasteur Institute. Part-time English. One of my students is a scientist. He arranged it."

Bolek remembered the Czech's attentions to Manya. "You're going with Kozak."

"No."

"Then why?"

Manya sat up and grabbed her slip. She examined it for a moment, then tossed it onto the bed. "My war is over. Yours is just beginning."

"All right. I'll make it easy." He pulled her around to face him. She looked frightened and drawn. "Just come with me. If it doesn't work out, you can leave."

"If you promise no more missions," she whispered "No more danger. No more risks." She stared out into the room. "And you can't."

"Everything is a risk. Will you give up a life together because it's a risk?"

She silently began to cry against his chest. He held her head tight, her soft hair entwined in his fingers, and tried to say more, but the words fell back into his mouth, hollow and misshapen. Bolek lay back and closed his eyes, but the image of Manya's face, pale and inconsolable, stayed with him. Nothing he could say would comfort her. He heard her moving around the room and her dress rustle as she slipped it on. Then the door opened, clicked softly closed behind her, and she was gone.

CHAPTER 22

"WE CAN GET ON A SHIP as soon as Simon gets a copy of his X-rays. They're clean now." Leila slipped her arm through Manya's. They continued down the street toward the mess hall. "He can finally get clearance." She bent to adjust her hat. It was made of navy blue straw and she had sewn a cheerful band of yellow to the brim. It sat alluringly on her soft blond hair.

"I wish I had taken a tailoring course," she continued. "I'd enjoy sewing — at least for a while. And it would come in handy." She hugged her short brown jacket, the one Frau Heinz had made. "Simon's uncle wrote that there are a lot of jobs in New York, but mostly manual work. Simon isn't used to that. And he's not strong yet." She looked up the street for a moment, then returned to Manya with forced attention. "And you? When are you leaving for Paris?"

"Sometime in the next week."

"Emmanuel's gone ahead?"

"He left two weeks ago."

"He wants to help you."

244

"I know."

"Let him."

Manya was about to scold her, but thought better of it. Leila was well meaning, but always opportunistic.

The night before Emmanuel boarded his train they had strolled down to the Lech, neither of them knowing how to say what was on their minds, neither of them able to pretend there was anything else of importance to say. They had walked in silence until they reached the Karolinen Bridge. Emmanuel had described the many bridges that crossed the Seine and how they linked the city's ancient quarters like jeweled bracelets. She could feel him waiting. "Please don't look for anything elaborate," she had finally said. "One room will be enough for me and the baby." He had nodded and gazed into the distance. She had taken a deep breath, resolved to say more, fearing her comment was too oblique, but his sad look told her he had understood.

She turned to Leila. "I asked him to look for lodgings for me as soon as he arrived," Manya said. "If I have to, I'll go to the Joint center until I find a place to live. But I won't stay with him."

"Does he know this?"

"I'm not going to marry him, Leila. I know you think I should, but I don't want to."

"He loves you. You could have a family."

Leila didn't ask about Bolek. He was not the kind of man she would have wanted for Manya. From the beginning, Leila had found Bolek unthinkable as a husband. He was too impulsive and unpredictable, and now that she and Manya were parting, probably for good, she couldn't help voicing her true feelings on the subject.

"You think you'll find someone else in Paris, don't you?"

Before Manya could protest, they heard shouting in the distance. People stepped out of offices and stores and stared down the street in the direction of the noise. Some leaned cautiously from doorways and craned their necks, more alarmed than curious. Then a line of moving people appeared in the distance and seemed to float up onto the horizon from the sloping street below. As it drew closer, Manya could make out demonstrators — refugees — walking shoulder to shoulder in columns that filled the entire width of the street. They chanted in Yiddish as they advanced, synchronizing their steps to the rhythm of the words. The people at the fringes held up large banners with inscriptions in English that read "Brits Out Now" and "England Wants to Finish the Job Hitler Started." Bystanders stepped into the group as it passed and for a moment the mass of moving people looked like a living organism eating everything in its path.

The marchers drew closer and Manya recognized Benjamin from the Joint warehouse walking in front. And there, behind him, was Tovah. Toward the back of the swelling crowd, cardboard signs bobbed up and down proclaiming "Alive in '45, a State in '48," and "A Homeland For the Surviving Remnant." And then a contingent came into view hoisting huge blue and white flags that unfurled over their heads as they moved forward. Behind them came the children waving paper flags in their small fists.

Manya was a veteran of marches, yet she filled with exhilaration just as she had when she was eight years old, singing *The International* at summer camp.

"That was fast," Leila shouted above the noise. "Simon told me he heard Bevin's speech this morning on the radio, but it's too soon to be in the newspapers. The camp paper doesn't come out till tomorrow morning. How did they organize so quickly?"

Manya shrugged. Ernest Bevin, the British Foreign Minister, had told the press the only reason Americans were in favor of a Jewish state was because they didn't want the Jews coming to the US. She had read that the Irgun had blown up some soldiers in Jaffa last week and that the minister had called them murderers.

The demonstrators were now moving right past her and the force of their singing was palpable. There had been other Zionist demonstrations during the seven months she had been in Landsberg, but none this large.

Leila had not taken her eyes off the crowd. "If I had known about this, I would have joined them sooner. They usually start with a rally in the German sector." She pointed down the street to where the barracks ended. "They'll probably stop at the Sports Hall for a closing speech. Come on! It's almost over."

The chanting had stopped and the marchers had begun to sing a song in Yiddish. Tears were rolling down many of their faces.

"What are they singing?"

Leila cupped her hand over her mouth and shouted, "It's the song of the Jewish partisans that was written in the Vilna Ghetto, *Never Say That This Will be the End of the Road*."

Manya and Leila stepped into the crowd. Manya couldn't pick up the words, but as they linked arms with other marchers, they moved to the rhythm of the song. The hopelessness of the past year lifted and Manya felt a powerful surge of conviction. She tightened her grip on her two companions and moved forward.

The group marched to the perimeter of the camp, then

slowed down and poured into an open area in front of the Sports Hall. A man stood at a podium erected at the top of the stairs. He wore a suit and glasses and held a megaphone in his hand. His name was Garber, Manya recalled, an official of the Camp Committee. She had seen him around Landsberg, usually rushing in and out of the administration building with a stack of files under his arm. He stood motionless for a moment and as he raised his hand, a hush fell on the crowd. It was then that she heard the sound of motorcycles. Turning, she saw they were surrounded by soldiers. The GIs must have been following the marchers from the beginning and had just now caught up with them.

Leila nudged her and motioned toward the Americans. "The stupid commander always sends his men to these demonstrations. If they stayed away, everything would be all right, but some hothead DPs always get crazy."

As if on cue, people began to wave their fists and yell out in Yiddish.

"What are they saying?"

Leila listened for a second. "Are you our liberators or our jailers?" "Go home. This is a peaceful demonstration."

The soldiers stood motionless, with their hands on their rifles and their inscrutable faces half-hidden beneath their helmets. But Manya knew they didn't understand any of this. They had not been in the war. They had probably just arrived from some remote farm in safe America and been told very little about the people for whom they were responsible. And what could they understand at eighteen or nineteen? That nobody wanted these glum refugees with broken teeth; that they smelled bad, were always angry, and had no place to go. The soldiers might even wonder why, two years after the end of the war, these people were still unwanted and why, after the nations of the world had displayed their indignation and outrage at the Nazi atrocities, none opened their arms to the survivors. She caught the eye of a boyish face framed by a steel hat. Then his gaze skimmed past her and he took in the group at large, as though it were one anonymous lump of trouble.

Garber lifted his megaphone high into the air, waved it and brought it to his mouth. "The British helped win the war against the Nazis," he said in a steady voice. "But they don't want us now. Nobody does!" A roar went up from the crowd. "Why do they stand in our way? If we had a homeland, there would be no 'Jewish Problem' for them — or anyone else."

Glass shattered behind her. There was a scuffle and the refugees began to hurl Coke bottles and rocks at the soldiers. Manya instinctively covered her head with her arms and yanked Leila to a crouching position. More refugees pulled bottles out from under their jackets and flung them at the GIs, who kept their heads bent and their rifles held stiffly across their chests. Someone gave a signal and the Americans moved toward the refugees. She waited to hear a gunshot, but the soldiers merely charged into the crowd, pushing the demonstrators into a tighter knot. Garber was now shouting into the megaphone, his voice a blare of noise that no one paid attention to. Manya saw a group of men leaning against a building with their arms up while MPs looked at their IDs and searched them. She thought the men must be the bottle throwers, but after the soldiers examined their cards, they released them. This seemed to be a police contingent looking for someone. She whirled around in the direction of Bolek's office, fighting her way through the crowd, pushing and elbowing people out of her way. Finally, she stood a few feet from the entrance and was able to see in through the window. The office looked empty. Just then a group of soldiers stomped out of the building and scanned the crowd.

"Go get that guy with the bullhorn," she heard an officer say, and his aide ran down the street.

A few minutes later Garber was standing in front of the officer.

"I have orders from Munich to arrest a DP named Bolek Holzer," the lieutenant said. "He's wanted for questioning about the murder of a Czech citizen."

"I don't see Holzer here," Garber replied without looking around. "And I would ask you to speak with our president before you take anyone from this camp." He removed his glasses and put them in his breast pocket. Without them he had the innocent, preoccupied look of a young student.

"I didn't ask your advice," the lieutenant said. "Everyone in this camp is under military jurisdiction, so don't give me that crap about 'president.' I did you a favor last month with that trainload of Jews from Poland. I want some cooperation now."

Garber smiled and gave him a small, formal bow. "I am deeply grateful that you permitted the refugees to come to Landsberg. They had been sealed in their cars at the border for just two days, Lieutenant, so only a few people had to go to the hospital for heat prostration. I thank you. But on this matter I cannot help you."

Before the lieutenant could reply, an MP shoved two more refugees in front of him and he paused to scan their IDs. Then another group of DPs was nudged forward for his inspection. Bolek was among them. His face had that half-smile he wore when he was trying to control the anger that was always so close to the surface. He passed near Manya and she automatically reached out. For a second, alarm flitted across his face, then he leaned away from her and kept his eyes straight ahead until he was standing in front of the officer.

The lieutenant scrutinized Bolek's face. "I've seen you before. You work for the JDC."

"No. I am an ORT teacher. Carpentry and printing. You see me at meetings."

The officer studied his papers. "Leon Bomberg. Well, Mr. Bomberg, I don't go to those meetings. And you seem to fit the description of a Mr. Holzer, so why don't you just come down with me to headquarters for a few minutes." Bolek looked puzzled, as though he couldn't understand what was being said.

Yankl, who had been standing in the crowd, suddenly stepped in front grumbling in Yiddish to the people around him. He pushed Garber aside and stood before the lieutenant.

"Excuse, sir. I am at Joint Immigration. Holzer works with me. It's two days now he left for Munich. He brings people and supplies. Gone two days. Returns tomorrow." He spoke softly, enunciating his halting English as though the officer could read lips. "And you see," he said gesturing with a sweep of his arm to the group of men standing behind him, "so many of us look alike." The men were all between twenty-five and thirty years old, all dark-haired, all gaunt.

"He's right," Garber chimed in. "You would use your time better if you called your Munich headquarters to look for Holzer. These accusations are serious. The committee cannot condone murder. If you have strong evidence, we would want to try him ourselves."

The officer frowned, looked at Yankl, then back at Bolek, who was standing with his hands in his pockets, his face just the right mixture of concern and incredulity. The lieutenant seemed to consider this for a moment when an MP brought up yet another group of men for inspection. The lieutenant gave their IDs a cursory glance and shoved them back at his aide. Then he spun around abruptly and headed toward his jeep while his men cleared a path for him through the crowd. Once the MPs departed, the marchers, who had been held back by the Americans, surged forward and began shouting at the departing soldiers.

Bolek was immediately surrounded by refugees. He spoke to them quickly in Yiddish, then tried to move toward Manya. But the crowd grabbed his arms and pulled at him, shouting what sounded like a combination of objections and commands. Finding Manya's eyes, he signalled in the direction of her barracks. She hesitated, and for a moment they stood staring at each other across a sea of shouting faces. Then she turned and fought her way in the opposite direction.

CHAPTER 23

BOLEK TAPPED on the barracks window. Tovah, who was taking a blouse off a hanger, spun around, startled. He motioned to her, and recognition filled her face. She came to the back door. She had barely opened it before he spoke.

"Tell Manya to come."

"I don't know if she's here," Tovah whispered. "I didn't see her earlier."

"Check."

She withdrew, letting the door shut gently behind her. He watched her disappear behind a partition in the middle of the room and reemerge with Manya at her side. Tovah pointed toward him; Manya glanced up, then hurried toward the back door.

She stepped into the night, stretching out her arms to find his form in the darkness. He could smell the sweet, pungent aroma of the perfumed soap she had bought from a street vendor soon after they had started their affair. It was called "Spanish Rose" and clung to his sheets so that every time he threw back the covers the fragrance floated up at him.

During the week since she had told him she was going

to Paris, he had been unable to resist badgering her — bullying her — into coming with him. He refused to believe she could part from him. And each time they battled, he felt the distance between them widen. Now, there was no time left. He was leaving.

She clutched his arm. "Is it safe?"

"I'm going tonight. I've been at Meyer's, in the storeroom, since the march. Paul's gone to get me an UNNRA uniform and new papers. I have to get back. A car is coming for me." He grabbed her hand. "Come."

He steered her through the dim alleyways between the barracks, avoiding the camp's main street. Even at this late hour, people would be returning from meetings and lectures and classes.

The night was warm and fragrant. Lilacs were in bloom. As they hurried past the open barrack windows, the sounds of camp life floated out and over them. Someone was singing "Raisins and Almonds," an old Yiddish song he hadn't heard since childhood, and a rush of nostalgia filled him. He turned to see if she, too, had recognized the tune, but her gaze remained steady and urgent as if she had abandoned nostalgia forever.

He stopped at the corner of the main street, opposite Meyer's Café and scanned the area. They walked toward the rear of the building, running the last few steps to the back door. He pushed it open and pulled her in after him. The small room was crammed with goods. Boxes of flour lined the shelves; sacks of coffee and tins of margarine were piled on the floor. It was dark except for the lamplight that came in through a window near the ceiling. He stood still, listening to her panting and waiting for his eyes to adjust to the new darkness.

"Paul will be here soon. Then I must leave." He paused. "You'll be able to join me within six months. Partition will happen. Paul will get you to Palestine, I guarantee it." He felt her stiffen.

"You'll go to fight the Arabs," she said, "and you won't come back."

"We'll win quickly."

"No. This war will drag on. I won't sit and wait till you get blown up."

"I won't get blown up."

"You're talking to me as if I were a child."

"Because you're not making sense. You can give me up because you're afraid to risk losing me? Either way you'll have nothing." Her face contorted, as though she were trying not to cry. "You love me," he insisted. "You do! And I love you!"

She shook her head.

"I can't come back." He took her face between his hands. "Did you hear what I said?" Her breath was on his lips. "You'll come."

"No."

He yanked her to him.

He slipped his hand around her waist and clasped her to him. He lay his other hand across her stomach and stopped. An image flashed before him of her standing in front of his house the day he returned from the hospital. The morning breeze had whipped her dress against her body, revealing her rounded form.

"You're pregnant!"

For a moment she looked frightened, then her cheeks filled with color.

"Yes."

He felt a ripple in time. "Mine."

"Mine too."

A child. His child. And she would not come. He heard her "no" again, like the echo of a verdict, and a terrible stillness filled him.

"You'll marry Kozak. You'll give him my child," he shouted.

"No!" She escaped from his arms. "But I can't go with you."

He stood still for a moment and then reached out and pushed her against the shelves. A box toppled and spilled at her feet. The room misted with a cloud of white powder. Flour hung suspended in the air, then drifted gently to the floor.

Then she was at him. She beat his shoulders and face and chest until he grabbed her wrists and held her against the shelves. More boxes toppled and fell around them. She struggled to hit him, twisting to get her hands free while she cried through clenched teeth. When her body went limp, he released her and stepped back. She was breathing hard. They stood facing each other, their breath like a palpable distance between them. Then she reached out to touch him, her fingers barely skimming his face. Bolek's heart twisted and he fell against her, kissing her eyes, her cheeks, her belly. "Please," he whispered.

She encircled him in her arms. "I can't," she said.

The words seemed an impossibility as she spoke, yet he understood their finality.

"I want this child," she said, pressing her face against his hair. "And I want peace."

"I do too."

"I don't belong in Palestine."

"Then where do you belong? You belong nowhere. All

256

your life you were mistaken about who you were and now you won't go with your own people." He felt the words explode in his mouth. "You're a casualty of the war and you want to take our child and bring it up with nothing."

"Nothing!"

Light streamed into the room. Paul was standing in the doorway.

"Holzer! Let's go." Bolek felt himself being pulled up. Paul hauled him to the door. A car engine droned outside.

Paul looked back at Manya briefly, then pushed Bolek onto the sidewalk. Bolek stumbled toward the vehicle, grabbed the door handle and lowered himself in. "Crouch down in the back seat!" The door slammed. Gears groaned and the car slid forward. Bolek twisted around and stared out the back window at the street corner under the lamplight. The café receded from view.

Only later, when they had stopped on a road near a small wood and he was changing into his UNRRA uniform, did he notice the floury streaks across the front of his shirt.

CHAPTER
24

THE TRUCK SPED through northern Austria toward the German border. The leaves were just coming out on some of the trees interspersed among the evergreens. Even though it was May, it had been a hard winter and spring was late. Two weeks earlier, when Bolek arrived in Romania, it had looked like the moon: a barren, ominous countryside, first war-ravaged, then famine-hit. Now, heading back across Austria again, there was a bit more hope in the landscape. Fields were dotted with tender vegetable shoots, like thumbs poking through the freshly turned earth. Occasionally, farmers looked up from their rusty plows with the same dogged, resolute expression he had seen on the faces of their German brothers. Austrians gave the air of being gentle, but underneath he sensed the same steely soul that had made unspeakable brutality, if not permissible, at least possible in their country. They had been willing disciples, although everyone seemed to be forgetting that now.

Bolek's jaw tightened. Not enough punishment. There had not been enough. The newspaper coverage of Nuremburg made the trials sound like a theatrical event with the Allies congratulating themselves for convicting the most obvious bad guys. Meanwhile, the little ones who had done all the dirty work were getting away, and the smart ones, the scientists who worked so long and hard to perfect the Nazi death machine, were being swept up, even fought over by the Allies. Well, in the end, people were practical. Why waste a clever mind? Why not exploit it? It made him sick.

Paul had told Bolek that Beneš's secretary had seen him slip from the building in Bratislava so many months ago and identified him from police photos. INTERPOL had notified the Americans and they traced him to Landsberg. It didn't matter so much that now he was a wanted man. He had been anxious to get to Palestine, anyway. Just living in Germany made him feel like a criminal and he was tired of being surrounded by goyim, of being a ward of the Allies, of being, at best, *tolerated.*

He adjusted his uniform, which was a bit too tight around the waist, and leaned back in the seat to rest. His body ached from the hours he had spent jammed into a truck with Romanian Jews barreling through Hungary, and when they stopped in Salzburg to transfer vehicles, he came up front to sit with Paul and the driver. Everything had gone on schedule. They would be in Munich in a few hours.

He had relived the scene in the storeroom of Meyer's Café over and over again during the past week. It sprang before his eyes as he stared at maps of Romania's scarred and desolate mountain routes. It tore through him as he searched the roads for a safe place to stop and feed the refugees. At night, just before he fell asleep on the floor of the Brichah mountain station, fragments of Abraham, his dead son, would unreel: a pink face floating atop a pile of carriage blankets; tottering towards him in the park, his tender, plump feet disappearing into the grass. These images were vague because, he realized with a sinking heart, he no longer remembered what his child had looked like. Whenever someone interrupted these ruthless visions he plunged back into the present with an abruptness that bordered on physical pain. He clenched his teeth. He would find Manya in Paris. He would *make* her come with him.

The work in Romania had been frustrating and had only added to his bitterness. At the hilltop station on the outskirts of Satu-Mare near the Hungarian border, he had found only twenty-five Romanians waiting to be taken out of the country. For weeks the Brichah agents had tried to collect the fleeing refugees, but it had been difficult to locate them in the remote mountains where they had been abandoned by their guides. An agent from the Brichah's Munich office said that some of these refugees had made their way to the Joint Offices in the bigger towns and that he could add them to his group. Bolek should have no trouble getting the Joint to hand them over, the man had added. The Romanian government was a vicious bureaucracy — all the Soviet regimes were — and Joint workers were happy to avoid the torturous red tape. Strange how hard the Romanians made it to leave, even though Bolek knew they were pleased to be rid of their Jews.

Within a week, Bolek and his agents had gathered over a hundred people from refugee centers in Satu-Mare and Bucharest. They were a rough-looking group, weathered like old barns. They didn't say much, but when his men handed round the first bowls of soup, they ate without pausing until the last spoonful was finished. He had not seen such hunger since the concentration camps. One of the refugees, a youngish man with sandy-colored hair told him he and his family had been eating hay for a week, and when he had finally resorted to begging in town, the Romanians, none of whom had ever seen him before, called him a Jew bastard and shut the door in his face. "Do we look so different?" he had asked Bolek. "How can they tell?"

"People know," Bolek had replied, feeling the old tightness in his chest. "You don't need a big nose or dark eyes. They know because their fathers knew and their grandfathers before them. They know because it's their most important legacy."

Most of the work for this mission had been done before he got there, and Paul's little speech about having become indispensable after Bratislava had been mere flattery. But after his close call with the American military, Paul had rushed him out to this assignment. Now, he was traveling back to Munich disguised as a UN official for a meeting of the International Refugee Organization, the agency slated to take over all relief work from the United Nations. Paul told him he would have to stop for a few days at one of the agricultural kibbutzim run by the Haganah and wait for a ride to Italy. Then, somehow, he would get to Palestine. His stay in Germany was over.

Paul nudged him and he sat up with a start. They had stopped in front of a building surrounded by farmland. In the distance, he saw a barn and several silos dimly outlined against the darkening sky. He must have been asleep since they crossed the German border in the middle of the afternoon. Lights came on in the main building. He knew this kibbutz. It was called Greifenberg. It was only eighteen kilometers from Landsberg, and Miriam, a Haganah member who worked in the mess hall kitchen, lived here. He had driven her home one night when her own small truck had broken down. In the dusky light he made out several smaller buildings, additional sleeping quarters and the chicken coops Miriam was so proud of. This had been an SS rest camp before the war, and right after liberation one of the Zionist groups had converted it into a farming collective. He slipped out of the front seat and stretched his stiff legs before walking into the main house. Miriam was standing in the middle of the living room obviously expecting him.

"Welcome, my little fugitive," she said, opening her arms and hugging him. She smelled of sweet vegetables, and when she pulled away, he noticed she was still in her food-streaked apron. Miriam was one of the few kibbutz residents excused from farm duties. She was too valuable working in the Landsberg mess hall and warehouses, where in a few months, she could skim from camp supplies enough canned goods to stock a small vessel leaving for Palestine.

Miriam linked her arm through his and smiled flirtatiously, as was her habit, even though she and Bolek had long ago settled on a friendship. "I'll show you to your quarters," she said, and he followed her into the hallway. He saw Paul come in with their rucksacks, toss them onto the floor and draw aside one of the kibbutz officials.

"Hello, Paul," Miriam called from the corridor. He nodded in her direction without looking up. "Well, at least one person needs some rest," she muttered and led Bolek into one of the bedrooms. There were five cots inside with scarcely any space between them. The one closest the window was unmade.

"You'll have to stay inside until we can get you to Italy." She pulled a sheet from a pile of linens and began to make the bed. "I don't know how long that will be."

Bolek took off his jacket and flung it onto one of the beds. He rubbed his aching shoulder, trying to remember the roadway that led to town. It was a narrow country lane and not heavily trafficked. He could walk it in a couple of hours. In the morning, before dawn, it would be safe.

"There." Miriam spread a blanket over the mattress. "Get some rest."

"I'm going into Landsberg tomorrow. Wake me at five."

Miriam grew somber. "Too risky." She slapped an already fluffed pillow.

"No risk at all. I have excellent papers."

She glanced towards the next room, where they knew Paul was talking with the group leader.

"Don't worry about him. He's not my father."

"Then how are you going to get there?"

"I'll walk."

"Is it that urgent?" Miriam knew about Manya—they all did—but no one asked directly.

He turned away, weary, and started to unlace his boots. His shoulder began to throb again, and he grimaced with pain.

"It would be easier by car," Miriam smiled.

"That's my girl."

Tires skidded outside and Miriam whirled around, a pillow poised in her hand. Bolek stepped to the window, pulled the curtains aside and looked out into the evening. Another vehicle had arrived. Two Brichah agents jumped down from the front seat and quickly walked toward the front of the building, where Paul waited at the open door.

"Looks like no rest for you. Off to Italy without even an overnight break. We thought it would take them at least a few days to get here." She turned to him with sad eyes. "I suppose this is good practice for what's coming. The war with the Arabs won't give us any rest either." She let the curtains slip back and sighed. "I'll pack you some food for the trip."

Paul leaned in the door. "They're here. Get dressed. We're on our way."

Bolek turned to Miriam. "Is she still in Landsberg?"

"Yes."

He opened his rucksack and found a note pad. Then he rummaged through his jacket pockets until he found a pencil, and crouching next to the chair, spread the paper on the seat and began to write. He scribbled hastily and folded the note several times before he handed it to Miriam.

"Will you give this to her?"

"Of course." Miriam took the paper and slipped it into the pocket of her apron. "If I don't see her at breakfast tomorrow, I'll go to her barracks."

"Make sure."

She smiled. "Have I ever let you down?"

CHAPTER
25

THE SUITCASE WAS OPEN and Manya's few clothes and books lay strewn across her cot. She had forgotten how little she had arrived with and now she saw how little she had acquired during her stay. The few articles of clothing that Rochel had given her would do nicely through the summer, she thought, smoothing out the wrinkles on a linen blouse, but come winter she would need warmer clothes. She wondered how cold Paris could be and saw herself walking along the icy banks of the Seine. Then she pictured herself holding a baby and her hand absently slid to her stomach. The skin beneath her clothes felt smooth and taut. Time was passing quickly. If she were to stay in Landsberg, what would her child's nationality be — International Refugee? Stateless Displaced Person? Or worst of all, German citizen? She knew that a birth certificate was only a document, but it would also be a tie to a piece of land, to a history, to old stones. She herself felt *her* homelessness complete. She was from nowhere and all she could think about was where she and her baby would be safe.

She turned her suitcase over and emptied the remaining

items onto the cot. Her grandmother's shawl, which had been tucked away at the bottom, fell out and lay crumpled on top of her clothes. She lifted it gingerly and pressed the old lace between her hands. Spreading it like netting on the bottom of her suitcase, she began to replace the folded items. She ran her fingers over a pilled cardigan. When would she have another?

She had recently received her first letter from Emmanuel. He wrote that the French economy was worse than he had expected and that his friend at the Institute was offering her less than originally promised. But, not to worry, he had added. Since liberation there was great enthusiasm among the French for learning English, and he could round up private students for her. He had found lodgings for himself on rue de Rosiers in the Jewish quarter; rooms were small, but not hard to come by. She could feel his optimism permeating the letter. For two days after receiving this news, she had awakened early, fearfully watching the cold, dark windows until dawn tinged them pink. Then, on the third day, she emerged from a dreamless sleep refreshed and filled with determination — no, with certainty — that all would be well. She had survived the war. She had survived the death of her family. And the death of her convictions. What did she have to fear? Shabby clothes? Cramped quarters? And there would be a child to love. Paris didn't have to be her last stop, she thought again as she refolded her worn cardigan for the third time.

Once she had decided on France, she remembered how happy her parents had been in 1936 when Leon Blum was elected to head a coalition government that included Communists. Even now the French government was made up of Communists and Socialists. It was not a crime to be an ex-

Party member or a Jew. Jacob was wrong. The French were certainly better than the Germans with whom he had chosen to live. Bolek was wrong too. She was a lover of cities and culture. She thought of Paris and imagined a university town filled with books and ideas. She might be a stranger to a place, but not to its atmosphere, and she could create her own life out of the richness there. She was only twenty-eight. There was still a future.

It would take several days for the last stages of her visa to be processed, perhaps even a week, and packing was premature since she would need to use some of the things she was so carefully folding away. But there was something reassuring about it, something absolute, as though the act of snapping shut the suitcase made her decision to go to Paris irrevocable. Each time thoughts of Bolek tugged at her, she looked at the corner near her cot where the suitcase stood.

And Bolek? She knew he was astonished that she had let him go, not only because he thought so highly of himself, but also because, as he often reminded her, neither of them had hoped to love again. She closed her eyes, wrenched by the memory of his pained face as Paul pulled him into the street. He would hate her forever with all the passion of his relentless energy.

"If I found a spring coat, I could probably fit it for you before you leave." Rochel appeared beside her cot. "Benjamin said he'd let me look at some boxes that came in yesterday — you know, before all the good things are taken."

"I have enough for the warm weather. It's winter I'm worried about."

"Why didn't you tell me! I could have made you something weeks ago. Remember those mildewed coats nobody wanted? We could have sprayed one of them and by the time I got through fitting it, it would have looked beautiful."

"I wasn't thinking ahead."

Rochel sat down on Manya's cot and fingered the loose threads on her blanket. "When do you think you'll be leaving?"

"Any day."

Rochel was silent. This was the first time she had alluded to Manya's departure since learning that her visa had been approved. "I could finish something if I found a good coat right away," she said at last.

"I guess that would be wise." Manya put down the blouse she was holding and faced her. "You're so good to me. I'll miss you."

"I don't write Polish well," Rochel said averting her eyes. "You may not hear from me — unless you learn Yiddish."

There was no use pretending they would ever see each other again. Rochel's application to Argentina had not been approved yet, but her brother had completed all the necessary papers. Buenos Aires was very far away.

Yesterday, Manya had gone to Peiting to say good-bye to Uncle Jacob and Helga. She had sat in the oppressive living room and written out the address of the Pasteur Institute. Although the brother, Erik, was conspicuously absent, there had still been an awkwardness among them. Jacob forced conversation about his fabric business and the possibility of traveling to Paris, but they both knew it was unlikely. At the doorway, Helga had kissed her on the cheek and Manya had clung to Jacob, her only remaining relative, and wept.

Manya moved closer to Rochel and put her head on her

friend's shoulder. Rochel sighed, then reached for her radio and began to fiddle with the dial. Piano music filled their small corner and Manya let her attention drift to the soothing sounds. It surprised her that Rochel preferred the classical station to the Yiddish programs that broadcast old shtetl tunes. This particular piece was sentimental, but sweet and familiar. Manya sat up. It was Mendelssohn, a piano concerto she hadn't heard in years. His music had been banned by the Nazis and now it was being played by the Berlin Philharmonic. By Germans.

"Mrs. Gerson?" A dark-haired woman with a round, cheerful face stood a few feet away. Manya recognized her as one of the mess hall cooks, also rumored to be working for the Haganah.

"May I speak to you for a moment?" she asked Manya. "Privately?"

Manya stood up, surprised, and walked with the woman to the reception area at the entrance to the barracks.

"I'm Miriam Gold," she said extending her hand. "I have a note from Bolek Holzer." She handed Manya a piece of paper and stepped back. Manya held the note and stared at it without opening it.

"He asked that I give it to you." Miriam nodded toward the paper.

Manya opened the note. She recognized the hasty scribble.

Contact me through the Jewish Agency in Tel Aviv. I'm known now as Dov Radner. Paul is still in Landsberg. He can arrange for your passage. Come. I love you so.

She folded the note and shoved it deep inside her skirt pocket.

"He planned to come to you this morning," Miriam continued, "but he had to leave last night right after he arrived at my kibbutz."

"Last night? You mean he was here?"

Miriam lowered her voice. "He brought some of our people out of Romania and came back to pick up a transport to Italy. He's headed there now."

Manya felt light-headed. She had assumed Bolek was well on his way to Palestine, but last night he had been so close, just a few kilometers away. And he had wanted to come to her. He didn't hate her after all. "Do you think he'll be back?" she asked. Her voice sounded small.

"In six months, after the partition is settled, everyone will be back to help get the refugees to Palestine." Miriam smiled. "It'll be Israel then."

"Not without a war first," Manya said.

Miriam pressed her lips together. "We're prepared for that."

"Prepared for all that dying?"

"You consider this living?"

"The war will be terrible," Manya said and looked away.

"Without the British blockade, more Jews will get to Palestine and we'll have an army. And then a home." She paused and gave Manya a hard look. "I can get a message to him. I can send it with a group leaving tonight. They're heading for the same port in Italy."

Manya's thoughts raced. Could she really leave Bolek to raise a child whose face would haunt her with his eyes, his mouth, the slant of his chin? Year after year she would be reminded of what she had given up. But did she have the courage, the strength, to take on a man who could never be counted on to be at her side when she needed him, who would love her in his own way, but never with as much passion as he would bestow on his homeland? For Bolek, his new country, a state of his own, would always come first, before wife, child, home. She, on the other hand, would be resentful and often, bitter. She paused. She loved him, and he loved her. Perhaps it would be enough. Perhaps she could live anywhere, make any kind of life, as long as he was with her. At least, she could try. She would write to Emmanuel that she couldn't come to Paris, not now.

She was seized by the need for Bolek. Joy filtered through her, and then that old familiar stab of fear. She walked to her cot and tore a paper from her class notebook. She wrote:

Come if you can. Or bring us to you.
Manya

She pressed the note into Miriam's hand and held it closed with her own. "Thank you," she whispered.

"Miriam, wait for me." Rochel was adjusting her shawl. "Walk me to the warehouse, won't you? There's a shipment of clothes I want to look at."

"If you're leaving right away," Miriam replied. "I have to set up for lunch. They get crazy if the food isn't hot." She shook her head wearily. "We still can't get warm enough or full enough, can we?"

Rochel ignored her, looking eager to leave. "If I find something, I'll be back right away so you can try it on," she said to Manya.

"I'll wait," Manya said. She slipped her hand inside her pocket and smoothed the ragged edge of Bolek's note. Then she leaned against the doorway and watched the two women step into the warm street — one, big-boned, young, with strong, graceful strides and sturdy arms swinging at her sides; the other, small, old, hurrying to keep up. She pictured Rochel in the warehouse sifting through the piles of used clothing, her expert fingers feeling fabric, touching a seam, looking for a winter coat intact enough to be restored.

"If she finds one," Manya thought, "Rochel will have to remake it for someone else."